ADVANCE PRAISE FOR *LAUREN'S EYES*!

"*Lauren's Eyes* is a triumphant debut. Sexy and compelling, it will keep you up 'til dawn."
    —Julianne MacLean, *USA Today* bestselling author

"A fantastic debut filled with steamy passion, gripping suspense, hot cowboys, and a little edgy paranormal action."
    —*Romance Reviews Today*

"An engrossing story that captivated from the first page to the last. Fast-paced, with a strong heroine, a hero who just oozed charm, and a mystery that needed to be solved. *Lauren's Eyes* is one not to be missed."
    —*Romance Reader at Heart*

LOVE ON THE RANGE

"I want to stir up a few things with you." Cal's gray eyes bored into hers. "Starting with that composure of yours."

She closed her eyes as his fingers tunneled into her hair. She wanted to deny his effect on her senses, but there was little point if she were going to stand there and let each new sensation wash over her. "You're doing a pretty good job of that right now," she breathed.

"Umm, but I want to do more."

She resisted the urge to lick her lips. "Like what?"

"Like this."

Her eyes sprang open at the first contact of his mouth to hers, then fell shut again as he kissed her hotly. Of their own volition, her hands skimmed up his sides, finding purchase in the belt loops of his jeans. Too soon, he broke the kiss, leaving her yearning for more, yet he didn't pull back.

His hands dropped to her shoulders, then brushed down her arms to grip her elbows.

"I want to stir your imagination," he said, lifting her arms until they circled his neck. "I want to stir your *blood*."

LAUREN'S EYES
NORAH WILSON

LOVE SPELL NEW YORK CITY

LOVE SPELL®

August 2004

Published by

Dorchester Publishing Co., Inc.
200 Madison Avenue
New York, NY 10016

ISBN 0-505-52600-X

The name "Love Spell" and its logo are trademarks of Dorchester Publishing Co., Inc.

Printed in the United States of America.

I want to dedicate this book to my family, whose ongoing tolerance for dust bunnies makes it possible for me to write.

I also want to thank my critique partners Kathryn Kelly, Barbara Phinney, Lina Gardiner, Dorothy Shepard, Carol Schede and Janelle Burnham-Schneider, all of whom helped me become a better writer. A special thanks to Deborah Hale for sharing her wisdom, Julianne MacLean for being such a champion of my work, and Julianne's M.D. husband Stephen for his medical expertise.

LAUREN'S EYES

Chapter One

She ignored the first tingle. After all, she'd been bent over the operating table for what felt like hours.

Then the second hot shard of sensation shot up her neck. Her hands stilled over the tabby whose abdominal incision she was closing. *Please, not here. Not now.*

Her prayer went unheeded. In the time it took to form the plea, she felt her scalp prickle. Soon, a shower of stars would appear in the periphery of her vision, narrowing it to a tunnel, and the tingling in her scalp would expand to a band of pain.

"Lauren, is something wrong?"

Lauren Townsend glanced at her assistant, Heather Carr. "Migraine," she lied. She gestured at the patient on the table. "This'll have to be the last one tonight. Why don't you break the news to the waiting room while I finish up?"

Heather grimaced. "They won't like it."

No, they wouldn't, but it was elective stuff. "Tell them I'll make it up Thursday night, for free." Already her tongue was getting thick. She'd have to be quick.

...ren finished the cat's sutures just as Heather returned.

"Riot averted," Heather announced. "Finished here?"

"Yes, thankfully."

"Gosh, Lauren, you look awful."

"Yeah, well, I don't feel so hot either." She peeled off her gloves. "Can you manage our post-op patients if I take off?"

"No problem." Heather removed the anesthetized cat's restraints and scooped its limp body up gently. "But you're not driving anywhere like that. I'll call a cab while you get cleaned up."

"Good idea." Lauren slumped against the table. "Tell them there's a good tip in it if they make it fast."

Twenty minutes later, Lauren stumbled into her house. Closing the door, she sagged against it. She'd made it. *Just.* By the time the cab had arrived, she'd been far enough gone to mildly alarm Heather. Her assistant had joked that Lauren should direct the driver to the ER instead of her house in this Halifax suburb.

But she didn't need a doctor. She just needed to lie down.

Rubbing damp palms on her khakis, Lauren pushed herself away from the door. Her legs felt shaky, but they carried her to her bedroom. Heart pounding, she crawled onto the bed to wait. *Deep breaths,* she told herself as the paralysis stole into her limbs. *You're okay.*

Yeah, right.

Abruptly, her vision went completely black. For a terrifying moment, the sound of her own harsh breathing was Lauren's only anchor in utter, lonely darkness. Then a vision exploded on her consciousness.

A blond woman dressed in Western wear stood on a ridge top, staring out across a canyon. In the background, the sun brushed the horizon, staining the sky pink. A lovely woman against a lovely backdrop. But Lauren had seen this silent picture before.

Watch carefully. Check the background this time.

She forced herself to see past the woman. Mountains rose against the sky, blue smudges in the distance. Over the woman's shoulder, Lauren noted four peaks, which aligned themselves like bumps on a dragon's back. *That's good. You can remember that.*

If only she could turn and scan the area. But she couldn't. She saw only what *he* saw, condemned to watch through his eyes.

Then the woman turned. She was even more beautiful than Lauren remembered. Her green eyes radiated a sultry welcome, an assurance in her own sex appeal that Lauren couldn't begin to imagine. Then the woman's lips moved as she mouthed a greeting.

She's not talking to you, Lauren reminded herself.

Helpless, Lauren watched gloved hands rise into her line of sight, one on either side, as though they were her own. *No, please,* she begged. But it was no use. She longed to close her eyes, flinch away, but she couldn't. The man's hands skimmed up the woman's arms, then closed suddenly over her throat. The sensual welcome on the blonde's face turned to surprise, then panic, then sheer terror.

As the woman fought for her life, Lauren fought to distance herself. Fought and lost. With her pulse pounding, she watched the life squeezed out of the beautiful stranger. Watched it up close and personal, as though the murderer's hands were Lauren's own.

Then it was over. As always, the link began deteriorating immediately, but this time Lauren clung to it. She ignored the shut-down signals from her battered mind and held on. *Show me something!* she screamed silently. He did.

Drawing a pack of cigarettes from his pocket, the man calmly pulled one out. Slowly, as though he hadn't just committed a murder, he produced a book of matches. Lauren shook, but the killer's work-gloved hands were steady as he lit his cigarette. Steady enough that Lauren had plenty of time to read the logo on the matches.

Foothills Guest Ranch.

Then he tossed the matches to the ground and turned away.

She let go then, exhausted, and started the slow climb back. Periodically, she tested her limbs until at last they obeyed. Stumbling to her office, she flicked on the computer. Anxiety gnawed at her as she waited for it to boot and for the modem to connect. Another delay while the search engine loaded. Finally, she plugged in "Foothills Guest Ranch" and almost sobbed her relief when she struck pay dirt on the first try.

Foothills Guest Ranch, Borland, Alberta. The logo was a stylized mustang over the ranch's name in black "wanted poster" lettering. It was exactly the same as the one on the book of matches. For the first time since the visions had begun, Lauren felt a stir of hope. Maybe she could do something this time.

But it was just a book of matches. There was no guarantee the murder would happen anywhere near the Foothills Guest Ranch. There was no telling how far those matches might have migrated, although the rugged country she'd glimpsed in the background couldn't be anything other than the foothills of the Rocky Mountains, could it?

Her meager hope fizzled again as another thought struck her. Though she made the season out to be high summer, who was to say it would be *this* summer? What if the murder wasn't destined to take place for years? What if she were doomed to living this horror for another year? She shuddered. It didn't bear thinking about.

No, she had to act, and act now. She wouldn't wait around until she read about the crime in the *Globe and Mail*. Not this time. Nor could she go to the police. Not after that nightmare with the DiGiacinto girl. Not only had Lauren failed to prevent the runaway's death, she'd found herself the main suspect. When she tried to warn the police, they'd dismissed her as a crank until the teen's body showed up in a Dumpster down by the docks.

Quickly, before doubt could set in, she registered at the Foothills Guest Ranch for an open-ended stay, starting next week. "You won't get her," Lauren vowed, then shivered as a faint echo of evil reverberated in her mind.

"Smile, Boss. Here comes another busload of wranglers."

Cal Taggart scowled at his foreman, Jim Mallory. "Would-be-wranglers, you mean. Hell, I wish there was another way outta this mess. I'm not cut out for this, Jim."

"It's not such a bad bargain, I don't reckon, long as you can hang on to the ranch. Whatever it takes, right?"

Cal grimaced as Jim threw his own words back at him. "Right." *Whatever it takes.* That was his credo, sure enough. Whatever it took to amass thousands of acres of prime ranch land. Whatever it took to secure the best breeding stock. And now, whatever it took to keep the whole damned shooting match from falling into the clutches of the bank.

"Whatever it took" these days meant throwing his back into making this guest ranch a success. If it took off, the profits would help Cal's cattle ranch through this downturn.

Downturn, hell. He'd had the worst run of misfortune of his life this summer. A grass fire in June claimed three

Norah Wilson

head, although in truth he counted himself lucky. It might
have destroyed his entire herd if he hadn't caught it in
time. Then what must have been lightning strikes claimed
a few more cattle.

But in the scheme of things, those were just aggrava-
tions. The real problem was that farm incomes had hit
their lowest point since the Depression. Foreign subsidies,
low commodity prices—if it weren't for the tourists he'd
have probably gone under.

As the two men pondered the price of survival, the first
of the passengers clambered off the bus.

"I'll handle this, Boss." With a grunt, Jim pushed his
arthritic frame off the fence.

"Stay put, Jimbo. I'll see to it." Cal tugged the brim of
his hat down and strode across the drought-scorched grass
toward the bus. Jim was the best wrangler he'd ever ridden with. Asking him to babysit tenderfooted adventure-
seekers on tame trail rides was bad enough. He'd not see
his friend reduced to the equivalent of Wal-Mart greeter.

No, that distinction he reserved for himself.

Dust rose from her sandals as Lauren stepped off the bus
into the punishing August sun. The black sun dress she'd
thought so perfect for traveling sucked up the sun's heat.
Her hands came up to shade her eyes despite the sunglasses she wore. She was definitely going to need more
protection. Back home in Nova Scotia, she'd have worn a
sun hat to protect her face, but she'd left it behind. Nothing short of a Stetson was likely to cut it here.

She glanced at the man making his way down the line,
greeting guests. Now, there was a working hat. Battered
and dusty, it looked custom-molded for its owner, a compact man who moved with what she imagined to be a typ-
ical cowboy cockiness.

Except he didn't really look much like a cowboy, Lauren realized. Shave off a few years, lose the hat, and she could picture him in a leather jacket, cigarette dangling James Dean–like from his mouth. Maybe he'd be astride a motorcycle.

She focused on his face. All planes and angles, it looked as though it might have been carved from the rock that rose in the distance. What would it feel like under her palm? The thought came out of nowhere, as did the answer. *Hard, but warm.*

Suddenly he was there, offering his hand. "Welcome to Foothills, ma'am. I hope you enjoy your stay."

"Thank you." As his big hand enfolded hers, she noticed his eyes. Sensual, hooded, they gleamed a silvery gray, like her beloved Atlantic Ocean under overcast skies.

They also gleamed with something else, she realized with another small jolt. Masculine interest.

Suddenly, she wished for her lab coat and trousers. The professional costume usually precluded this kind of thing. Not that she minded a little male appreciation. But from this cowboy, it made her unaccountably nervous. Maybe because she felt an answering twinge, a twinge she couldn't afford to indulge. She hadn't crossed a continent to flirt with a cowboy. She had one purpose here, and one only.

Turning toward the growing mountain of luggage, she dragged her duffel bag and overnight case from the pile. A hand closed over hers on the duffel bag's handle.

"Let me help you with that."

Damn. The gravel-voiced cowboy. "I can manage, thanks."

"Allow me. You're really not dressed for it."

"I've got it, thanks."

7

At her tone, he released his grasp. "Ma'am." He tipped his hat, the barest suggestion of amusement flickering in those gray eyes. Then he was gone, helping a family of five drag their luggage from the pile.

Check-in, handled by a capable middle-aged woman, went smoothly. Another employee, a handsome young man of maybe nineteen or twenty, showed Lauren to her cabin. It was a fair distance from the lodge, and he insisted on carrying her bags. Not wanting to puncture his youthful machismo, she allowed it.

En route, they encountered the cowboy, who looked pointedly from Lauren's empty hands to the overburdened Brad Pitt wannabe. She shrugged, averting her flaming face. After she'd turned down his help only to accept it from this handsome youth, he had no doubt concluded the worst.

A moment later, her young escort left her at her cabin. It was tiny, nothing more than a small kitchenette, a single bedroom and a tiny bathroom. The bath, she noted with relief, was modern. Equally pleasing was the sunny bedroom, its double bed draped with a hand-sewn quilt. On a scarred dresser, a bouquet of wildflowers trembled in the breeze from the open window. She fingered the blooms, inhaling their sweet scent. Prairie mallow and some fragrant purple thing.

Lauren crossed to the bed and stretched out on it, testing the firmness of the mattress. Exhaustion tugged at her. She'd have loved to pull the colorful coverlet over her shoulders, but she couldn't. If she succumbed to sleep now, she'd be dead to the world until tomorrow, and that wouldn't help. She had a job to do.

She'd pumped the young man who'd shown her to the cabin for information. The best way to meet other folks, Brady had said, was to take meals in the ranch house's dining room. Sooner or later, all the guests turned up there. Groaning, she rolled off the bed and hit the shower.

When she walked into the dining room an hour later, she was among the first of the diners. She picked a table by the door so she could keep an eye on the comings and goings.

Dinner was buffet-style. The dueling aromas of beef and freshly baked bread tantalizing her, Lauren strolled over to the big table. She could only gape at the volume and variety of food. Hip of beef, baked potatoes, molasses-baked beans, garden salads . . . After six or seven dishes, she stopped counting. And carving the beef, a white chef's hat on her head, was the same round-faced woman who'd handled the registrations.

"You sure get around," Lauren said.

The other woman smiled. " 'Round here, nobody has just one job."

"And what are yours?"

"Registration desk, cook, and housekeeper." She poked the beef with the tines of her fork. "How do you take your beef?"

"Medium." Lauren's mouth watered. "It looks wonderful."

"It *is* wonderful."

At the masculine voice, she turned to find the cowboy, minus his hat and with plate in hand.

"It's our specialty," he continued as the cook handed Lauren back her plate, which now bore a sizeable hunk of meat. "Rolled and aged before being cooked in a big ol' barbecue oven. Nobody does it like Delia." He winked at the cook.

"Go 'way with you." The older woman blushed to the roots of her red hair.

He grinned at Delia. "Not without some of that beef."

9

Lauren almost dropped her plate. He'd smiled when he greeted the tour group, but it hadn't changed his face like this. Good thing, because she might have melted into an embarrassing puddle.

"I've got just the piece for you, Boss. It still moos when you poke it."

Boss? This hard-edged cowboy was the proprietor? Lauren watched as the woman forked a slab of rare beef onto his plate. She should have figured it, out. He did exude an undeniable air of authority. Not conventional authority—she'd bet he didn't have much use for that. More like an aura of confidence that came from competence.

She'd bet, too, that he harbored a wide streak of cynicism. It was there in the set of his mouth, as attractive as it was. Yes, his character was certainly set in his bones. High, intelligent forehead, strong cheekbones, stubborn chin. What in God's name drew a man like this to the hospitality industry?

He cleared his throat, and she realized he was waiting for her to move on. She'd been standing there studying his face as though it held the key to some ancient secret.

"Oops, sorry. Woolgathering." She smiled, then moved on leisurely. No small feat when she felt like bolting. As it was, she felt a flush climb her neck as she added food to her plate. Skipping dessert, she escaped to her table.

She'd barely regained her composure when a pair of pointed boots stepped into her downcast vision. *Wonderful.* She didn't need to make the journey up his spare frame to know it was him.

"Mind if I join you?"

Did she mind eating her meal with him watching her through those hooded eyes? Absolutely. "Not at all."

He drew up a chair. "Cal Taggart."

10

"Lauren Townsend."

"So, did I pass inspection back there?"

Of course, he would mention it. She refused to be embarrassed at being discovered. And if she played it right, he'd be the one blushing.

"I don't know yet." Her gaze swept his torso visible above the table. "I didn't get past the face."

A glint in those gray eyes was his only reaction. "And how'd the face rate?"

She pursed her lips, tilted her head consideringly. "Too strong, but good around the eyes."

He raised an eyebrow. "You an artist or something?"

"Or something."

He smiled the same smile that jerked at her senses when he'd used it on Delia. *Good around the mouth, too.*

"So, do I get a turn?"

She sipped her water. "I guess it would only be fair."

He studied her. "Good hair, good bones, good diction." His gaze fixed on her eyes. "Proper East Coast lady."

His assessment stung slightly. She let her lips part on a smile. "Boring, you mean."

He shrugged, reaching for his own water goblet. "Could be, I suppose, if I believed it."

She arched an eyebrow. "And you don't?"

She waited while he chewed an ice cube. "Mouth makes a lie of the rest of it."

Her pulse leapt. "Maybe it's the mouth that lies."

He made no remark, just watched her with those steady eyes. She suppressed the urge to swallow.

"To faces, then," She raised her water goblet.

He clinked her glass in a salute. "To faces."

"Okay, now that the obligatory bantering is out of the way," she said, conscious of her proper East Coast diction, "can I ask you some questions about the ranch?"

11

Something flickered in his eyes. "Sure. What would you like to know?"

For the next half hour, as they ate, she questioned him about his operation. How many guests could he accommodate? How many were currently registered? How often did new guests arrive? Did most of them come on the shuttle bus from Calgary, or did they just drive up? What about customer demographics? Mostly men, or did he get lots of women too?

But talking about business, and by extension himself, didn't seem to be Cal Taggart's favorite pastime. His answers grew progressively shorter until he clumped his coffee cup down.

"Ms. Townsend, if you're looking to start your own ranch, you'd be better off pickin' someone else's brains. There are plenty of more established, more successful outfits in these parts."

"Oh, no! I have no desire to get into the business."

"Then why the twenty questions?"

What to say? *I'm conducting a homicide investigation—before the fact?* Lauren licked suddenly dry lips, searching for inspiration. Then the solution came to her.

"I'm a writer," she lied. "My publisher thought it would be a great idea to set my next book on a guest ranch," she said, warming to the idea. "It's research of a sort."

"A writer?" He sat back in his chair and wiped his mouth with a napkin. "Should I know you, then?"

Yikes! She'd as much as said she was published, hadn't she? "Oh, I don't think so."

"Despite my too-strong face, I have been known to read the occasional book."

"Not these books."

There was that eyebrow again. "And what kind is that?"

She searched her brain feverishly for something. Romance? No, too risky. Just her luck he'd have a mother or a sister who was an avid fan of the genre. Then inspiration struck. With a perfectly straight face, she said, "Female erotica."

Chapter Two

Cal double-checked the saddle on the small mare, then gave the paint a reassuring scratch on the shoulder.

Female erotica. The words might as well be etched in neon in the forefront of his mind. He shook them away again, along with the image of Lauren Townsend's cool blue eyes skimming him. *Concentrate.* A riding clinic was no place to let his mind drift.

"Okay, pal, let's get you up there," he said to the kid at his elbow. Despite his fear, the boy followed Cal's bidding. A moment later, the kid sat astride the mare, beaming. This was a part of the job Cal actually liked. If things had been different with his marriage, he might have had his own child to teach. . . .

Dammit, he was wandering again. Snapping back to the task, he showed the boy the basic commands, then watched him practice.

Out of the corner of his eye, Cal caught a glimpse of Lauren, who'd landed in a brush-up clinic. One of his wranglers was helping her mount her horse, a dun gelding. Help she didn't particularly need, he decided, as he watched her spring into the saddle. But when she tried to bring the side-stepping gelding back in line, it veered off in the other direction. The harder she tried to correct him, the more the horse danced off.

Cal stepped forward and grabbed the dun's reins. "Whoa, Buck." He glanced up at Lauren. "Having trouble?"

"What was your first clue?" A blush stained her face.

"I think I know your problem." He eyed the English riding boots that hugged her calves. A bit of a style clash with the white Stetson they handed out to all their guests, but nice.

"Do tell."

He liked looking at her from her imperious position atop the horse, he decided. He had to blink back a sudden image of Lauren wearing those black riding boots and little else. Was that the kind of stuff she wrote about? Probably not. Something told him the fantasy he'd just had was a distinctly male one.

"So what am I doing wrong, Einstein?"

"You're used to English-trained horses, am I right?"

"Of course! That's why he won't move toward my hand."

"Exactly. They're all Western-trained. They respond to the touch of the rein against the neck, not the pull of the bit in the mouth. Try it," he urged, releasing the bridle. "Touch the rein to the right side of his neck, and he'll turn left."

She did, clearly pleased when her mount obeyed. "It feels so strange." She wheeled Buck again. "What about the legs?"

Yes, what about them? Yesterday, it had been her face he couldn't drag his gaze from. Cool blue eyes and that generous lower lip she kept so primly compressed. But since he'd seen her mount the horse, he couldn't stop thinking how her slender legs would feel wrapped around him.

"He'll move away from the leg," he croaked.

Damn, why did she have to tell him she wrote erotica? That must be why he couldn't get sex out of his mind.

"Good, that's the same as English."

She seemed oblivious of the carnal nature of his thoughts. He tipped his hat back. "Since you don't need any more lessons, I'm gonna move on to the folks who do."

Lauren was glad to see Cal go. Now she could use her energy to block the almost overwhelming vibrations coming off of Buck. Though she did appreciate Cal's help straightening out the cues. She'd felt the horse's swelling confusion recede immediately.

She'd been five when she realized other people didn't tune into animals the way she did. She'd remarked to her mother how funny it was that their lazy cat had such quick thoughts, like darting beetles. Her mother had explained it was impossible to know what a cat's thoughts were like. When Lauren persisted, her mother had grown annoyed. After that, she kept it to herself.

Not quite thought, not quite emotion, it was something of both. *Vibrations*. She picked them up from all animals to some degree, but never as strongly as when she sat astride a horse.

Which was why she hadn't been able to jump horses like the other girls in her family's social sphere. Riding was fine, but she'd been expected to graduate to eventing, and she couldn't cope with the horse's fear at being cajoled into jumping flashy rails or sparkling water. To Lauren's relief, her disappointed parents had turned their attentions to her more socially promising sister.

Though she'd never breathed a word of her "gift," it was the reason she'd gone into veterinary medicine. Thankfully, everyone, including her assistant Heather, accepted that she had extraordinary instincts. The visions were enough to brand her a freak; she didn't need to be dubbed some kind of Dr. Dolittle.

Too bad her talent didn't extend to humans. She chewed her lip as anxiety churned in her gut. She'd feel a whole lot better about her chances if she could pick up on the killer's thoughts. Unfortunately, people were as impenetrable as lumps of lead.

Beneath her, Buck's eagerness surged. Man, she hoped she'd get used to all this sentience under her, because it looked as if she was going be spending a lot of time in the saddle.

Her best bet to meet everyone, she'd decided, was to go along on the trail rides. She'd discovered last night that she couldn't hang around the dining room until every guest had come and gone. She'd be stuck there for hours at every meal. Besides being unbearably boring, it would arouse notice. Although it looked as though today would be a bust. The woman she was looking for, the potential murder victim, was nowhere in the group.

Finally, the trail ride started. Cal and the other cowboys—wranglers, he'd called them—marshaled the group out of the paddock and across the meadow. She felt a rush from Buck, but checked him, wanting to hang back in case new riders joined them.

An hour later, Lauren was among the last of the riders to emerge from a narrow, well-traveled pass onto a grassy ridge top. Not until the riders fanned out again did she get a look at the spectacular view they'd been promised. She gasped aloud.

Foothills rose in the distance, glorious against the magenta sky. And four of them huddled on the horizon like the ridged back of a sleeping dragon. *This was it.*

Clumsy in her haste, she dismounted and led Buck

closer to the lip of the canyon, her stomach churning. She knew she should be relieved—was relieved—that she'd found the spot so quickly, but standing here brought the horror home anew.

"Scared of heights?"

Lauren whirled to find Cal Taggart behind her. "No," she denied, pressing a hand to her thundering heart.

"You don't look too thrilled with the view."

"Oh, no, it's beautiful. Really." Then, because he looked skeptical, she said, "Well, maybe I am a bit scared of heights."

"Not too scared, I hope," he drawled. "Sunset Ridge is our nightly destination. You'll be seeing a lot of it."

Tipping his hat, he moved off to caution the others about staying a safe distance from the cliff's edge. Lauren let her breath escape. If they'd be riding out here often, she'd better get used to it. Tethering her horse, she joined the group.

Twenty minutes later, they started home in the gathering dusk. As soon as they cleared the pass and started descending the ridge, Lauren felt her anxiety ease. But no sooner did she relax than another wave of agitation assaulted her. Cal, atop a dancing chestnut mare, fell in beside her.

"So how does Buck suit you?"

"Oh, we'll get along fine, I think. He's very patient."

"Yeah, they have to be pros in this business," he said.

She cast him a sidelong glance, and caught her breath. Oh, but he sat a horse nicely. He looked weightless, settled in the dip of the saddle, his back erect but loose. So natural, he could be an extension of the horse. She'd been a good horsewoman herself, at least in her teens, but nothing like Cal. She closed her eyes and felt for that same harmony, letting her shoulders drop to take the stiffness

18

out of her straight-backed posture. Buck brightened immediately with gratitude, which made her smile.

"I was thinking, maybe you'd like a livelier mount, since you're obviously a skilled rider."

She glanced at him sharply. The fact that he'd paid her a compliment was quickly lost at the thought of a more forceful mount under her. Physically, she knew she could handle a stronger-willed animal, but the thought of trying to filter its psychic vibrations intimidated the heck out of her.

"Thank you, no. I think I'll stick with slow and steady."

His hooded eyes suddenly took on a sleepy, sensual look. "That's a sensible decision, ma'am. But if you should get a yen for fast and wild, just give me a shout."

Before Lauren could react, Cal urged his mount into a gallop. He was a quarter mile away before she thought to close her mouth. Despite herself, a thrill forked through her. There was something about his brand of swagger that worked, dammit. Especially after glimpsing that heated look in his eyes.

She chewed the inside of her lip. Too bad she wasn't here for a genuine holiday adventure. She had no doubt the maverick cowboy could provide it, if she had the courage to take him on. Which she didn't. She had neither the tools nor the experience.

Besides, she had a job to do. She couldn't afford to be sidetracked.

Cal firmly believed that anyone who presumed to ride a horse ought to be made to care for it. Which was why trail rides ended with the guests grooming their mounts. Fortunately, most guests enjoyed the ritual. Today, with this new group, he demonstrated the basics on his horse, Sienna. Afterward, he made the rounds, showing each rider how to signal the horse to raise a foot, how to cradle it, and how to clean it with a hoof pick.

When he reached Lauren, she was expertly wielding the pick on Buck's hind right hoof. "Looks like you've done this before."

She glanced up at him, then back to the task. "Yeah, I've done my share, I guess."

She dropped Buck's hoof and stood, pressing a hand to her lower back as though to ease an ache. A jolt went through him as he imagined his own hands on her, kneading the small pain away.

Damn, what was it about her that drew his eye? She was tall, but not underfed like so many of the stick women who came through here these days. Yet she didn't have the hourglass figure he usually went for. Her hips were narrow, her breasts small. Even her hair, black as a raven's wing, was cropped short. She should have looked boyish. Instead, she exuded an athletic femininity that excited him.

She'd be a good match for him when he finally convinced her to lie down with him.

The thought was just there, hardening into resolution. And persuading her shouldn't be too difficult, judging by the way she caught her breath at his frank appraisal.

"He likes the currying," she said with a breathless quality that made Cal smile, "but he truly appreciates getting his feet cleaned. He could hardly wait for me to get to them."

He could hardly wait? She sounded like some kind of cross between an animal mind reader and a horse aesthetician, he thought. "Buck tell you that himself, did he?"

She colored. "It just makes sense. It'd be like us not being able to clean under our nails after digging in the dirt."

20

The analogy made him grimace. He wished he had a reason to prolong the conversation, but she'd finished with Buck, and he had grooms-in-the-making who needed supervision.

"If you're finished, just hand him over to Brady."

Did he imagine it, or did she brighten when he gestured toward Brady? An ugly emotion knifed his gut, bringing him up short. Jealousy. When had he last felt its acid burn? Not since Marlena. And not for long, even then. Anything he'd felt for her died a quick death in the face of her infidelities.

To experience jealousy in this situation, to place himself in competition with a kid half his age . . . well, it was ridiculous. Sure, Brady had that Hollywood face, but he was just a boy.

No competition, Cal decided as he moved on to the next guest.

Unless, of course, she preferred boys.

Lauren cursed inwardly as she handed the reins over to Brady. The last thing she wanted was to draw attention to herself and her unusual gifts. She had the feeling that if the killer really noticed her, he'd *know* her. Just as she prayed she'd know him. The man had been in her head. Surely she'd sense him.

But when she'd spied Cal's hungry look, she'd said the first thing that came to her.

Yes, she'd have to keep her lip zipped and give that cowboy with the hot promise in his eyes a wide berth.

Crushing down an appalling and unwarranted disappointment, she headed toward her cabin to soak her sore muscles.

* * *

For the next four days, Lauren managed to keep to her resolution to steer clear of Cal. Of course it helped that he wasn't there. He'd taken an all-male group on a wilderness pack ride. Instead she pumped Delia for information, ignoring any guilt she might have for abusing the woman's trusting nature.

And each day, Lauren joined the shorter trail rides, searching for the blond woman from her vision. By Friday, she had a sore backside, but she was afraid if she begged off a single ride, she'd miss her only opportunity to save the woman's life. On the up side, Sunset Ridge no longer made her so dizzy with anxiety.

Then Cal returned. Stupidly, her spirits lifted, though she was still determined to avoid him. He let her hide among the other riders for two more days, but the glint in his eye told her he knew she was ducking him.

Today, however, she couldn't dodge him. This ride was an overnighter, though nothing like the sleeping-under-the-stars pack ride Cal had taken the macho-types on. By comparison, this trip offered the height of luxury. They would ride all morning, stop for lunch, then press on to an old cabin where they would overnight with real beds and, thanks to propane, lights and hot water. Still, she suspected the number of takers would be small.

She was right. When she reported to the paddock with her canteen and binoculars, there was no one there but Cal. Lounging against the fence, one booted foot hooked on the bottom rail, hat brim pulled low on his brow, he looked all cowboy.

Lauren blinked. "What? Am I early?"

"No, you're right on time."

Her pulse leapt. "We're it? Just you and me?"

"Does that bother you?"

Damn right, it bothered her. And excited her, too. "Of course not. But it's hardly a good use of your time, is it?"

"Depends how you define good."

She wasn't going to touch that one. "But I'm just one guest. If no one else is interested, we should forgo it. The wants and needs of the majority should rule, after all."

He dropped his foot and pushed away from the fence, moving closer to her. She resisted the urge to step back.

"Ah, but we're concerned about the wants of all our guests."

His eyes held a mocking light, which fascinated her more than the blatant sexual innuendo. For the first time, it occurred to her that the derision she'd glimpsed in him from time to time might be directed as much at himself as his patrons.

"You don't like this gig much, do you?"

Barely moving a muscle, his face turned expressionless. "Believe me, I take this gig very seriously. I put all my energy into it, and nothing will stop me from making it a success."

"I didn't question your commitment to it," she pointed out tartly. "I asked you if you liked it."

"And I gave you the only answer you're likely to get. Now, it's your turn to give me an answer. Do we go or stay?"

Lauren was about to utter an emphatic, "Stay," when Cal cursed. Following his gaze, Lauren found herself watching a woman approaching them.

It was her. The blonde.

More beautiful than she'd been in the visions, the woman projected raw sex appeal as she led a sorrel mare across the paddock. The mare was saddled, Lauren noted. She also noted that the usually self-possessed Brady, who followed closely behind the woman, wore the look of a deer caught in headlights.

"Hell, Marlena, go back to bed. It's too early for this."

Instead of shrinking from Cal's tone, Marlena just laughed. "Don't worry, Cal, honey. I haven't come to play with *you.*"

Her voice was husky, a good match for that killer body.

"I'm relieved to hear it. I offered you shelter, not entertainment."

At his words, Lauren swivelled to look at Cal. If he was tense, he didn't betray it, except perhaps for a little stiffness in his shoulders.

"The least a husband could do, I would think."

Husband? Cal was married? To the victim in her vision?

"*Ex*-husband."

"Whatever." Marlena shrugged, as though her exact status were of no import. "But I don't expect you to entertain me, sugar. I'm quite capable of finding my own diversions."

"Don't I know it."

This time, his clipped words seemed to find their mark. For a fleeting moment, she looked hurt. Then she was smiling that knowing smile again. "Brady here is going to keep me company."

Cal cast a glance in Brady's direction. "That a fact?"

"It's my day off," said Brady, blushing.

Cal shrugged. "Your funeral." Turning his back on Marlena, he pinned Lauren with a fierce look. "You coming or staying?"

Dear Lord, she didn't want to go anywhere with this volatile triangle of people, let alone into the bush, overnight. In just these few short minutes, the emotion roiling among the three had caused a hard knot of anxiety to form in Lauren's stomach. Which was precisely why she couldn't stay behind. If she were looking for a motive for murder, she'd found one. An ancient one.

Not to mention two suspects.

Lauren took a deep breath. "I'm coming."

Chapter Three

Beneath Lauren, Buck swayed gently. The soft drone of insects filled the air. Brady and Marlena rode a few dozen yards ahead of her, and Lauren could hear Cal following behind. Above them, the sky was a cloudless blue dome.

Eventually, the hot meadow scents gave way to secret wood smells as they moved through a copse of trees. Then, with a creak of leather, Cal pulled abreast her. *So much for peacefulness.*

"How's your backside holding out?"

Lauren grimaced. "A little numb."

"Well, you'll get to rest it before too long. Dinner'll be waiting for us on the other side of this little stand of trees."

They rode in silence. Lauren tried to recapture some serenity of mind, but was too conscious of the man beside her. His hands on the reins looked hard and capable, and the sleeves of his shirt were rolled up to reveal tanned forearms. Very nice forearms, with a shimmer of blond hairs. Did those blond hairs match the rest of his body hair, or were they merely bleached from the sun? Her stomach clutched with excitement.

Then another thought occurred to her, making her stomach clench for an entirely different reason. In her vision, there'd been a band of dark skin between rolled-up sleeves and the top of the work gloves. What color had the hairs on those arms been?

"So what changed your mind?"

She blinked. "Sorry?"

"About coming out after all."

Lauren glanced over at him, but he was gazing straight ahead. "Well, I'm not the only customer anymore, am I? It's not like I was dragging you out here for my sole entertainment."

He snorted. "You mean Marlena? She's no customer. And she'd have been happy enough to ride out alone with Brady."

"Really?" She feigned surprise.

The look he sent her was skeptical. "Yes, really. As I'm sure you picked up, Marlena is my ex wife. She knows these trails well enough to ride 'em alone. And you probably also gathered that she plans to screw young Brady cross-eyed."

"Cal!"

"You mean you missed that little nuance? I'd have thought you'd pick up on that stuff, considering your line of work."

"It's none of my business."

"And none of mine, for that matter, but if you're going to be here any length of time, Marlena's . . . adventures . . . are bound to be in your face, like it or not." His upper lip curled. "My ex-wife's sense of discretion is not very highly developed."

"I'm sorry." Was that what his marriage had been like? Had he suffered the humiliation of a wandering wife?

Because Lauren needed to gauge him as the potential

murderer, and maybe, if she were honest, because she couldn't help herself, she asked, "Did she . . . I mean, is that why . . . ?"

Cal stopped, and Lauren reined in her own mount. His face was hard, his eyes flinty. "Is that why I divorced her, you mean? 'Cause she spread it around?"

She resisted the urge to squirm in the saddle. She'd asked, after all. "I wouldn't have put it so crudely, but yes."

His mouth was a grim slash. "Yeah, that's why."

Now that they'd stopped, she could see the stiffness in him. Out of nowhere, she felt the urge to touch his face, to soothe away the lines of tension. She fisted her hands on the reins instead.

"Marlena's a spoiled child when it comes to men. They're like surprise packages she can't keep from unwrapping."

"I'm sorry," she repeated.

"So was Marlena, or so she said, but it didn't stop her. There was always a next time. She wasn't really sorry until I packed her bags and drove her to the bus station."

Lauren studied his bleak profile. So, he'd been cheated on more than once. She wouldn't have thought him the type to be so . . . forbearing.

He must have loved her very much.

Or not at all.

"Why'd you let her come back?" Lauren held her breath, hoping he wouldn't clam up now, hardly believing he'd said this much.

He shrugged. "She's got trouble, needs a place to stay."

"And she felt she'd be safe with you?"

He shot her a glance. "Safe as a woman like Marlena can be. Safer than in Calgary, with a bone-breaker on her trail."

"Bone-breaker?"

"Loan shark's thug. Seems like she breezed through the fifty large I settled on her a trifle faster than expected."

Lauren's jaw dropped. "You gave her fifty thousand dollars after what she did?"

Cal lifted an eyebrow. "Considering the value of this ranch, I got away lightly. Though that little outlay could still cost me the ranch if beef prices don't stabilize." He lifted his hat and mopped his brow with the sleeve of his shirt, then replaced the hat. "What say we pick it up, Lauren? I'm starved."

Just like that, the subject was closed. She'd been lucky to get that much out of him, but there was so much more she wanted to know. Was he in this racket strictly to save his cattle operation? Did he blame his ex-wife for his predicament? But she was loathe to push. Cal was the last guy she wanted getting wary. Right now, he was looking pretty good as a suspect—a suspect who made her knees go weak just because he'd said her name for the first time in that raspy voice.

"Yeah, let's go," she said, urging Buck forward.

Cal cursed silently as he trailed the small procession. Whiskey and women. He didn't know which was worse. They could both loosen a man's tongue and make a fool out of him. He'd certainly made a fool of himself with Lauren. Looking into those blue eyes, he'd told her the whole sordid story of his lousy marriage. For the life of him, he still didn't know why.

Not for sympathy, that was for damn sure. It had taken a long time before people stopped looking at him with that infuriating mute pity. He never wanted to see it again.

So why had he spilled his guts?

Because you want to know her, he answered himself. *Because you want her to know you.*

29

"Jesus," he breathed. For a moment, the idea scared him spitless. Then he remembered what he really wanted—to get into those sexy jeans—and relaxed. Yeah, that was it. That's why he'd told her all that stuff. Women liked that stuff, right?

Hell, who was he kidding? What did he know about women like Lauren? His experience had been gleaned from rodeo groupies. All they'd cared about—besides how long he could last on a twisting ton of malevolent animal—was how long he could last between the sheets. Mind you, that had been enough for him. Hell, he'd gone and married a rodeo Annie, hadn't he?

Brady's shout brought Cal's head up. He scanned the terrain ahead as it sloped to the valley floor. He spotted the problem immediately. Marlena was hurtling down the ridge, pushing her mount recklessly. Exultant laughter rose up to goad him.

"Dammit, Marlena!" At his command, Sienna sprang forward. Lauren's face was a blur as he raced past her. Reaching the steepest part of the slope, he eased up, letting Sienna pick her path. The mare hardly slowed.

He caught Marlena a minute later. Snatching the sorrel's reins, he brought both horses to a dust-churning halt. He was so angry that his sides heaved almost as deeply as the horses'. Marlena glowed with excitement, but her mount's eyes rolled.

Seeing red, Cal gripped one of her wrists. "What the hell do you think you're doing?"

"What's it look like I was doing?"

"It looked like you were trying to kill yourself. Which is fine by me, as long as you don't drag my horse into it."

"Cool down, Cal. I was just having some fun."

"Find something else to amuse you." Jesus, she was a piece of work. Her erratic behavior had only gotten worse over time. He dropped her wrist before the desire to squeeze it harshly got the better of him.

Scowling, Marlena rubbed her wrist. "What's your problem? These mustangs are as sure-footed as goats, and you know it."

"Yeah, and I'd like to keep 'em that way. That was just plain stupid." Behind him, he heard Brady and Lauren ride up. "You will not endanger one of my horses again. Got it?"

Marlena glowered back at him. There was a time when all that temper would have turned him on. Now it left him stone cold. "I mean it, Marlena. Push that mare again, and you'll walk home."

"You wouldn't do that!"

"So help me God, I'd like to do a lot worse, so don't push me." He turned to Brady. "Take the lead, kid."

"Sorry, boss."

"Not your fault."

Brady responded with alacrity. After a last baleful look, Marlena fell in behind him. Lauren, however, made no move. She just sat there in the saddle, looking at Cal.

"You coming?" he growled.

Her answer was to urge Buck after Marlena. Taking a deep breath, he took up the rear again. This could be a long trip.

To Lauren's relief, the rest of the ride was quiet. They reached the log cabin by late afternoon. Nestled at the base of a scrub-dotted slope, the structure looked as though it had been there forever. In fact, according to Cal, it was some seventy years old. Its age certainly showed, but it had been carefully tended.

Marlena made herself at home immediately, dragging ready-made sandwiches and cold salads out of the refrigerator. The four of them sat at the kitchen table and devoured the food. As Lauren polished off her sandwich, it struck her that it was little wonder Marlena seemed so at home. She and Cal had probably laughed here, fought here, made love here.

Ignoring the way her stomach clenched, she stole a look at Cal. His face was shuttered. What was going on behind that cool expression? He glanced up then, catching her studying him.

"Can I offer you dessert?" he asked. "Delia's apple pie."

Lauren realized her appetite had fled. Not even Delia's pastry could resuscitate it. "No, thanks, but did I see a shower in the bathroom? I wouldn't mind washing the trail dust off."

"Sure, help yourself."

"What about me?" Marlena protested.

"Guests first." Cal didn't even glance sideways at Marlena.

Lauren wasted no time heading for the bathroom.

"Hey, save some hot water for me and Brady," Marlena called.

Lauren winced as she closed the door. Marlena and Brady showering together. That should go over well with Cal.

She showered in record time. The old shower head barely emitted a trickle, but it was hot. It sluiced away the dust, but couldn't touch her tension. Dressing quickly, she returned to the kitchen, only to find it deserted. For an instant, dread rose up, closing her throat. *Marlena*. Had she gone out?

She laid a hand on her chest to hold down the panic while her mind raced. The time of day was certainly right. In her vision, the sinking sun had provided an obscenely beautiful backdrop for the murder, turning the foothills into a smoky bruise on the delicate pink horizon. Had she found the victim only to lose her? How could she have been so stupid?

Lauren was on the point of rushing out into the dusk when a sound arrested her. Marlena's laugh, seductive and clear, from the front bedroom. Limp with relief, Lauren sank down at the kitchen table and sent a quick thank-you skyward.

The next moment she heard a masculine growl and a crashing sound, followed by a feminine squeal. Flushing, Lauren fled to the porch, the screen door banging shut behind her.

"At it already, are they?"

She jumped at Cal's voice, which came from the vicinity of her feet. She looked down to see him sitting on the steps.

"Never mind. I can hear for myself." He stood. "How about a walk? If we climb that ridge, sunset'll make it worthwhile."

She weighed her options.

One, she could go back inside and try not to think about the fact that Marlena might be sowing the seeds of her own demise.

Two, she could shake Cal off and leave him to brood alone to the accompaniment of the noisy lovers

Or three, she could walk with him, try to distract him, maybe even defuse the rage he must be feeling.

"Sure, I'd love a walk," she heard herself say.

Are you crazy? She tried to ignore her inner voice as she descended the steps to join him. *He could be a murderer.*

She quieted the voice with logic. While he might be capable of such extremes with the headstrong Marlena, she doubted he posed a threat to anyone else.

Wordlessly, they set off. When after a few minutes Cal still hadn't spoken, Lauren took the lead. "Tell me about these foothills."

He obliged readily enough, naming the peaks that rose in the distance. He told her how the meadow looked in spring and how the now-dry streambed could swell in a flash flood. To her relief, he wasn't the tangle of angry emotion she'd expected.

On the other hand, he had a very good poker face, she thought as they reached the top of the ridge and stopped. The streambed wound away from them far below, and the sun was a fiery ball dipping toward the horizon. "It's beautiful," she said.

"Hmmm."

She glanced at him then. Expecting to see his poker face, her heart took a bounding leap. There was nothing inscrutable about his expression just now. He was looking at her hungrily.

Suddenly, he was too close, too immediate, too tempting.

"Lauren, I think I have to kiss you. Now's the time to dodge if you don't want it."

His husky words electrified her. She should protest, *would* protest, but the seconds ticked by. In that short span, her imagination slipped its leash. Already she imagined what his lips would feel like, how they'd taste. When his hard hand cupped her face, an involuntary shiver raced up her spine, but she made no objection. Then his lips were on hers.

It wasn't what she expected. Instead of hot demand, there was testing, tasting. He shaped her lips with his, tilting his head this way and that, as though searching for the best angle. Her heart pounding, she conceded they were all good. But she wanted more. Without thought, she opened her mouth against his.

She felt him stiffen, but instead of deepening the kiss, he started to pull back. Abandoning any pretense that she didn't want this, hadn't thought about it since the first moment she'd laid eyes on him, she caught his head and really kissed him.

His mouth was dark and male and sinful. For a few seconds, she gloried in the taste of him. Then she realized he wasn't responding. For several horrifying heartbeats, he just stood there rigid, accepting the sweep of her tongue in his mouth.

Good grief, how was a girl supposed to handle that?

She was still grasping for a graceful way to extricate herself when he groaned and yanked her against him. Finally, *finally*, he kissed her the way his eyes had promised.

It was like being hauled up into the funnel of a tornado, she thought dazedly. His mouth robbed her of breath, seeming to pull the very essence from her. His hard hands flashed over her, heating her flesh and making her head spin. Fueled by equal parts relief and lust, she arched into him, welcoming him. With another deep-throated sound, he ground himself against her. Already her insides were liquefying, ready to accept him. It was madness, but she prayed it would never end.

He splayed a hand inside the open V of her shirt to explore the hollows of her collarbone. She made a small protesting sound when he abandoned her mouth, but it turned into a sigh as his lips found the leaping pulse at the base of her throat. All she could think was how good that hot mouth felt, how it might feel on her breasts. Then it was back on her mouth, kissing her even more urgently than before.

Anywhere, she thought. He could touch her anywhere with that talented mouth, those clever hands. She'd do anything as long as he didn't stop. On a surge of raw lust, she caught his lower lip between her teeth and bit. His groan thrilled her, but then he flexed a powerful thumb against her throat.

He could snap my neck like a twig, choke the life out of me without any trouble. The thought came from nowhere, jerking her out of the madness. Desire was snuffed out by fear as the images from her vision surged into her mind. "No."

Suddenly, being crushed against his chest felt like being suffocated. She couldn't draw a proper breath. Like a drowning woman clawing her way to the surface, she fought him.

Cal felt the change in her, but before he could turn her loose, she was clawing at him like a madwoman. Even after he let her go, she continued to flail at him, seemingly unaware she was free. Cursing, he captured her wrists and held her fast.

"Dammit, a simple no would have done!"

"Let me go." Her voice was high and thin, her eyes wild, her chest rising and falling rapidly. *Fear.* That's what it was. She looked, he realized, like a mustang at the point in the breaking process when it recognized its spirit was in jeopardy. The thought filled him with impotent fury. He'd never broken a horse's spirit in his life. The horses couldn't know that, so he accepted their fear. But Lauren should have known better.

"I'm not an animal," he bit out. "I understand no."

She bowed her head. "Please, let go of my hands."

"Why? So you can tear another strip off me?"

That brought her head up. "I won't. I swear."

"Good, because it stings like a bitch." He released her and stepped back in one motion. From a safe distance, he pressed a hand to his neck, relieved no blood came away on his fingers. Still, he'd have an ugly weal to explain. Damn, but it burned. He glanced up to find her watching him with stricken eyes.

"What?" he growled.

"Your neck . . ."

"I'll live."

"I'm so sorry."

She did look sorry. Crazy woman! Kiss him like that, then claw hell out of him. "Mind telling me what that was about?"

"I can't."

He lifted an eyebrow. "You can't tell me?"

Her gaze slid off. "I don't know if I can explain it."

"Try." He invested the single word with all his anger and frustration. She looked completely miserable, but he had no intention of letting her off the hook. She was on her own.

"Well, we were kissing and it was so good and I didn't want to stop. I mean, I really didn't want to stop. In another few minutes . . . I was afraid it was going to go too far."

"Not, by God, if you didn't want it," he gritted, forgetting his resolve to make her stumble her way through. "Though I might add that you were giving a pretty good impression of wanting it."

"Oh, I *did* want it."

That verbal confirmation gave him a jolt, which he instructed his body to ignore.

"But then I thought, *who is this man?*"

A choking noise was the best he could do.

"Well, it's true, isn't it? I don't really know you. I don't know you, yet I was almost ready to have sex with you. It happened so fast. I guess I just got scared."

"Of me? That's very flattering."

"No, I scared myself."

He searched her face, found her blue gaze unwavering. She spoke the truth, he realized. Or part of it. Something inside him unclenched. "Okay, I'll accept that you don't know me very well." He took a deep breath and exhaled. "But you can start with this: I'd never force myself on a woman. Got it?"

She nodded. "Got it."

"Good." Because she still looked so miserable, he added, "And while we're at it, I'm rarely cruel to animals or children, either." That earned him a wan smile. "Come on, we better go. We don't want to be tripping down this ridge in the dark."

Cal hung back, letting Lauren lead the way back down the ridge to the cabin.

She was an enigma, that one. She'd been just as hot as he'd fantasized. Hotter. But then, out of nowhere, she'd fought him like a virgin whose virtue was under attack.

Scared her, she'd said. Fair enough. It scared him, too.

Oh, not the speed and power of it. He'd known she'd be all fire and passion. What scared him was touching her and finding her there, right there beneath the surface, so real and complete and present. He'd wanted to kiss that mouth, feast on every inch of that tall body, but he hadn't counted on her being so damned . . . *alive* in her skin.

He'd tried to pull back then, but she'd latched onto him and kissed him senseless, and all the while he'd felt *her*, not just her silky skin and woman-taste. His mouth went dry, half in arousal, half in fear. That wasn't how the game was played. She wasn't supposed to bring all that other . . . *stuff* to the party.

If he didn't know the kind of stories she spun to titillate readers, he'd think she didn't know the rules. He almost snorted aloud at the thought. More likely she preferred to make her own. As he watched her descend the steepest part of the incline, a thought struck him—maybe that was how she spiced up a diet gone flat, by investing the casual encounter with artificial meaning.

This time, he did snort. When she glanced back at him, he disguised it as a grunt of exertion as he climbed over a boulder. They'd have to straighten that out if they were going to get horizontal. Personally, he didn't need any playacting. If she did, she'd be out of luck, 'cause he couldn't act worth a damn.

Just ask his ex-wife. A dull ache gripped his gut. *Failure*. If he'd been a better actor, maybe Marlena could have stayed faithful. She needed to have a man crazy in love with her all the time, and to his enduring shame, he'd had neither the commitment nor the stamina to be that man.

Of course, everyone expected him to be wild with jealousy, and for a while, he was. But it had quickly resolved into bitter acceptance. He'd told himself he'd sent her packing to keep order among his men, and there was truth enough in that. But on those occasions when he allowed his mind to be still, he suspected his decision had more to do with getting rid of the evidence of his failure.

And now she was back. Though she wasn't his wife anymore, she was still a living reminder of his shortcomings. And like a mare in season in a corral full of stallions, she could still be trouble. Maybe it was just as well she'd singled out one man. Cal hoped the much younger Brady could keep her preoccupied.

Yeah, he'd have to keep an eye on Marlena. The eye that wasn't fastened on Lauren's mile-long legs.

Cripes, if he could get through the summer without the ranch going to hell, it'd be a miracle.

An hour later, the four of them sat awkwardly around the table. When Cal announced he would sleep outside to keep an eye on the horses, Lauren almost sighed her relief.

"I can split the shift with you, Boss," offered Brady.

"You're not on the clock, kid. Don't worry about it." Cal stood. "Anything I can do for you before I go, Lauren?"

She shot him a quick look. There was nothing in his expression to suggest that he was offering anything more than normal courtesy toward a guest, but she blushed anyway.

"No, thanks. I'm just about ready to turn in."

Lauren watched Cal's profile as he turned to his ex-wife.

"I trust *you* won't want for anything, Marlena."

To Lauren's ears, the insult seemed automatic, without heat.

"Thanks, Callum, sweetie, but I can take care of my own needs quite adequately."

Marlena's rejoinder was equally reflexive, requiring no conscious thought. . . .

Wait a minute . . . *Callum*? His real name was Callum?

" 'Night, then." Cal collected his bedroll and left.

Despite her assessment that the exchange had contained more habit than heat, the tension in the cabin dipped with Cal's exit. Maybe Marlena was a better actress than Lauren thought. Maybe better than Cal thought. For that matter, maybe they were both Oscar contenders.

Or maybe the threat to Marlena came from an entirely different source. According to Cal, his ex-wife was apparently being sought by a loan shark's thug. Could the thug find her here? And even if he did track her down, would defaulting on a debt earn her a death sentence? It didn't seem likely. Putting a scare into her, sure. Maybe even hurting or disfiguring her pretty face. But *murder?*

Suddenly, she couldn't think about it any more. She said her goodnights and headed for the back bedroom.

Her mind numb from the strain of the evening, she

slipped into a nightshirt, studiously ignoring the frustrated ache in her belly and the tingle in her breasts. She was not going to relive tonight's mortification by replaying that kiss in her mind.

But what must Cal think of her?

She could hardly have told him the truth—that for a few seconds, she'd been fighting for her life, that she'd had a flash of him choking her with those big, work-hardened hands.

Instead she'd told him that she'd been frightened by the suddenness of the passionate explosion between them. There was enough truth in it that he'd bought it, or seemed to. Still, she'd felt his speculative gaze on her back all the way down the ridge. He'd test the waters again. She had no doubt of it.

What she did doubt was her own ability to deny him.

Face it, she chided herself. *You're vulnerable. You haven't had a relationship since Garrett broke off the engagement almost three years ago.*

Okay, sure, but she could have picked someone she didn't suspect of murder to fantasize about, couldn't she?

No, that wasn't fair. Despite her hysterics tonight, every minute she spent with Cal persuaded her he wasn't the villain of her vision. But he could still be a powerful distraction when she could ill afford to be distracted.

Nothing had changed. Yet everything had changed. She'd touched his face, kissed his mouth, felt his sex stir. . . .

"Aaargh!" Pure thoughts. Pulling the quilts over her head, she tried to channel Mother Teresa.

Lauren woke to the smell of bacon frying. Groaning, she fumbled for her watch and peered at it in the half-light. Six-o-five. Too early to crawl out of her warm nest. She settled back again, but before sleep came, the scent of perking coffee reached her. Hunger she could have ignored, but the siren call of caffeine snared her.

Both men sat at the table. She paused a moment in the doorway to watch them. Cal was dressed but rumpled. He'd probably slept in his clothes. Brady wore his shirt open, and his bare feet poked out from beneath faded jeans. Nice body. She could see why he'd caught Marlena's eye.

Her gaze drifted back to Cal. No, Marlena was crazy. How could she have wanted anyone else when she'd had Cal?

Brady spotted her first. "'Morning, Lauren. We wake you?"

She stepped into the kitchen. "It was the coffee."

"Sit." Cal was already on his feet. "I'll pour."

"I can do it. Just show me where the mugs are."

"You're the guest, remember?"

To her surprise, it stung to be reminded that she was paying for this privilege. She sat. "Black, no sugar." If that was the way he wanted it, she could do her part. "And I'll have one egg over easy, a slice of toast and two pieces of bacon."

"Coming up." If he was ruffled, he hid it well. He handed her a steaming mug of coffee, then turned to Brady. "Why don't you wake Marlena? Since Lauren's up, we'll get an early start."

Brady blushed, but manfully managed not to squirm. "Sure," he said, then left the kitchen.

Cal's gaze followed him. "Kid's still worried I'm gonna come aboard him."

"Not worried enough to leave trouble alone."

"They never are. Marlena packs too much of a punch." His expression flat, he turned back to the gas range.

"Cal!"

The anguished shout came from Brady. Before Cal or Lauren could react, the young man came skidding into the room.

Cal put up a hand to stop him. "Whoa, man, what is it?"

"Marlena! She won't wake up. I think she's dead!"

Chapter Four

No. Lauren watched Cal roll Marlena's sheet-tangled body over. Her blond hair spilled over the pillows like Barbie doll hair. *Not like this. It's not supposed to happen this way.*

Then a moan issued from Marlena's pale lips.

"Oh, thank God! She's alive." Brady looked as though his grip on the bedpost were the only thing keeping him standing.

"Thank God is right. That'd be just what I need." Cal lifted one of Marlena's eyelids, and she shrank away, groaning. He lifted his gaze to Brady. "Did she take anything last night?"

"Huh?"

"Drugs, Brady. Did she take any drugs?"

"Yeah, she did." Brady's Adam's apple bobbed. Suddenly, he looked less like Brad Pitt and more like a scared kid. "She said it was nothing bad, nothing illegal."

"What was it?"

"I don't know. Some pills."

"She took them to get high, I presume?"

Brady blushed furiously. "She said it would make it better for her. She offered me some, but I didn't take any. I was afraid I wouldn't be able to . . . you know, to . . ."

"Okay, okay, we get the picture." Cal sighed. "Bring me her backpack."

Brady complied, his gaze downcast, shoulders slumped.

"Empty it," Cal instructed as he removed the pillow from under Marlena's head and rolled her onto her side.

Again, the younger man did as he was told.

"There! That cosmetic bag—dump it on the bed."

Brady hesitated at the invasion of Marlena's privacy.

"Come on, Brady, just dump it. We'll make our apologies after we make sure she's not gonna die."

He dumped it. Lauren gasped.

"Damned walking pharmacy." Cal scooped up a handful of drugstore-issue pill bottles and scanned the labels. "Uppers, downers, sleeping pills, painkillers. Jesus, she must have double-doctored her way through greater Calgary to collect this much junk." For the first time, he looked as though he might not have the situation completely under control. "What do we do now? She might've taken a freaking cocktail of this stuff."

"Let me have a look at her," Lauren heard herself say.

Brady perked up. "You a doctor or something?"

"Or something," she muttered.

Cal glanced up. "You know first aid?" When she nodded, he shifted out of the way. "She's all yours."

"Brady, have a look at the pills and see if you recognize what she took," Lauren said, before perching on the bed. Brady jumped to the task, and Lauren turned her attention to the exam. It turned out to be more reassuring than she'd anticipated. Despite first appearances, Marlena wasn't unconscious, just very drowsy and reluctant to open her eyes. Her pupils were responsive, heartbeat regular, reflexes good. Through the whole exam, Marlena mumbled curses, trying to twist away into sleep.

Lauren sat back. What could Marlena have taken? She didn't display the slow respiration and poor reflexes of a barbiturate overdose or the excited vitals of an amphetamine high. It looked like a hashish overdose, but Brady said pills. . . .

"Found it!" Brady's voice was excited. "This is the one. I'm sure of it. It starts with an X."

Lauren took the bottle from him. "Xanax." Her shoulders sagged with relief. "Benzodiazepine. Good."

"Good?" asked Cal.

"It's a nervous system depressant. It can cause profound drowsiness, impaired coordination and so forth, but normally not coma. At least, not in a reasonable quantity, and not in the absence of alcohol or some other substance." She glanced up at Brady. "Can you be sure she didn't inhale or inject anything in addition to this?"

"Just the pills. Nothing else."

"No booze?"

"No, ma'am."

"What time did she take it?"

"The last time?" Lauren didn't think Brady could redden any more, but he did. "An hour ago. Maybe a little longer."

"Then stand clear." Lauren rolled Marlena closer to the edge of the bed. Hoping that her patient had a healthy gag reflex, she slipped two fingers into Marlena's throat.

"Damn!"

Both men leapt back in unison as Marlena vomited neatly on the small braided rug beside the bed. With arms that trembled more from relief than exertion, Lauren maneuvered a suddenly vocal and decidedly furious Marlena back onto the pillows.

Lauren grimaced, holding her hands in front of her. "I'm going to clean up, after which I think I'm really going to need that coffee." She strode to the bathroom on shaking legs.

When she emerged five minutes later, she found Cal at the table with the flowered cosmetic bag. Her trembling finally conquered, Lauren filled a coffee mug and carried it to the table without sloshing a drop. "She all right?"

"Judging by the abuse she's heaping on our boy right now, I'd say she's well on the road to recovery. Thanks to you."

Lauren shrugged. "The effects are a lot like alcohol. If we hadn't tried to wake her up so early, she'd likely have slept it off. We'd have been none the wiser."

"Jesus, that's scary." He raked a hand through his hair, making it stand up. "So how'd you come by all that knowledge if you're not a doctor? ER nurse? Pharmacist?"

Her mind raced as Cal refilled his mug. She'd known this question was coming. While she'd busied herself cleaning up, she'd toyed with the idea of telling him the truth—that she'd done a year of med school before deciding to thwart her parents' ambitions for her, and to pursue her own love, veterinary medicine. But it was a little late now. He'd find it pretty strange that she hadn't previously mentioned that she was a vet. Worse, he'd probably think she made the erotica writer bit up to titillate him. How humiliating would that be? She'd painted herself into a corner.

"EMT," she said, then took a hasty swallow of her coffee. Well, she wasn't lying. Her knowledge of poison control did come largely from her EMT experience. "Emergency medical technician. Before I moved to Halifax, I worked with a volunteer ambulance service. But I haven't worked on people in years."

Lauren almost bit her tongue at the last bit, but if Cal wondered what she did work on these days, he didn't ask. Instead, he gestured toward the cosmetic bag.

"What do you make of this stash?"

She pursed her lips. "It seems fairly comprehensive for a young, healthy woman."

"Diplomatically put." He extracted one of the tiny bottles. "Personally, I'd say my ex-wife has a honkin' big drug problem."

"She wouldn't be the first to abuse prescription drugs."

"No doubt." He rolled the bottle in his hand. "But I've got a hunch the prescription route wasn't her first choice."

"Why do you say that?"

"I doubt she spent her whole settlement, plus whatever she borrowed from the loan shark, on drugstore highs. I'm thinking she must have developed a taste for the recreational stuff, then turned to prescription drugs when the money ran out. Not that it matters." He poked the bottle back in the bag with the others. "She'll be doing without all of it as long as she stays here."

Lauren said nothing, merely stared into her coffee cup.

She heard the legs of Cal's chair scrape across the floor as he pushed back from the table. "What?" he demanded roughly.

"I didn't say anything."

"You don't have to." He snapped up the cosmetic bag, dangling it by its grip. "You think I should give this back to her?"

The intensity of his gaze was jarring, made her want to look away. But she held her ground.

"I have the impression you're planning to hustle her out of town again as soon as this loan shark thing blows over."

"Damn straight I will."

Lauren strove for the right words. "Underneath her . . .

exuberance, she seems very . . . I don't know . . . emotionally shaky. Do you think it's fair to set yourself up as her keeper when you're planning to cut her loose?"

"Fair?" He pinned her with that gray gaze. "How about just keeping her alive? With a stash like this, we could find her OD'd in her bed any morning. Or she could kill herself pulling some reckless trick like she did yesterday, flying down that bluff." He pushed his coffee cup aside and blinked. "What if she hurt someone else while under the influence? It would ruin me."

Lauren felt the last of her doubts about Cal fall away like a stone she didn't have to carry anymore. There was no question he meant what he said. He'd do everything in his power to keep Marlena safe while she was on his ranch. With so much on the line, he wouldn't let bad publicity kill his business.

"Hell, Lauren, I know what you're thinking, but this isn't some kind of power trip." He stood and deposited his empty mug in the sink, then turned to her, his posture rigid. "I can't give those drugs back to her. Besides the fact I don't want to see her kill herself, I'd be putting other people at risk every time she put a foot in a stirrup. The ranch . . ."

"I understand."

"And there'd be no confining her to the house. She'd sooner give herself up to that thug who's chasing her than sit around inside."

"I know. You're right."

"She's a good horsewoman, but ripped out of her head on—" He stopped, blinked at her. "Wait a minute, did you say you understood?"

"I did. You're right."

"I am?"

"The stakes are high. I guess I can understand."

His smile started slowly, then spread over his face. "Saints be praised. A woman who can admit she's wrong."

The smile was devastating. Because she felt dangerously close to grinning foolishly back at him, she turned away, picked up the carton of eggs from the counter and shoved them at him. He accepted them reflexively.

"You still owe me an egg. Easy over, one slice of toast. I'm going to get dressed."

His surprised bark of laughter followed her into the bedroom, where she had trouble wiping the grin off her own face as she regarded her reflection in the mirror. Lord, the man could make her insides melt with a mere smile. Imagine the kind of fire he could start if he really tried.

The face in the mirror sobered. In the interests of her mission, she sincerely hoped he wouldn't try.

At least, the rational part of her mind hoped he wouldn't. Unfortunately, the rest of her longed to taste him. She studied her own eyes in the mirror and read the truth—the urge to press her body against his was growing. What had started as a pulse of awareness had swelled to a drumbeat in her blood.

God help her, she didn't think she could resist him.

God help them all.

Cal pulled the brim of his hat down against the glare of the sun. So far, the trip back to the ranch had been quiet. Marlena had been spitting mad about Lauren making her sell the Buick in front of loverboy, and her mood hadn't improved when she found out Cal had confiscated her drugs. She had since graduated to full-fledged seething, but was doing it quietly. Brady was subdued as a whipped puppy, and Lauren was in her own world.

For a change, Cal's mind wasn't on Lauren as he followed the small train of riders. For once, it was where it belonged: on the herd. The cattle were in the high pasture now and would be until fall when the men rode out to round them up and drive them back to the homestead. It was a dusty, miserable job driving cattle, yet Cal couldn't wait. He loved that part of ranching.

The summerlong race to put up enough winter feed to see the cattle through until spring wasn't so wonderful, though. It was hard, endless work, but he'd choose it over baby-sitting doctor-cowboys and lawyer-cowboys any day.

Hell, he'd choose it over managing the ranch, or at least the business end. He liked the office part little enough to begin with, but now, with the big agribusinesses moving in and further destabilizing things, he was really starting to hate it.

It was just as his daddy said when Cal had left home for good at the age of sixteen. "You'll never amount to nothin', boy, 'cause you can't settle to nothin'. You'll wind up broken in that damned rodeo you love so much, or busting your hump for wranglers' wages."

Well, the bulls hadn't done him in, and he paid the wages around here as opposed to collecting them, but his father had been right about one thing. He was a wrangler at heart, not a cattle baron.

But just because the old man was right didn't mean Cal couldn't prove him wrong. He'd make a success of this ranch if it killed him.

"Cal!" Brady's shout dragged him out of the past. "Rider at two o'clock."

"I see him." Brady had stopped, and the others pulled up, too. Cal reined in Sienna, cursing as the rider on the handsome palomino changed course to intercept them. Just what he needed to cap the day. He glanced at Brady. The kid's face was stony, eyes hard.

"Well, come on," Cal growled. "Let's keep moving. It's not a ghost rider. Just my neighbor, Harvey McLeod."

Cal's irritation grew as Harvey closed the gap between them. White Stetson, white hair, white teeth—he looked like a Hollywood cowboy. A Hollywood cowboy who coveted Cal's ranch.

"'Morning, Cal," called the other man.

"McLeod." Cal nodded an acknowledgment. "You looking for me or are you just lost?"

Harvey flashed those preternaturally white teeth in a fierce grin. "Just passing through to visit my new property." He gestured vaguely to the northeast. "Hope you don't mind."

Cal glanced in the direction Harvey indicated. Damn. "MaKenny's spread?"

"Yep." Harvey nodded. "Hinchey place, too."

MaKenny and Hinchey both. Poor bastards. A chill went up Cal's spine as he realized he was sandwiched in between McLeod's holdings and the mountains. Not that it made any difference to his operations. But it still gave him a bad feeling.

"Well, don't let me keep you. It's a long ride."

McLeod bared his teeth again. "Just thought I'd let you know my offer's still open. Your land and your herd."

Anger surged through him, but Cal was careful to keep his expression flat. "The answer's still no."

"Times are tough. If you change your mind, let me know. I'll give you a fair price."

That much was true. McLeod *had* made a decent offer. If he'd offered as much to Tom and Dan, they probably counted themselves lucky. They might have lost it all to the bank and gone away empty-handed. Still, Cal couldn't feel terribly well disposed toward a man who made no secret that he wanted his land. "Appreciate your concern, McLeod. That's right neighborly of you."

His sarcasm appeared to be wasted on the older man, whose attention had shifted to Marlena and Lauren. With a gallantry that grated on Cal's nerves, Harvey swept his hat off. "Ladies."

Gritting his teeth, Cal realized he wasn't going to get away without introductions.

"This is Lauren Townsend, a guest here. Lauren, my neighbor, Harvey McLeod." When they'd exchanged greetings, he nodded toward Marlena. "And you'll remember Marlena. She's here for a short spell of R and R."

"Marlena Taggart? *The* Marlena?" McLeod's perfect smile widened. "I'm afraid I never had the pleasure. You left just after I bought the Hoyt place, but I've heard a lot about you."

Hadn't had the pleasure? He was one of a select few, then. And Cal could well imagine what he'd heard.

With effort, he clamped down on the thoughts. It was done and over.

Marlena took her own hat off and shook her hair free, running a hand through it. "I certainly would have remembered a cowboy who sits a horse as nicely as you do, Mr. McLeod."

"Call me Harvey, please."

"Harvey, it'd be my pleasure."

Cripes, Marlena was turning it on. Beside her, Brady was going red in the face. Just like old times. Life wasn't interesting enough for Marlena unless she had at least two men in a lather.

Unfortunately, things could get uglier than usual between these two men. Harvey was Brady's father.

Not that Harvey acknowledged him as such. When the

kid's mother had died two years before, her journal fingered Harvey as Brady's father. Unfortunately, when Brady'd come around looking to connect with dear old dad, Harvey not only denied paternity, but bounced the kid off his land. Cal had pulled Brady out of the bottle he'd crawled into and given him a job.

."Well, it's been nice seeing you, Harvey. I expect you'll want to be moving along. You got a fair piece to cover before you reach McLeod ground again, and daylight's burnin'."

Harvey's smile was a slash of white in his tanned, handsome face. "So it is, Taggart, so it is. Ladies." With a nod to the ladies, he jammed his white Stetson back on and galloped off.

"What a charming man." This from Marlena, whose gaze was glued to McLeod's retreating back.

"He's a vulture," pronounced Brady. "Just waitin' for another cattleman to go down so he can swoop in and pick the bones. Right, Cal?" He turned to Cal for confirmation.

Cal wished he had a cigarette, an indulgence he rarely allowed himself. "He's waiting for his chances all right, but he does pay a fair price. Can't fault him there. And at least he's a rancher, of sorts."

"Yeah, the sort that puts men out of work," Brady scoffed.

"I don't get it." Marlena wrinkled her nose. "How can running a lucrative operation put people out of work?"

"Technology." Cal lifted his hat and let the breeze cool his sweat-soaked hairline. "You don't need a branding crew, for instance, if you can staple a computer chip in a newborn calf's ear." He squinted against the sun, then replaced his hat. "But it could be worse. They could have sold out to a developer for a helluva lot more money."

Marlena snorted. "What's wrong with development? I'd sell in a minute if it was mine."

"Don't I know it," Cal muttered under his breath.

"What *is* wrong with development?" asked Lauren. "Don't you have to accept a certain amount of it?"

He shot her a sharp look. She was just like the rest of them, knowing nothing about this ancient ecosystem and caring less. And she wondered why he hated this gig. The rawness of his disappointment surprised him. Somehow he thought she'd share his views.

"What's wrong with development?" His disappointment lent his voice a sharper-than-usual edge. "How about because this is one of this freaking planet's last intact bioregions? How about because we need agricultural balance for clean watersheds, wildlife, even weather? Developers would throw up fences and the big game would disappear overnight. There'd be more recreational vehicles and people disrupting things. Few years, it would be ecological disaster. California North."

"He must be awfully rich," Marlena said.

Cal suppressed a sigh, not because his rant had flowed around his self-absorbed ex-wife like so much prairie wind; he'd expected nothing less. No, he sighed at Brady's reaction, a reflexive fisting of the reins. His mount jumped at having her bit bumped for no good reason. Why'd Marlena have to pick herself a kid? Especially this kid.

"Harvey McLeod can likely afford everything from the prairie grass to the Rockies, but he's not getting this piece of Alberta." Cal spat, but he couldn't quite get the taste of fear out of his mouth. "Let's go."

Without looking back to make sure they followed, he urged Sienna into a ground-eating gait.

* * *

It was mid-afternoon before they got back to the ranch. Lauren felt limp as soggy lettuce, and Marlena looked worse. Out of the corner of her eye, Lauren watched the other woman tend to her mount. Cal was right. She was a good horsewoman, and even in her hungover state she didn't stint on the rubdown. The mare gleamed by the time she was done. Afterward, to Lauren's surprise, Marlena stopped to talk to her.

"I'm not suicidal, you know," she ground out.

"I didn't imagine you were. Most overdoses are accidental."

For an instant, it was as though a curtain lifted and Lauren could see the depth of Marlena's loneliness, the breadth of her fear. Then the veil dropped again. "I'd have been all right."

Lauren nodded. "I think so, too, but I was following protocol, and I'd do it again."

By the time she got the words out, she was talking to Marlena's back. Lauren watched the other woman go, her stride exuding confidence and sexuality so at odds with the haunted look Lauren had glimpsed so fleetingly in those green eyes. For just a few seconds, Marlena had looked more like a little girl than a siren.

Lauren shook her head to dislodge the notion. Geez, she must be more tired than she thought. There was nothing remotely childlike about Marlena. Besides, she had more important things to think about, including the way both Cal and Brady had reacted to the appearance of Harvey McLeod. Was McLeod the wild card here? Would he be the catalyst to set the violence in motion? And what about the man, the "thug" as Cal had called him, on Marlena's trail?

Brady had been fiercely jealous. Automatically, Lauren's gaze sought him out. He was still in a sulk, working it out with long strokes of the finishing rag. The horse's coat shone, but Lauren didn't need psychic talent to feel the animal's anxiety. The mare's ears were laid back, a sign anyone could read.

Biting her lip, she approached the nervous mare carefully from the side. Brady's motions slowed when she came into his peripheral vision.

"I think she's done, Brady. You're going to wear her hide off at this rate."

He stiffened at her words, then dropped his hands in defeat. "You're right. Sorry, girl." He gave the mare's neck a scratch, his fingers finding the spot where horses nuzzle each other. Lauren felt the horse relax under the familiar, soothing caress. She couldn't say as much for Brady.

"Brady, if you want to talk some time . . ."

"No!" His face reddened in obvious mortification. "I mean, no thank you, ma'am. I can handle myself."

"Of course."

As she watched him lead the mare away, a sense of helplessness assailed her. Why me? Why did I inherit this stupid job? she wondered, her hands fisted at her sides in frustration. She wasn't adequate to this, had no idea how to go about trying to defuse these strong emotions.

"Best leave the kid alone."

Lauren glanced up to find Cal watching her. "I guess you're right. But he's so upset."

"Upset?" He hefted his saddle and gathered up the bridle in his free hand. "He's like a bronc with a burr under his saddle."

She shifted her attention back to Brady's retreating figure. "I thought if I could distract him, he might cool down."

"There's no distracting a man in his condition. Once you've climbed on and that gate swings open, you just gotta ride it out. Anyone can see he's in for a gravity check, but there's no point telling him. He'll know it soon enough when he hits the ground."

"A rodeo reference. How apropos." He was right, and she knew it, which made her words sharper than she intended.

Cal regarded her through narrowed eyes. "I know what you're up to, you know."

Her heart jumped. He knew? How could he? Heart pounding, she gathered up her own tack. "Really? And what's that?" Without waiting for his answer, she headed for the tack room at the back of the barn. Brady passed her on his way back to the house. Averting his eyes, he acknowledged her with a nod.

Cal fell in beside her, shortening his stride to match hers.

"You're a fixer. You can't stand all that conflict and riled-up emotion, so you run around putting everything right."

His words hit too close for comfort. It had taken some doing, but she knew she came across as confident and self-assured. And for the most part, she was. She'd had to develop a certain amount of assertiveness to forge her own path against the wishes of her parents. She'd come a long way, but there was truth in what Cal said. She still hated turmoil.

"What's wrong with a little peace and harmony?" She surged ahead of him, exasperation fueling her strides. "Why do people have to be stirring things up all the time?"

Her momentum carried her into the relative gloom of the tack room, where she stopped short. Her arms ached with the weight of the saddle, and she longed to dump the damned thing, but the sudden darkness after the blinding sunlight had stolen her vision. Cal didn't seem to be hampered—the squeaking and jangling told her he had stowed his own tack. Of course, he probably knew every inch of these barns in the dark anyway.

"I can't see a damned thing," she groused.

Suddenly he was next to her in the gloom. Her heart started to thud again in her chest, this time in awareness, as he took the heavy western saddle from her. Her tired arms wanted to levitate of their own accord as soon as the burden was lifted, which made her want to laugh out loud. Instead, she clamped her arms firmly to her sides.

When he turned back to her, her eyes had adjusted enough to make out his face. He'd taken his hat off, and her pulse kicked again at the sight of him. Belatedly, she realized she should have turned and walked back into the safety of the sunlight while he dealt with the tack. But it was too late now. He was wearing that hungry look again. And so, she feared, was she.

He closed the distance between them with a step. "Stirring things up doesn't have to be a bad thing."

He was close enough that the breath stirred a tendril of hair on her forehead. In her heightened state of awareness, it felt like a caress. She registered, too, the dust motes that danced behind him in a shaft of sunlight and the smell of horse and oiled leather combined with the sharper odor of the pine tar.

Four heartbeats, five, six, but still he didn't kiss her, though she was all but straining toward him. Then he brought his hands up, but instead of cradling her face as she expected, he tipped her hat off, then touched her hair gently.

"I want to stir up a few things with you." His gray eyes bored into hers. "Starting with that composure of yours."

She closed her eyes as his fingers tunneled into her hair. She wanted to deny his effect on her senses, but there was little point if she were going to stand here and let each new sensation wash over her. "You're doing a pretty good job of that right now," she breathed.

"Umm, but I want to do more."

She resisted the urge to lick her lips. "Like what?"

"Like this."

Her eyes sprang open at the first contact of his mouth to hers, then fell shut again as he kissed her hotly. Of their own volition, her hands skimmed up his sides, finding purchase in the belt loops of his jeans. Too soon, he broke the kiss, leaving her yearning for more, yet he didn't pull back.

His hands dropped to her shoulders, then brushed down her arms to grip her elbows.

"I want to stir your imagination," he said, lifting her arms until they circled his neck. "I want to stir your blood."

Her answer was to pull his head down and kiss him blindly. He responded with a ferocity that thrilled her, backing her up against a wall. It was just like the other time on the ridge. Desperate. Frantic. The need to surrender to the wild sweetness, to him, grew urgent, building intolerably with every second.

Then, without warning, he stepped back.

His solid frame no longer supporting her, she stumbled forward in confusion.

Cal swore to himself as the chatter of children drew closer.

"What's wrong?"

Couldn't she hear them? "Kids. Quick, this way."

60

Grasping her hand, he pulled her to the back of the tack room and through a door to the stable area. He muttered another curse when he spotted a stable hand at the far end.

"In here." He opened the first box stall and gestured for her to precede him. She stopped abruptly when a big bay gelding lifted its head to contemplate them curiously.

"Cal! It's occupied," she hissed.

He laughed. "I wasn't proposing anything kinky," he said, guiding her inside. "It's just that I've got a bit of a problem below the belt that I'd rather not explain to Earl over there. Maybe we could visit with Cosmo here until it passes."

At his words, her gaze immediately dropped to the telltale bulge in his jeans. When her wide-eyed gaze finally climbed back up to his face, he groaned laughingly.

"Come on, Lauren, have a heart. Don't look at me like that. You gotta help me out here."

Her lips quirked. "It *is* a pretty big problem."

He stifled a laugh, then shot a look toward the end of the stables. "Save your compliments, sweetheart, and ask me something about this nag. Earl's working his way toward us."

With a smug smile, she turned to look at the gelding.

"Oh, this is the guy no one rides, isn't it?"

"That's right. He hasn't been worked in a while, which is downright criminal. He's a Tennessee walker with a gait as smooth as butter."

She held out a hand to be nuzzled. "What's wrong with him?"

"Headshake. A couple of months ago, he started tossing his head continually. Now he couldn't pay mind to a rider's signals if he wanted to."

She slid a hand up the bay's neck and stroked him. She

didn't pat or thump, he noticed, as so many weekend warriors did in the mistaken belief they were communicating approval. Rather, she scratched and stroked in a way that had the gelding delirious with pleasure.

Cal knew how he felt.

"I think I can stop his head-shaking."

Her words jolted him back to the subject at hand. They also astounded him. "You think you can cure him?"

"Not cure, exactly. He'll probably always be susceptible. But I'm pretty sure I can curb the behavior."

"And how long would that take?"

"I could do it tomorrow."

He snorted. "Sweetheart, this is the worst case I've ever seen. You've got horse sense, I'll give you that, but no one's gonna cure Cosmo in a day."

"Want to make a bet?"

The gleam that had come into her eyes made him suspicious. Could she have some fancy English riding school trick up her sleeve? So what if she did? He couldn't lose, could he? If he won, he might just get what he wanted. If she won, he'd get Cosmo back.

"Sure, I'll bet you, if you're not afraid of a real wager."

Her eyes widened. "A real wager? What'd you have in mind?"

He moved closer, lowering his voice so his words wouldn't carry beyond her ears. "If your cure doesn't work, you'll invite me to share your bed—*tomorrow night.*" Her breath hitched, but he wasn't sure whether it was his words or the desire that thickened the air between them. "That's where we're going to wind up eventually. This way, it'd be sooner rather than later."

Those pale blue eyes went wide but she didn't deny his assertion. "What if I win?"

He grinned. "Name your wager."

She touched her lip with her tongue as she considered her options. In the background, Cal could hear Earl moving closer.

"If I win," she said at last, "you'll tell me how you wound up in the guest ranch business."

Chapter Five

Cal felt a muscle flex in his jaw. Damn the woman for her curiosity! With effort, he unclenched his teeth and smiled. "That's not much of a wager. I could tell you that right now."

"Oh, I don't want the pat answer." She moved even closer. Close enough for him to inhale the clean shampoo smell of her. "I want the real story. I want to know how a man like you got into a business like this."

Under her unwavering gaze, he let his smile broaden, as though the idea of talking about himself didn't cause his stomach to knot. Didn't matter anyway. She couldn't win. "Darlin', you got yourself a bet."

"Great! When can we do it?"

She stepped back, and his breathing eased a fraction. "Well, I've already put my money on tomorrow night," he drawled, then watched as she blushed.

"I meant the test with Cosmo."

He paused to consider. "I've got some new folks coming in tonight. What about right after dinner tomorrow, while the new crop of cowboys are resting their backsides?"

"High noon?" Her brow pleated in a small frown. "It'll be a tough test."

"What? You want to back out already?" He half hoped she did. Chances were good he could talk her into bed tonight, and to hell with waiting for tomorrow.

"No, noon is fine. Now I'd better go rescue my hat before someone steps on it."

He opened the stall door for her and watched her go, those long legs of hers inspiring erotic ideas. Twenty-four hours, he reminded himself. Twenty-four hours and she'd be his.

Across the way, the stable hand backed out of a box stall with a wheelbarrow full of dirty straw and manure. "Hey, Earl," Cal called, then set off with a distinct bounce in his step.

Lauren skipped the morning trail ride the next day. She had work to do. As soon as Cal left, she went out to the barn. A quick word with Earl, and she knew who could help her—Cal's trail boss, Jim Mallory. She found the old man cleaning tack, surrounded by the gentle odor of saddle soap.

"Jim Mallory?"

He glanced up from his labor and smiled. "Miz Townsend."

"Lauren." She returned his smile.

"What can I do you for, Miz . . . Lauren?"

"Earl tells me you're quite skilled at leatherwork."

"Naw, I'm just a mender." Lovingly, Jim touched the cantle of the saddle he'd been cleaning. "Now this is skill."

"It's beautiful." Lauren fingered the intricate design.

"So what do you need in the way of leatherwork?"

"Blinders," she said, lifting her gaze from the saddle.

Jim's mouth fell open. "Blinders? You mean, like we slap on the Percherons when we harness them up?"

She nodded. "Same concept, but we want to shield more of the eye, like so." She showed him a rough drawing she'd done.

"Horse won't like it."

"This one will."

"Which one?"

"Cosmo."

Jim eyed her consideringly. "Think it'll help?"

Lauren explained her theory, then went on to tell him she'd made a bet with Cal and needed to be ready to test her theory by noon. When she was done, Jim's eyes had narrowed thoughtfully.

"You seen this work before?"

"Well, no, not personally, but I understand it's worked for other horses."

"What if it doesn't work for Cosmo?"

"Then I lose the bet." A jolt of raw excitement knifed through her at the thought. It wouldn't really feel like losing. She pushed the traitorous thought aside. She wanted to win this bet. Not that she genuinely expected to learn anything from Cal to help her with the investigation. She'd admitted that much to herself last night, just before slamming the door on that line of thought. She didn't want to analyze why it was so important for him to open up to her.

Jim's voice yanked her back. "Well, I guess I'd better get busy, then, hadn't I? You fetch a bridle and I'll get my kit."

Cal leaned his chair back with a sigh as Delia removed his plate from the worn pine table. "That was a fine meal, Delia."

Across the table from him, Lauren added her compliments.

"Well, for two people who enjoyed lunch so much, neither of you cleaned your plates very well," Delia observed tartly.

"We're in a bit of a hurry, that's all," said Cal.

"I know," she replied, gesturing to the empty dining room. "The whole bunch of them have gone out to the corral to see if Lauren's cure works."

Cal's chair clumped back onto all fours. "Everyone knows about the bet?"

Lauren fingered her napkin. "I mentioned it to Jim Mallory."

"Jim?" Was the whole ranch speculating about them? Cal waited for Delia to move away before continuing. "Chrissakes, why?"

"I needed his help with the bridle."

A ghastly thought struck him. "Oh, hell, you haven't devised some wicked contraption to curb poor Cosmo, have you?"

Her mouth fell open, then snapped shut. "Of course not!"

Cal sat back in his chair. "But you did modify the bridle?"

"He still has full range of motion," she assured him. "He'll be able to toss his head just fine, if he's so inclined."

Well, that was a relief. But Cal still couldn't relax. He had one more question. "Does that mean the whole ranch knows what's riding on this little wager?"

"No, of course not . . ."

"Despite our necking in the barn, I've got this quaint idea that what passes between a man and a woman oughtta be private."

"As do I." She leaned closer, her eyes flashing. "You think I'd purposely expose myself to that kind of attention?"

67

Norah Wilson

Marlena had. Damn, but it still rankled. He thought he was over that. "No, I guess you wouldn't." He passed a hand over his eyes. "Look, I'm sorry. It's just my experience being what it is . . ."

"No, I'm sorry." She cut off his apology. "I shouldn't have taken offense." She took a deep breath and smiled. "So are we ready to do this?"

"I'm ready."

Delia wasn't lying. Everyone was there. Cal and Lauren crossed the paddock together. Lauren paused at the stable door.

"You want to ride him?" she offered.

"No, you go ahead." He scanned the spectators. "Need some help to saddle him up?"

Jim Mallory stepped out of the barn. "He's already saddled and wonderin' what all the fuss is about. Go git him, Lauren."

Lauren disappeared into the dark doorway, and Jim headed for the paddock fence to take up his favorite leaning posture. Cal followed. "I hear you been conspiring against me, old man."

Jim was predictably unruffled by the complaint. "I think she might be onto somethin'. This just might work."

"What's she rigged up?"

Jim bent one knee and hooked the heel of his boot on a rung. Comfortable, he reached for his tobacco pouch to roll a smoke. "She swore me to secrecy. You'll have to wait and see."

He didn't have to wait long. Lauren emerged first into the sunlight, but all eyes were on the bay she was leading.

"What the hell?"

His prize Tennessee walker was wearing . . . Christ, what was he wearing? They looked like some kind of goggles. They covered the sides of the eye like blinders, but arched up around.

Lauren sprang into the saddle. With a glance at Cal, she gave the gelding a pat on the neck, then walked him around the paddock. Fifteen minutes later, she'd put him through his paces. He'd tossed his head a few times, but Cal had to concede it was normal tossing, not his usual uncontrollable thrashing.

The crowd, realizing there'd be nothing more to see, dissipated.

As Lauren rode up and dismounted, Cal wasn't sure how he felt. Jim had no such ambivalence. He clapped Lauren on the back, his weathered face splitting into a wide if tobacco-stained grin.

"You done it, girl! You fixed 'im."

Lauren's smile was just as wide as Jim's. "I didn't really fix him. Take the blinders off and he'll go right back to tossing his head. It's a photic thing."

Cal lifted an eyebrow. "Oh, a *photic* thing."

Jim took the reins from Lauren. "That means the effect light has on somethin'," he said helpfully as he passed Cal.

"I knew that!" he called after Jim. He turned back to Lauren to see laughter dancing in her blue eyes. "Okay, so maybe I didn't, but I figured it out when I saw Cosmo's shades."

"It's a lot like the impulse we humans get to sneeze when we look into the sun."

"Makes sense. So Cosmo's really back in business?"

She nodded. "With the shades, as you called them. And I imagine you could work him after sunset without them."

"So it looks like you win," Cal said, his gut clenching at the thought. How had she known the shades would work?

The memory of how Lauren handled the scare with

Marlena popped into his head. She'd been Johnny-on-the-spot with the medical knowledge that time. Come to think of it, she was an ambulance attendant, an accomplished rider, a writer of erotica, and now a freaking horse whisperer. What else could she do?

"So you'll talk to me?"

Lauren's question straightened his spine. Damn, he hoped she wasn't an amateur shrink, too, wanting to dig around in his head. He shook the thought away. "I'll make good on the wager, but first tell me, how'd you know the blinders would work?"

She answered with only the merest hesitation. If he hadn't been studying her face, he might have missed the wariness that crept into her eyes. "I'm a veterinarian," she said. "Small animals, but I do have some experience with large animals. I did a stint with Agriculture before setting up practice in Halifax."

"A vet?" Cal inhaled sharply. He couldn't have been more surprised if she'd hauled off and belted him one.

"Yes, a small animal vet. I've got someone covering my clients right now."

He pushed his hat back on his head. "I thought you said you were a writer."

She lifted her chin. "Can't I be both?"

He ignored her question, but he couldn't ignore the dismay blossoming in his gut. She wasn't the footloose writer he'd imagined her. She was a veterinarian with a practice waiting for her two thousand odd miles away. No way would she hang around here after her little holiday was finished. Suddenly his chest felt tight.

"Well, aren't you a regular MacGyver."

Her eyes narrowed. "You find that threatening, do you, Cal? That a woman can have multiple competencies?"

"I don't find it threatening; I find it pretty damned

dodgy," he shot back. "Why, for instance, didn't you tell me you were a vet when I first asked you what you did?"

"You didn't ask me what I did," she countered. "You asked me what my interest was in your ranch operations. If I'd been interested in my capacity as a veterinarian, I'd have said so."

Cal took a deep breath. She was right; he'd accused her of conducting market research and she'd replied she was just researching a book. There was absolutely no basis for his anger.

Except that she had concrete ties to the East Coast, responsibilities that would call her home when her holiday, or her research, or whatever the hell it was she was doing here, was done.

His anger dissolved, fear seeping in to take its place. Why the hell should that thought upset him? The whole appeal of an affair with Lauren was the very transience it offered, wasn't it?

Worried, he did a split-second lust check—did he still want to get her between the sheets, given this new knowledge? His body's answer was emphatic, and vastly reassuring.

Whew.

"Sorry. Guess I'm a little sore about losing the bet." He gave her his best good ol' boy smile. "I had my heart set on winning, as I'm sure you can appreciate." The way her breathing accelerated made his pulse leap. Maybe they could both get what they wanted. "So where and when would you like to do this little debriefing?"

"I get to choose?"

"You're the winner; you get to call the shots."

She licked her lips, a gesture Cal was certain was as unconscious as it was sexy.

"What about tonight, in my cabin, after the sunset ride? Or later," she added, "if you've got stuff to do first."

"After the ride would be fine," he said, an ironic smile tugging at his lips. "I'd already cleared my schedule."

She blushed at that, but held his gaze. "Tonight, then," she confirmed, then turned and strode away.

Tonight, he echoed silently as he watched her go.

Lauren's nerves were stretched to the point of snapping. The sundown ride had been gorgeous but uneventful. Afterward, Cal wanted to get his guests settled with Brady for the Friday night bonfire down by the creek, so she'd come back here to wait for him. Big mistake. She was so wired up that her breathing was keeping time with the clock as she paced her living room.

She wiped damp hands on her jeans. Meeting him here after dark was probably not the wisest move. Not that she'd had much choice about the time. If she were going to keep an eye on Marlena, she had to stay vigilant until after nightfall. But she could have picked a safer location. Why, oh, why had she chosen her cabin?

You know why.

A soft tap at the door arrested her pacing. Taking a steadying breath, she crossed to the door and opened it. Right away, she was glad she'd taken a big gulp of air, because she seemed to have forgotten how to breathe. There in the soft glow of the porch light stood Cal, dressed in fresh jeans and a soft blue shirt. As good as he looked in a Stetson, he looked better without it. His hair, still damp from the shower, was slicked back to his finely shaped head.

"Are you going to invite me in?"

She stepped back, blushing. "Of course."

He handed her a bottle of wine she hadn't noticed he

was carrying. "I swiped this from Delia, so I guess it's decent."

She eyed the label. "A French merlot. What's not to like?"

"I'll take your word for it. I tend to gravitate to the Canadian lagers myself."

Lauren grinned. "Shall I open it?"

Cal glanced around the small room. "That's the general idea. I could use a little Dutch courage."

She was rummaging in the utensil drawer for a corkscrew when those words jerked her head up. "You're nervous about this?"

"Maybe a little." He rolled his shoulders. "I don't much like talking about myself."

"So I noticed." Lauren's own apprehensions abated in the face of his confession. "It'll be painless, I promise."

"I doubt it."

She'd found the corkscrew and he took it from her, along with the bottle, which he opened with an ease that belied his earlier claims of ignorance. She found two wineglasses, which he filled expertly.

Back in the living room, he sat on the couch and she picked a chair. She took a sip of her wine. "Mmm, very nice."

"Can we do this backwards? Q and A first, niceties later?"

Lord, he was practically vibrating with tension. She thought briefly about letting him off the hook, but decided he wouldn't thank her for it. A bet had to be honored.

"Sure. We could do that," she said. "Why don't you pick it up wherever you want?"

"My mother died when I was three."

Good gracious! Lauren didn't know what she'd expected, but it wasn't that. He was going back some. "I'm sorry."

He didn't even look up from his contemplation of his wine. "I don't really remember her, except maybe for her voice. Sometimes I think I can remember that." He swirled the ruby liquid, as yet untasted, in his glass. "But the point is, my daddy pretty much raised me. He wasn't mean, I don't guess, but he didn't have much softness in him either."

Lauren had a sudden image of Cal as a motherless child, all solemn gray eyes. With effort, she clamped down on the emotions the image evoked. Cal wouldn't thank her for her pity, either.

"By the time I was fifteen, we were butting heads pretty regular. I wanted to ride broncs and drive fast cars, and I didn't much care for the day-to-day grind of ranching." Finally he sipped the wine, but it might have been water for all his expression gave away. "The day I turned sixteen, I split."

"Because you were bored?"

"No, because I had an awful fight with my dad. It was my birthday and I was planning to go into town with the boys. As usual, the old man forgot. Anyway, he told me I couldn't go, said he had a fence that needed mending. The long and the short of it is that we fought, I left and didn't look back. His parting words to me were that I was no good, that I never would be any good, because I couldn't settle to anything. Said I'd wind up busted up in the rodeo or working for wrangler's wages."

"I'm sure he didn't mean it."

"Oh, he meant it all right."

"So you set out to prove him wrong by starting this ranch?"

"No." He gave her a crooked grin. "I set out to prove him right. Made a name for myself on the bullriding circuit."

"Bulls? Those big Brahmans, you mean?"

74

His grin widened at that. "Brahmans make good bucking bulls all right, but they got all kinds. Far as I know, they just have to be big enough, athletic enough and rank enough."

"And you did that for how long?"

"Too long. I've broken more bones than I can remember, some more than once. But it's hard to leave. Paycheck's real good, if you can stick on the bulls long enough to get into the money. You gotta be young and foolhardy to do it, and healthy to win at it. By the time I called it quits, I was neither."

"So you took your winnings and bought the ranch?"

"Yes, ma'am. Right after I convinced Marlena to be my bride."

His voice was laced with self-mockery. Again, Lauren hurt for him. "I'm sorry it didn't work out."

"Wasn't her fault." He shook his head and laughed. "Man, I don't know what I was thinking. I really don't. The poor woman went from running with one of the top-ten bullriders in North America to being a struggling rancher's wife." He tipped up his glass and drained it. "The mistake was mine. I didn't even stop to think what the adjustment would be like for her."

Lauren could certainly empathize with Marlena, but she couldn't let that pass. "No more of an adjustment for her than for you, surely."

"I was more than ready to give up the adrenaline rush, but Marlena wasn't. I should have left her in Calgary. She'd have snagged herself another rising star, no problem."

Lauren frowned. "If that were true, what's she doing here? Why isn't she on some cowboy's arm in Calgary?"

"My fault, too." Cal twisted the stem of his glass. "As beautiful as Marlena is, her youth is behind her, and the rodeo is for young bucks. Young bucks who have their pick of beautiful women. She was already on what she called the wrong side of thirty when we met. She ran with me for a couple of years, then after we were married she stuck it out here for another couple. All in all, it was a poor investment for her, hooking up with me. By the time the dust settled, she wasn't top-drawer anymore."

Something inside Lauren lurched precariously. She'd never known a man so ready to accept responsibility for . . . well, for everything. She took the empty glass from him, afraid he would snap the stem as he toyed with it. She refilled it for him and passed it back, topping her own off at the same time.

"It seems to me you've taken all the blame here."

He shrugged. "It was my fault."

"All of it?" she asked quietly, meaning Marlena's betrayal, praying she didn't have to spell it out. She didn't.

"Marlena had no trouble staying faithful when I was at the top of my game." He stared into his wineglass again. "Even most of the time when I was hurt. It wasn't until I dragged her out here that our real problems started. And that, as I've already said, was my fault. She needed more attention than I was prepared to give her, and . . ." He glanced up sharply. "Oh, hell, how'd I get side-tracked? Marlena's got nothing to do with why I'm running a dude ranch for yuppie cowboys."

"Then tell me what does."

He put his wineglass down. Lauren got the distinct impression he wanted to stand, or pace maybe, but there was no room in her tiny cabin. Instead, he slouched back on the sofa and stretched out his legs in a semblance of relaxation.

"Well, since I couldn't rub the old man's nose in it by keeping my name in the winners' column anymore, I changed tactics. I decided I'd get myself a bigger ranch and a bigger herd than he ever managed to build. I sank everything I had, plus everything the banks would lend me, into this ranch and the breeding program. But since then the market has gone from bad to worse. Then this summer I had a run of bad luck. Brush fire in May claimed some animals, and a rash of lightning strikes took some more. The economics are brutal. Fact is, I'm teetering on the brink. That's what led me to the idea of giving this guest ranch thing a try."

"And is it everything you'd hoped?"

"It's only just started to turn a profit. Not enough yet to stabilize the other operations, but it will." He leaned forward, nabbed his drink, and took a swig. "No matter what I think of this dog and pony show, it's gonna be my salvation."

The image of Marlena's dead body on a rocky outcropping flashed through Lauren's mind. Cal's salvation could well evaporate, or stall to the point that he couldn't hang on to the ranch, if her premonition came to pass.

Cal was still talking. "Then I can concentrate on building the herd. I've got land enough to graze twice the cattle, but I've got to get through this downswing first."

Lauren hid a smile. This was a different Cal when he talked about ranching. Gone was the tight look around his mouth. "Herefords, right?"

"Nothing but."

She smiled at his obvious pride. "So why Herefords?"

"They're about as efficient as you can get."

"Efficient?"

"They turn grass into pounds faster than other breeds. They're hardy—they'll thrive anywhere. They're gentle-natured and easy to work with. And as a bonus, they make good eating. Nice marbling without excess fat."

"Gee, why would anyone raise anything else?"

He grinned. "You got me."

She sucked in a breath. Lord, that smile was deadly.

Right up there with Dennis Quaid's. "Well, cowboy, it sounds like you've got it made," she quipped. "A cattle ranch you love and a sideline to tide you through the market downturns."

His face sobered instantly, gray eyes cooling. "No, I don't have it made. I won't have it made until I've doubled the herd. I won't have it made until I find some kind of financial stability." He raked a hand through his still-damp hair, making it stand up in spikes. "When I can look the old man in the eye and tell him to goddamn well choke on it, that's when I'll have it made."

The bitterness in his voice dismayed her. Somehow, with his laconic telling of the tale, she hadn't grasped how volatile his relationship with his father must have been. Even more troubling was his apparent inability to savor his accomplishments to date. She groped for the right words.

"Success is relative, Cal. You've got a beautiful ranch here. Just because you haven't surpassed your father's stature as a cattleman doesn't diminish what you have achieved." She laid a hand on his forearm, the better to impress her words on him. "You can't let someone else define success for you."

He surged to his feet. Two strides carried him across the room. "Haven't you been listening? I *am* defining my own success in the clearest of terms. It'll be enough when I beat the old man at his own game." He pivoted to look out the window, though there was nothing to see but the lights of the main ranch house. "Some things are easy to measure, and this is one of 'em."

His short hair stood boyishly on end from shoving his hands through it. Unbidden, a picture sprang to Lauren's mind of a younger, more vulnerable Cal, a boy who'd had to make do without the tenderness of a mother's love.

She saw him again in her mind's eye as a rebellious young man, chafing against his father's cold authority.

Another image, this time of a handsome bullrider whose beautiful girlfriend was faithful when he was winning and "mostly faithful" when he was broken.

Her heart squeezed painfully, but with more than mere pity. She was amazed at the man that he'd become in spite of those things. In those few short seconds, she made her decision. She knew it was probably foolhardy, but she wanted this man. She wanted to give everything that she had so he would know he was wanted.

And he wanted her. He'd made no bones about it. He wasn't looking for forever; he knew she had to go home eventually. So where was the harm in it?

Suddenly, she couldn't remember.

Before her courage deserted her, she stood and crossed the worn softwood floor to where he stood. Heart trembling at her own audacity, she slid both arms around him from behind. He drew his breath in a hiss, and for one horrifying second, she thought he'd pull away. Then she felt the angry tension in him change to something else. His hiss turned to a groan when she pressed herself against his back. She smiled her relief into the soft fabric of his shirt.

"You're absolutely right," she murmured, taking heady pleasure in the small shudder that went through him. "Some things are easy to measure, like how much I want to make love with you."

Cal almost jumped out of his skin when she slipped her arms around him. Only the soft crush of her breasts against his back stopped him from breaking away. Then she said it, the words he'd been aching to hear. *I want to make love with you.*

As he'd shaved that night, he'd practiced the words of seduction he'd use on her to bring her to that confession, but now he didn't know what to say. Words had deserted him.

With a wry smile, he lifted her right hand and settled it palm-down in the center of his chest. "Can you feel that?"

She trembled slightly. "It feels like it's going to explode," she breathed against his back.

"Only if you don't let me turn around."

"Oh. Of course."

The warmth of her body retreated. She tried to drop both hands, too, but he kept the one he'd pinned to his chest. It made for an awkward turn, but no way was he letting her go now.

His breath caught again at the look on her face. Desire sharpened every feature and put a flush on her cheekbones. It also made her very soul shine out of those blue eyes. Her warm, generous, fix-the-world soul.

She's too good for you.

The thought blindsided him. He'd had his share of success with women, but they'd been much like him, just looking to get themselves through. Lauren was different somehow. He didn't know how he knew, but he did. Those other women understood exactly what they were getting in him. And more importantly, what they weren't getting. He seriously doubted Lauren did.

Dammit! He was going to give her a chance to back out. He could feel the words welling up in him. To stop them from bursting out, he tipped her head up and pressed his mouth to hers. Damn, she tasted good. Like sin. Like red wine and night and woman.

He lifted his head and the words escaped despite the desire burning in his gut. "Are you sure?"

She slid her hands down to ride the waistband of his jeans. "I'm sure."

He rested his forehead on hers, breathing heavily. "You understand it's just sex? No bride and groom on a wedding cake, no happily-ever-after?" He felt her nod, but he had to have the words. "Still want to?"

"Only as much as my next breath."

That was all he needed to hear. Taking her at her word, he hauled her against him again and cut off her next breath with his mouth. It was not a tasting, testing sort of kiss. It was a devouring. For long moments, there was nothing but the pounding of his own heart and the harsh sound of their breathing.

When he released her mouth at last, she sagged against him. "Take me to bed, Cal."

He didn't need another invitation. Hoisting her high, he let her slide down his body, the exquisite friction making him tremble. "Put your legs around my waist," he urged hoarsely, and when she complied, he groaned. "There's one fantasy down. I've wanted to feel those legs around me since I first laid eyes on you."

"Glad to oblige." She'd wrapped her arms around him too, and the soap scent of her rose up to further torture him. "But I hope that's not the only fantasy you've been entertaining."

"No, ma'am, it's not," he assured her as he headed for the small bedroom at the back of the cabin.

"Good, 'cause I've got a few fantasies of my own."

His legs almost locked at that. Chrissakes, she wrote erotica! Heaven only knew what shape her fantasies took. His probably looked pretty unimaginative compared to hers.

He reached the bedroom and suddenly he didn't know what to do with her, or what to do with his own self-consciousness. Drop her on the bed and follow her down? Stand her on her feet and ravage her mouth? He'd never been accused of a lack of imagination in the bedroom, but what would she expect? This was a helluva time for a crisis of confidence. Despite his near panic, he wanted to laugh.

Unlocking her legs, he let her slide down the length of him. As soon as her feet touched the floor, she went for his mouth, and that was his salvation. He forgot his indecision in the fiery heat of her. In a move that was pure instinct, he gripped her bottom and pulled her closer, taking a savage satisfaction in her gasp.

She broke the kiss to tug at his shirt. "Get this open. I want to touch you."

"Gladly." His fingers flew over the buttons. With each one he freed, she spread the shirt wider, her cool hands sliding greedily over his exposed chest. When he'd undone the last button, he reached behind his head, intending to yank the damn thing over his head by the collar, but she stopped him.

"Not so fast."

She pushed the shirt back so the fabric confined his arms, her hands like delicate birds on the points of his shoulders. For agonizing moments, she just looked at him in the dim light cast by the small bedside lamp. Then she pushed the shirt all the way off his shoulders. One shrug and it fell to the floor.

Cal couldn't take his eyes off hers. And Lauren, it seemed, couldn't take her eyes off his chest.

"Perfect."

Her breath stirred against him, making him shudder. "Perfect? I think you need another light in here, sweetheart."

She lifted one hand and trailed it across his pectorals, her touch as light as the brush of a butterfly's wings. He sucked in a breath and the muscles of his stomach contracted. That ripple of motion drew her other hand, which seemed intent on mapping the ridged terrain of his abdomen. Then her fingers stopped. They'd found the hard diagonal furrow under his rib cage.

"What'd I tell you?" he said. "Not perfect after all."

"Scar tissue?"

"A shaving nick."

Her hand was moving now, measuring it. "I'd say it was a little more serious than that. What happened?"

"Souvenir from my bullriding days." Her hand hovered over the spot, the merest kiss of flesh on flesh, and damned if he didn't feel a soothing energy flowing into him.

"A bull gored you?"

"Not intentionally. Not that some bulls won't try to stick a horn in you, but that time it was my fault. I got my hand stuck in the bull rope. He was just trying to shake me loose."

She lifted her gaze to his face at last. "Are there more?"

" 'Fraid so." He covered her hand and guided her fingers to another scar. "This one's a lot smaller, but it was a more serious injury." Her fingers seemed to freeze, and a ghastly thought struck him. What if she were squeamish about that kind of thing? No, surely not. She was a vet, after all. On the other hand, maybe she had expected perfection. She could sure as hell command it.

"You know, Lauren, now's the time to bail if you're gonna "

"Bail?" Her eyes sprang wide. "Why would I want to bail?"

"If the scratches and dents bother you . . ."

She stepped back and pulled her sweater over her head. "They don't bother me."

"Apparently not." His voice was little more than a croak. She stood before him, her midriff bare above the waist of her jeans, her small breasts cupped lovingly by white lace. Cal took one step backward and sat down on the bed.

"Come here."

She just smiled a slow, sexy smile, then reached behind her back to unhook her bra. Cal held his breath as she peeled it off and tossed it aside. Her breasts were beautiful, small, high and firm, their nipples dark. Lord, how long had it been since he'd been with a woman? And how much he wanted this one.

"You are so beautiful," he said when he remembered to breathe again.

"You like?"

"I like." Cal didn't know how much more of this long, slow build-up he could stand. "Come here and I'll show you how much."

He circled her waist with one arm, pulling her close between his legs. The other hand he used to shape one breast, to learn its texture and weight. *Slow,* he reminded himself at the leap in his groin. *She wants to take it slow.* With deliberateness, he nuzzled his head between her breasts, watched her nipple stiffen. For long minutes, he tortured her with his breath and his callused fingers, the hitching of her breath in the silence his reward.

She broke first. Her hands grasped his head, guiding him to her thrusting breast. Gripping her hips, he closed his lips around the tight bud he'd been tormenting. The sounds she made were a prayer of relief and gratitude. He didn't know if it was the sweet noises she was making or the taste of her that did it. Either way, his own self-control was swept away like a twig in a flash flood.

He pulled her down onto the bed. The delicious shock of chest-to-chest contact was enough to slow them, but only for a moment. Then they were rolling, tangling, mouths mating, hands seeking, finding. He undid her jeans, dragging them off without ceremony, leaving her with just a small triangle of white cotton. Then, as he watched, she peeled the last barrier away and tossed it on the floor.

He might have found control enough to savor the picture she made, but she wouldn't be slowed. She was intent now on getting his buckle undone. Afraid he'd embarrass himself if she touched him with those butterfly fingers, he rolled away and shucked his jeans off himself, underwear and all. Before discarding the jeans, he extracted a condom from a pocket. Flopping back on the bed, he held it up for her to see.

"Don't hate me for bringing this. I really wasn't presuming anything—"

The look in her eyes—Lord, had they always been so blue?—stopped him. Her eyes didn't despise him. Nor did the fingers that skimmed his forearm. She took the condom from him with a wolfish smile, and he felt something break loose inside him.

"I sincerely hope it's not the only one you brought."

He grinned. "No, darlin', it's got some friends."

She tore the packet open and knelt beside him. As she sheathed him, her touch was a curious combination of the sureness of a surgeon's hands and the reverence of a lover's. He groaned, half in arousal and half in self-mockery.

"Good thing I brought spares. I think I'll have to make it up to you next time. This is gonna be way too fast."

She laughed, a clear joyous sound. "Race you, cowboy."

She did.

He rolled her underneath him and entered her swiftly and without preamble, eliciting a muffled half-scream from her. He froze in confusion. Had he hurt her? Then he felt her muscles begin to contract around him and understood.

With a growl of his own, he withdrew and filled her again, exulting in her cries. Once, twice, three times, and each time she sobbed her pleasure. He wanted to go on stroking her forever, but she was flying apart. Then she locked her legs around him and he came apart, too. Mindless, he hammered into her until his world shattered.

Lauren came back to herself slowly, a piece at a time. In her arms, Cal still shuddered, and she marveled at how helpless he seemed. Somewhere in the region of her heart, a well of tenderness sprang, as sweet as it was unexpected. She stroked his heaving back as he regained control.

"Sorry, I must be crushing you," he said at last.

"Mmm, but in the nicest possible way."

Reluctantly, she let him pull away, but he didn't go far. He rolled onto his back, insinuating one arm under her. Without conscious thought, she curled into him, her lips curving as his arm came up to smooth her back possessively.

"I guess it was embarrassingly evident that I needed a good . . . crushing, eh?" she said.

There was a pause, and his fingers stilled. "I'm not very good at reading between the lines, Lauren, so I'll just ask. Are you saying it's been a long time?"

"Almost three years."

Another pause. "But I thought . . . I mean, you write erotica. . . ."

His presumption took her breath away. She hadn't stopped to think how her lie had colored his perception of her.

"Ian Fleming wrote James Bond. That doesn't mean he ran around killing bad guys and seducing women."

"Good point," he conceded. "Just for the record, it's been a long time for me, too, if you hadn't already guessed from that performance." He grimaced. "I should be thanking you for saving me some serious face."

Mollified, she lifted her head and traced one finger along his smooth chin. He must have shaved tonight. For her.

"Mmm, and what a nice face it is," she said. He grazed the callused tips of his fingers across her hip just then, causing her to suck in a breath, but she refused to be distracted. "Do you know, the first time I saw you, I wanted to touch your face."

"Yeah?"

"I wanted to see if it felt as hard as it looked." God, she couldn't believe she was telling him this stuff.

He treated her to that devilish, cocky grin. "See anything else you liked?"

His hand had slid down to explore the indentation of her waist. Desire mushroomed again in her belly. And something else, something more tender.

"Yes, I've seen plenty I like. I've seen your patience with kids when you're teaching them to ride. I've seen your forbearance toward Marlena, in spite of the problems she poses. I see your loyalty to Jim, who anybody can see is too crippled up with arthritis to do the work he used to do. I see—"

He rose on one elbow. "Yeah, yeah, and I open doors for ladies and help old folks across the street." He tipped her head up and kissed her mouth hard, almost angrily.

"What was that about?" she asked when he let her breathe again

"You'd pretty much reached the end of my redeeming qualities, so I thought I'd save you from floundering."

Lauren wanted to protest that she hadn't even begun, but the hardening of his eyes told her to let it go. Instead, she gave him what he'd been fishing for, the physical stuff.

"Okay, I confess. It was your back."

"My back?"

With the flat of her hand, she pushed him back down. Then, before she lost her nerve, she wriggled up to a sitting position, then moved to straddle him. Her own fluidity surprised her. Geez, with any luck, he'd think she'd done this before! Far be it from her to explode his fantasies about erotica writers. Especially when his eyes blazed with such carnal approval.

"Yeah, your back," she said as his hands came up to smooth the outside of her thighs. "There's this thing you do when you're riding sometimes. Your back is slightly bent and your shoulders are really loose. You look . . . I don't know . . . weightless, I guess, like you've become part of the horse."

"Cutter's slump," he rasped. His hard hands grazed a path along her hips, then closed on her waist. "We use it when we're working cattle. And stragglers on trail rides, too, it seems."

"Cutter's slump—that's a good description." She drew a finger down his chest to his abdomen, delighting in the way his muscles bunched under her. She could get used to this position. "There's just something about the angle of your shoulder blades, the way your neck slopes into your shoulder . . ." She leaned forward, bracing herself against his chest, to touch her mouth to that very confluence of sinew. The salt taste of him bloomed on her tongue, sharp and exciting, so she worked her way along the cord of his neck with open mouth. Then he tangled his fingers in her hair and lifted her mouth to his.

His kiss was fierce, devouring. Beneath her, his heart thundered and she felt the urgent press of his arousal against her buttocks. Instinctively, she rotated her hips and gasped as his penis nudged her most intimate flesh. Desire spiraled out of control. She would have reared back then to accommodate him, but he locked his hands on her and held her firm.

"Condom!" he managed in a strangled voice.

Condom! Of course. How could she have forgotten? "Where?"

"Jeans. Front pocket," he gritted.

She dove for his jeans, retrieving a packet. "Got it."

He took it from her. "Better let me do it this time."

He was too intent on the task to see the flash of her smile. Should she tell him today was the first time she'd ever put a condom on a man? Nah, let him keep his illusions.

Illusions that might be the sole reason he wanted her.

The thought dampened her humor, and her ardor, a little. She was tall, with good legs, but otherwise unremarkable. Boyish, even. Her waist didn't dip enough, her hips didn't swell enough and her breasts didn't jut enough. And Cal was definitely the kind of guy who went for all that dipping, swelling, jutting stuff. Even if she hadn't met Marlena in the flesh, she'd have known that much.

"Come back to me, baby."

His words silenced the neurotic voice in her head. That, and the powerful erection he sported. Whatever his reason, there could be no denying he wanted her now.

And now was all that mattered, wasn't it? All they had.

He waggled his eyebrows suggestively. "Now, where were we?"

That dispelled her wistful mood instantly. Laughing like a hyena, she dived onto him. He caught her, grunting as he absorbed her weight.

"Laugh at me, will you?" His hands skimmed her sides

teasingly. "You realize I'll have to make you pay for that?"

"Mmmm." She lifted her hands to his and guided them over her breasts. "And pay, and pay, and pay . . ."

Chapter Six

Cal caught himself whistling as he wielded the paint-brush. Grinning, he slapped varnish on the last two-inch slat in the cedar tub surround he'd constructed to house the new hot tub. Finished, he stepped back to admire his handiwork.

He'd resisted the idea of an outdoor whirlpool—this was Alberta. Two months of summer and ten months of hard sledding. But he had to keep up with the trends, and hot tubs were in demand. Besides, he was developing an appreciation for them.

For about the millionth time today, he pictured Lauren in it, steaming water caressing her breasts. . . .

"Ooh, hot tub. Is it operational yet?"

Marlena. "Sorry to disappoint you. Need a visit from the electrician first." He put his brush on the newspaper and capped the can of stain. "But by this time Friday, you could be just as pruny and sunburned as you like."

"You know I never go out without sunscreen," she murmured.

Cal felt her eyes on him as he gathered up his materials

and glanced up. "Was there something I could do for you, Marlena?"

She squinted at him. "There's something different about you. . . ."

"Yeah, I'm deeper in debt. You have any idea how much these units cost?" Not waiting for a reply, he strode to the shed.

"That's it!" she exclaimed. "That's your sex walk."

He stopped. *"Excuse me?"*

"Don't even try it, Taggart. I know that walk, like everything's been lubricated. We were married, remember?"

Something in her tone made him look closer. She looked, he realized, as though she might splinter into a hundred pieces.

"I do remember," he said gently.

"It's that black-haired one, isn't it? That Townsend woman."

"Marlena, I don't think we should be talking about this. . . ."

"No, it's okay. It's good. Good that you've found someone. I'm happy for you, Callum."

"It's not like that." He stepped into the shed. If he thought he'd discouraged her from continuing the conversation, he was mistaken. She entered the shed right behind him.

"I'd say it's exactly like that. I've seen how you look at her, you know."

He didn't argue, just set about cleaning his brush.

"You know what's funny?"

Geez, why did women want to talk about this stuff? "What?"

"After all this time, it feels like I've just lost you."

"Marlena . . ."

"Oh, I know, I lost you long ago, after the things I did. But through it all, you never took up with other women."

Aw, hell, she'd sprung a leak. Cal pulled a handkerchief from his pocket and passed it to her. As always, he was helpless in the face of tears. "Don't cry. I hate it when you cry."

"I'm sorry. I know it doesn't make a lick of sense, especially after my own conduct, but it feels like you've been unfaithful." She blew her nose and took a deep breath. "Crazy, eh? Not that she's the first, I'm sure. It's just my being here, seeing you . . ."

"She *is* the first," he heard himself saying. "And I understand how you feel." He did. Sort of.

She wadded the handkerchief up into a ball. "You're moving on."

"I guess." Cal wished he could find the words to help her. He'd loved her once, or thought he had. "We all have our demons, Marlena. Lord knows you had it rough growing up. We had that in common. It was the thing that bound us."

Marlena dabbed at her eyes, which, Cal noted thankfully, were now dry. "Yeah, but you didn't make a mess of your life like I did."

That was arguable. "You can stop running, you know. Rest up. We could get some help to get you off the chemicals. . . ."

"Stop running?" Marlena laughed. "Oh, Cal, you know I can't stop. If I stand still, it all catches up with me." She touched her hair as if to assure herself it was unmussed. When she spoke again, she sounded much more like herself. "Which is why I'm going to saddle up and drag Brady out for a ride."

A scraping noise from outside caught Cal's attention.

Then he saw the Stuart boys fly by the open door. Just kids chasing a barn cat. He stuck the paintbrush in a bottle of solvent.

"Sunset ride's just a few hours away."

"I can't wait that long. I'm crawling inside my own skin, Cal. I need to ride *now.*" Marlena folded her arms across her chest, her fingernails raking her forearms. "You can spare Brady for a few hours, surely."

She really was in a bad way, and he'd help put her there by withdrawing her cache of drugs. "Sure, I can spare him."

He gestured for her to precede him, and they stepped out into the sunshine together, right into Lauren's path.

"Lauren!" he said.

"Hi."

His pulse leapt like a jackrabbit as their gazes met. She'd been hard to resist before he knew how she tasted, what her skin smelled like, how sweetly she fit under him. Now, when he looked at her, his senses sizzled. For a second, an answering heat deepened the blue of her eyes, then her gaze slid away.

"Marlena, did I just hear you say you're going riding?" she said.

"Mmmm. Me and Brady."

"Where are you headed?"

Marlena was clearly surprised by the question. "I don't know. Open horizons, I guess. Why you askin'?"

"I'm feeling pretty restless myself. Mind if I tag along?"

Marlena shot Cal a look, but he was too surprised to react.

She turned back to Lauren and shrugged. "Sure, if you want. But pick a fast mount, not that nag you usually ride. I've got some steam to blow off." Marlena cast Cal another speculative look, but he kept his face blank. Then she turned back to Lauren. "I'm going to find Brady. Meet us at the stables in ten if you're coming, otherwise we leave without you."

Marlena strode off. Cal grabbed Lauren's arm before she could follow suit.

"Don't go. I've got an hour before I have to start tacking up horses." He relaxed his grip to caress the sensitive skin at the crook of her elbow. "Maybe we could put it to good use?"

Lauren suppressed a groan at the leap of need. It wasn't fair that he could call up so much desire in her with that tiny stroke of a thumb. And it wasn't fair that she couldn't stay here and luxuriate in it. Their time would be so short. . . .

"I'm sorry, Cal, I can't."

"Of course you can." He pulled her around to face him, toe to toe. "I've been thinking about you all day. About us."

She felt herself tremble. "Me, too."

"I want to peel your clothes off real slow, in the full light of day. And every inch I uncover, I want to taste." He leaned his forehead on hers, as shaky as she was.

"Oh, God, that sounds good." She sagged against him, inhaling the clean scent of aftershave and man, knowing suddenly that she'd remember the smell of him as long as she lived. Then she remembered Marlena, and jerked away. "But it'll have to wait. Come see me after supper."

With that, she spun and hurried off toward the stables before she—or *he*—could change her mind.

She passed a miserable afternoon. True to her promise, Marlena rode hard. It was all Lauren could do to keep up, even with the faster mount, a blue roan whose psychic vibes all but overwhelmed her.

Then they began to encounter streams crisscrossing the grassland, and the pace slowed. Though neither Marlena nor Brady complained, Lauren knew she was very much a fifth wheel. Lauren rewarded their civility by pretending to doze under a tree with the horses while they took themselves off to "swim" just around the bend in one of the rivers they forded.

Being an unwelcome chaperone wasn't the biggest of her miseries. No, her biggest preoccupation was the frustration that pulsed in her blood. She could be in Cal's arms right now, making slow, soul-stirring love with him. She'd felt as though she were being torn in two back there when he'd implored her to stay.

This is why you were supposed to steer clear of him. How could she protect Marlena when her senses were filled with Cal?

With discipline, she answered her own question. *Just like you showed today.*

A less manic Marlena led the trek back to the ranch. By the time they got there, the sun was already riding the horizon. Marlena was safe for another day. Cal would be steering the guests home right about now, which meant he was probably a half hour away. Time enough for a bath before slipping into one of the dresses she'd brought with her, a simple black wraparound.

And still he didn't come. Eventually, hunger drove Lauren up to the house, where Delia made her some sandwiches and a carafe of tea to take back to her cabin. She ate slowly, her nerves jumping with excitement. Cal should be back any time. Any minute, she'd hear his boots on the wooden porch, his soft knock at her door. Any minute, she'd be hurling herself into his arms.

Except the minutes turned into hours, the anticipation into crushing disappointment. When the hands on the old clock showed nine o'clock, she accepted the inconceivable. He wasn't coming.

After all that had passed between them the night before, he wasn't coming. She leapt to her feet. How could he do this to her?

That's probably what he thought when you went after Marlena.

The thought had her sinking back on the sofa. Was this how he'd felt? Deflated? Confused? Hurt?

Well, there was only one way to find out.

She marched up the path to the main house and found Delia.

"I need to talk to Cal. Where can I find him?"

"Try downstairs. I think he's in the bar with the boys."

Lauren had no trouble finding the place; once she got downstairs, she just followed the mournful voice of the Cowboy Junkies' Margo Timmins caressing an old Hank Williams tune. The "bar" was neither dark nor overly smoky, but she supposed it approximated a honky-tonk. A young woman Lauren recognized as a sometime waitress from the dining room stood behind the small bar reading. A handful of men sat on stools watching football on a wall-mounted TV. A glance told her that Cal wasn't among them. She eyed the other end of the room, where a group of men and women crowded around a pool table. She didn't see him there, either.

Then she heard the unmistakable sharp crack of the cue ball breaking racked balls. When the shooter straightened so she could see him over the heads of the small crowd, Lauren's jaw dropped. *Cal.*

A lit cigarette dangled from his lips as he contemplated his next shot with narrowed eyes. He looked so . . . different. Yet hadn't she pictured him like this the first time she'd laid eyes on him? Tonight, he exuded a sort of restless, ragged cool that stole her breath away. Whatever it was, it was sexy as hell.

He leaned down to bridge his shot, shirt stretching taut along his back. Lauren had to crane her neck so as not to lose sight of him. He made the shot. Moving quickly now, he chalked his cue and lined up the next ball. It dropped, too. And the next and the next until he'd cleaned the table.

Cheering erupted among the few onlookers. Cal spread his arms, palms up, in a mocking show of acceptance, then removed his cigarette from his lips and stubbed it out. A woman touched his arm and spoke directly into his ear. White-hot jealousy shot through Lauren as she watched the other woman with her head so close to Cal's. Laughing, he pulled away from the woman, tossed his drink back, then headed for the bar. Lauren intercepted him.

"Cal."

"Lauren." He sidestepped her without missing a beat and spoke to the woman behind the bar. "Another one, Katie."

The barkeep's eyes widened, but she took his glass.

"And one for the lady, too." Cal turned to her. "What'll it be?"

Lauren's skin chilled as he turned his gaze on her. She'd forgotten how glacial those silver eyes could look.

"I don't want a drink."

Katie slipped an old-fashioned glass in front of Cal. It looked like straight whiskey, but he tipped the glass and took a swallow without grimacing.

"So, what did you come here for, then, if not for a drink?"

His breath fanned her forehead. Yep. Whiskey, all right. "I thought you might come by tonight."

"I wanted to come by *this afternoon.*" For a moment, his disaffected air slipped just enough to give her a glimpse of the hurt beneath. Then the mask was back in place. He pushed away from the bar to leave, and she clutched his sleeve.

"You're angry with me."

He pulled his arm free but didn't walk away. Neither would he look at her. "I'm angry with myself for getting tied up in knots over something that doesn't have you tied up the same way."

A savage surge of elation shot through her at his admission. Hard on its heels came confusion. She shouldn't want him to care so much. But she did. And she owed him similar honesty.

"You don't think I was torn over this?"

"Torn, yeah. I could tell by the set of your back as you rode away." He angled a look at Katie, who'd been watching the exchange, and she quickly retreated to the other end of the bar.

Lauren chewed her lip. "I don't know if I can make you understand. . . ."

"Tell you what. I'll save you some time and awkwardness. You regret it already. It was a mistake, a lapse in judgment, and you don't want to repeat it but you're not sure how to tell me." He swallowed the last of the whiskey and placed the glass on the bar. "Consider me told."

"No! That's not it at all." She laid a hand on his chest to prevent him leaving. "I don't regret a minute of last night. Maybe I should, but I don't."

His heart raced under her palm, disproving his detachment.

"You needed some space, then? That it? I'm crowding you?"

"Of course not."

He passed a hand over his eyes. "Okay, then it must be

that you don't want anyone to know that we're involved. You want to keep this strictly an after-dark activity."

She could have screamed. "I didn't say any of that. Stop putting words in my mouth. Can't you just accept that I had to go?"

"No," he said flatly. "No, I can't. I need a sound, logical explanation. Come on, Lauren," he growled, turning to face her squarely. "Give me something I can work with."

She bit back a laugh. How logical would he find her visions? How sound would he think her motivation for traveling thousands of miles to babysit a woman she didn't even know? How understandable would he find it that she harbored suspicions about one of his hands? About *him?* Could he "work" with that?

"That hard to think of something I might swallow?" With an impatient noise, he brushed past her, heading for the door.

"I had a premonition, dammit."

Her words arrested him. He turned slowly. "A premonition?"

"Yeah, a bad feeling about Marlena riding out today."

Cal's eyebrows shot up. "But why? She wouldn't have been alone. She had Brady with her."

"I know. But remember the day she almost killed herself flying down that ridge? We were all with her that day, and she could easily have killed herself."

"She was high as a kite that day, which won't happen again," he said, looking unconvinced. "I flushed her pills, remember?"

"I know, but I still couldn't shake the feeling."

He let his breath out in a gust. "Hell, is that all? Christ, Lauren, I imagined all kinds of scenarios. . . ."

"I think I've just heard a few of them," she said dryly.

"Well, you could have just flat out told me."

His forehead had smoothed, but his posture still looked a little stiff. She gave him an exaggerated eye-roll. "Yeah, right. You'd have laughed it off, then seduced me into staying."

A glint of humor lit his eyes, and his lips curved upward, making her catch her breath. "Okay, maybe you have a point there."

"Besides which, you'd think I'm a flake."

He snorted. "I'd hardly brand you a flake over a little premonition. I've never met a woman yet who didn't think she had a leg up on men in that department. Which, of course, they do."

His shoulders were starting to lose that stiffness, warmth slowly replacing doubt in his eyes. It wouldn't take much to fan that warmth into something hotter. Not much at all.

"It's true, we are more intuitive," she said, drawing her tongue over her upper lip. "In fact, I'm having a premonition right now."

"Is that so?" She felt his gaze on her mouth like a touch.

"Absolutely. I was thinking that if I were to turn around and walk out of here and back to my cabin, you'd follow me."

This time, his smile was slow and lazy, lighting her up from the inside out. "How very perceptive of you, Miz Townsend."

She didn't get far. Cal caught her outside the house, spun her into his arms and kissed her thoroughly in the crisp night air. Lauren melted against him. Dear Lord, where did it come from, this dizzying excitement? Maybe he breathed it into her, infused it with his mouth, his hands. Euphoria popping along her nerve endings like champagne bubbles, she twisted loose and dashed away.

His muffled oath made her laugh, but when she heard his feet pounding behind her, she put on another burst of speed.

He caught her again on the porch of the cabin, his momentum carrying them up against the door.

"Gotcha!" he growled before dipping his head to kiss her again, hard. She thrilled to his taste, which was familiar, yet strange with the tobacco and whiskey influences. His hands took full advantage of having her pinned against the door, and roamed her body wildly. Desire mushroomed in her belly. It was heaven, but it wasn't enough. *Too many clothes. Too vertical. Too public.*

Reaching behind her, she twisted the knob and they all but fell inside. Cal kicked the door shut and dragged her back into his arms. When neither could breathe anymore, he released her.

"Whoa, we better slow this down," he rasped, running his hands up and down her arm from shoulder to elbow.

"Slow down? Why?" She pressed close, nipping at his chin.

His laugh rumbled through her. "I seem to remember promising slow and thorough this afternoon."

"How about fast and reckless? You offered me that, too, I believe, about a minute after we met." She caught the lobe of his ear between her teeth and bit gently. "Remember?"

His answer was a feral growl as he crushed her against the inside of the door. He kissed her with a ferocity that shocked, then excited. Only when he eased away from her to rake her dress open did she realize he'd managed to untie it. He palmed her breasts, abrading them gloriously through the lace of her bra. Her gratified sigh ended on a sharp gasp as he roughly swept the cups aside. Then his fierce, hot mouth was suckling at her.

She tried to hold it together, closed her eyes against the

carnal picture of his head at her breast, but that only served to drag her further into the inner world of sensation. She needed him inside her, *right now*.

She dragged his head back up for another soul-searing kiss, sliding a hand down between them to skim the hardness straining against his jeans. Using both hands now, she tugged his belt free, slid his zipper down. His sex sprang into her hand, ready. Somebody groaned, but she wasn't sure if it was he or she.

"Now, Cal. Right now. I can't wait any—"

He cut off her words with another kiss, pressing her hard into the door as he raked her panties down. She stepped out of them when they settled at her feet. Then he lifted her until she felt his erection nudging her.

"Wrap your legs around me," he commanded hoarsely.

She complied, knowing that was all it would take to get him inside her. The shock of the joining stilled them briefly, then he surged against her, his movements edged with the same ferocity as his kisses. All she could think was, *I did this. I made him crazy like this.* Then all thought was gone, her world dissolved in a powerful climax that carried him over the edge with her.

Cal inhaled deeply. She smelled so good. Felt good, too. Her body was limp as she clung to him, trembling. She was growing heavier by the minute, but he didn't want to let her go

He didn't want to open his eyes, either, and see his self-disgust reflected back at him. Hell, what was he thinking? He'd nailed her against the damn wall like a common streetwalker.

No, correction—the hooker he'd turned to after his first scared weeks in Calgary he'd treated with more respect. Of course, at thirty to his sixteen, she'd been more mother than lover. But the point was, he liked to think he treated all women with respect, even the rodeo Annies who'd tussled over him.

Lauren wriggled, reminding him he was still crushing her against the door. *Way to go, Romeo*. Groaning, he set her back on her feet, pulling the edges of her dress together. He tried to read her face, but her eyes were just a glint. The only light in the room was that spilling in from the sentinel light outside.

"Oh, hell, I'm sorry, Lauren," he said, adjusting his own clothing, wishing there were some more discreet way to do it. "I didn't mean for it happen like that."

"Me, either. That's the first time I've ever forgotten."

Cal's mind was blank. "Forgotten?"

"The condom. I've never forgotten before."

Oh, hell. Oh, God. Oh, no.

"Don't worry, I've been doing a little mental math." She traced a delicate finger over his lower lip, seemingly oblivious to his shock. "We're safe."

He pushed her hand down. "Oh, hell, I forgot the condom."

"It's okay, really." She looked at him oddly. "I may not have finished med school but I was paying attention while I was there. I doubt I could get pregnant right now if I tried."

"You're sure?"

"As sure as I can be."

Well, that was something, at least. Now the rest of it.

"You don't have to worry about disease," he blurted out. "I mean, after Marlena . . . Well, you might be thinking . . ." He shoved a hand through his hair. Geez, he was no good at this. "What I mean is, I got checked when she left. I'm clean."

A pause, then: "And since?"

"And since, nothing."

Silence for a moment. "You mean, I'm the first since . . ."

"Yeah, that's right. I guess the rust is showing, huh?"

She laughed softly. "Mine, too. We should have had this talk the first night. For the record, I'm 'clean,' too. I don't make a habit of sleeping with men on my holidays. Or much of any other time, for that matter. And never without a condom."

Yes! He knew it. Well, part of him knew it, even as he'd speculated about the probable pastimes of pretty erotica writers.

He laughed. "Man, I'm so lousy at this."

"You're not doing so bad. But I've got one question."

"What's that?"

"If you hadn't yet realized we'd forgotten the condom, what were you apologizing for?"

He blinked. "That's pretty obvious, isn't it?"

"Not to me."

She was touching his face again, making it hard to think. "You don't think what I did just now was just a little . . . barbaric?"

She laughed, a low, musical sound. "Cal, you were an animal. And I loved every minute of it. The only thing that remains to be seen is, what kind of animal." She pressed close again. "I was sort of hoping you're the water-loving type so I could talk you into that big antique tub with me."

She touched her mouth to his chin, but he didn't lower his head to give her the kiss she was angling for

An animal? Like his prize bull? Like the stallions he kept? A weight seemed to land on his chest, squeezing it.

Chrissakes, Taggart, grow up. That was always the way of it. And a good thing, too. He had little else to offer a woman.

Besides, that's the way it was supposed to be with Lauren. Wasn't that why he picked her? Honest sex with no strings. And wasn't Lauren-in-the-water exactly the subject of his fantasy this morning?

Damn right it was. He pushed the confusing stuff to the back of his mind and bent to kiss her slowly, thoroughly.

"Lead the way to that tub of yours, sweetheart. I'll do my best impersonation of an otter."

Some time after two o'clock, Cal jolted awake. Lauren's bed. Lauren's cabin. He'd been going to rest his eyes for just a minute before leaving, and he must have fallen asleep. But what had woken him?

Cold, he realized, as a crop of goose bumps rose on his arms. Odd for August. It should be cool but not cold.

Beside him, Lauren's breathing quickened. Maybe the cold had wakened her, too. Well, he could warm her. Smiling, he rolled over, looping an arm around her waist.

She was rigid as a fence post.

He shook her gently. "Lauren, what is it? Bad dream?"

She didn't acknowledge him with even a flicker of movement.

He sat up with a start, swearing as he groped for the lamp. After a few fumbling seconds, he located the switch and flooded the bed in a circle of light. When he turned back to look at her, the apprehension in his gut erupted into full blown fear.

Her jaw was clenched hard, her teeth ground together, and her hands were clenched at her sides. Hell, it looked as though her whole body was clenched. But that wasn't the worst of it.

It was her eyes that struck fear into him. Wide and terrified, they seemed to look right through him. He actually turned to see if she were watching some horror behind him.

"Lauren, can you hear me? Wake up!" He shook her again, this time less gently, but to no better effect. It was as though she wasn't even there, as though she'd slipped right out of her body.

He needed to call an ambulance. He lunged for the phone on the night table and dragged it back to the bed. "Hang in there, darlin', I'm going to get you some help."

"No."

Just a whisper, but he heard it. He dropped the receiver. "Oh, Lauren. Are you okay? You *did* speak, didn't you?"

"No doctor." The words were stronger this time, but still little more than a whisper. He put the phone back.

"Look at me," he commanded. This time she did focus on him. "Thank God! You really are back. Now, let's see you move."

The fingers of her right hand fluttered feebly.

"Lauren, that isn't funny."

"Comes back," she said, sounding as though she had a mouthful of marbles.

"What comes back? The movement?"

"Yes."

He dragged a hand over his face. "For the love of God, what is this? What happened to you?"

She made no answer this time, just stared at him mutely. Then one fat tear broke from her eyelash and slid down her temple into her hair.

Groaning, he crawled back onto the bed beside her. "I'm sorry for yelling. You just scared me." He brushed her hair back from her face. "Would it be okay for me to hold you?"

Another tear slid silently into her hair, but she gave a perceptible nod.

He gathered her carefully into his arms, tucking her head into his shoulder and aligning her frozen limbs with his. She felt stiff enough to shatter, but bit by bit her muscles began to relax until she lay pliant against him. Pliant and sleeping. It didn't take very long. Maybe fifteen minutes.

Fifteen minutes for her to regain herself.

Fifteen minutes for him to lose himself.

Lauren smiled. She was having the nicest dream, cocooned in a warm nest. She stretched luxuriously. So warm, so hard . . .

So hard? Her eyes flew open. Cal. He was still here. But it was full daylight. She glanced at the clock radio by the bed.

Ten o'clock! She shot up. "Cal, wake up. The riding clinic . . . you're late."

"I've been awake for hours." His hand came up to trace the curve of her naked back. "You're the sleepyhead, darlin'."

"But the guests . . ."

"I called Jim around five and told him I planned to have a little lie in. He'll have things in hand."

She blinked. A little lie in? She'd bet he'd never slept in once in his adult life. He had too much vitality for that. She groaned. "Oh, Lord, what must Jim think?"

His hand fell away. "I expect he's thinking I'm getting some hot sex, but I figured you'd rather I didn't tell him about your little rigor mortis routine."

Rigor mortis routine? What . . . ?

Oh, God, yes. The vision.

She'd actually forgotten about it. Once wakened by a vision, she usually huddled wide-eyed on the couch under a blanket until dawn, reliving as much of it as she could. But last night she'd fallen into a profound sleep. Cal's strength and toughness had seemed to radiate right into her along with his body heat, robbing the vision of its usual harrowing aftermath.

"You remember now. I can see it."

"It's nothing." She clutched the sheets to her breasts and felt the force of her own heart pounding.

"Nothing?" His gaze pinned her. "I almost called 911."

Should she tell him? Could she? The voice in her head screamed, no! Every experience she'd had—from her mother to her doctor, from her fiancé to the police—taught her there was nothing to gain and everything to lose from telling that truth.

She lowered her head. "The doctors describe it as a seizure." That, at least, was truthful.

"Like epilepsy, you mean?"

Her head snapped up. "No, not epilepsy." Though the family doctor had mistakenly treated her for it when she was a teen. She'd tried to tell him it was visions, not epilepsy, but her efforts earned her a session with a psychiatrist. After that, she'd learned to stay quiet about it and palm the pills.

"I always know when it's coming. I have a good half hour's notice, plenty of time to get to a safe environment." She lowered her eyes and plucked at the blanket. "I'm not an insurance risk, if that's what you're thinking."

"This happens regularly?"

"No, not regularly. Occasionally." She looked up at him then. "I *am* safe, Cal. If I can work around it well enough to perform surgery, I can handle myself here."

He raked a hand through his hair. "Hell, Lauren, I wasn't thinking about me, I was thinking about you. You couldn't move, couldn't talk. You were so . . . vulnerable. I hate that."

"I hate it, too, but I can work around it." She ran a hand along his stubbled cheek. He looked so appealing, his eyes clouded with concern and his hair tousled. Unexpectedly, her heart squeezed. "I should have told you this last night, but I guess I zonked out on you. You really didn't have to stay."

"It was no hardship." He turned his face into her palm and the slight rasp of it sent a shiver through her. "That is, if you don't count the part about letting you sleep unmolested. I didn't know I had that much saintliness in me."

She laughed, then drew him down with her. "Such saintliness should be rewarded, don't you think?"

"Mmm, I sure hope so."

Before she could claim that lush mouth with her own, someone rapped on her door, hard, and a male voice sounded.

"Cal, are you in there?"

Chapter Seven

"Spider. Dammit." Cal leapt up and dragged his jeans on.

"Spider?" Lauren blinked up at him.

"Spider Jenkins, one of the cowhands. He wouldn't track me down unless something's wrong." He shrugged into his shirt, then went to get the door. Spider stood on the threshold, the brim of his hat clutched tightly, his balding head gleaming in the sun.

"Come in, Spider, before you mangle that hat."

Spider stepped inside. "Sorry about this, boss."

Cal shrugged. "If Jim sent you, it's gotta be important."

"You got a dead yearling on the west boundary, right close to the old MaKenny spread."

Hell, there went another chunk of change. "What happened?"

"Well, that's why I'm here. I never seen nothin' like it."

"Grizzly?"

"No, it weren't nothin' like that. Seems like it died from the inside out."

Cal's heart skipped a beat. "What do you mean?"

"Billy says it couldn'ta died more than a day ago, but it's

111

bloated something wicked. And blood. Looks to me like it bled pretty bad from its nose or mouth or somethin'."

Oh, no. Not disease. "How long to get there?"

"Not long at all. We can take my truck."

Cal exhaled, forcing down his apprehension. "It's not far off the track, then?"

"You can see it from the road. That's how Billy knew it musta died recently. He swears it weren't there yesterday."

Cal looked around for his hat, then realized he didn't have it with him. To hell with it. "Let's go."

"I'll come with you."

At Lauren's voice, Cal glanced up to see her in the doorway, fully dressed, a set of binoculars around her neck and a backpack slung on her shoulder. Of course she'd want to come.

He nodded once. "Right."

Spider's eyes bulged at Cal's easy acquiescence. "You're the boss, boss, but do you think that's a good idea? I almost lost my breakfast, and I've seen some ugly stuff in my day."

Despite his anxiety, Cal smiled. "I imagine she's seen more things die 'from the inside out' than we have. Spider, meet Lauren Townsend. She's a veterinarian."

Spider grinned. "You must be the gal had that bet with Cal over Cosmo, then? Ain't often the boss loses a wager."

Cripes, they'd heard about his lost bet in the farthest reaches of his ranch. Somehow, he couldn't muster much pique, though. Not after she'd made losing so gratifying. "Come on. You two can trade laughs at my expense once we get on the road."

Twenty minutes on the main road and another fifteen on a number of back roads put them in the vicinity of the MaKenny property. They crested a hill and Cal saw the carcass even before Spider touched the brakes.

They climbed out of the truck, ducked under the fence and headed toward the fallen steer.

"Wait, guys," Lauren said. "Let me get a look before we get any closer." Lauren raised her field glasses. Cal watched her face intently. Her lips compressed into a thin line as she focused the binoculars. Then she proceeded to scan the area around the animal. Damnation, he wished she'd say something.

"What do you see?" he asked when he could contain himself no longer.

"You can look for yourself," she said, passing him the binoculars. "But first, Spider, did I see a tarp in the truck?"

"Yes, ma'am."

"Would you fetch it, please?"

Spider looked to Cal, who nodded his sanction, and the cowboy trudged back toward the road.

"Did you really need the tarp, or did you just want to get rid of Spider?"

"Both. Now lift the glasses and have a look."

He obliged. The steer was hugely bloated, its white face bloodied. The drought-yellowed grass around it was splotched with brownish blood. "Hell." Cal's stomach dropped. He could think of only a couple of things that could kill a cow like that, but one in particular leapt to the fore. The stories from the outbreak in Red Deer last year were still fresh in his mind.

"Anthrax?"

"Rapid death, with bloating and epistaxis. You'd have to suspect it."

"Epis-what?"

"Bleeding from the nose," she said absently, obviously lost in thought. "Though I believe there's a strain of botulism . . ."

He lowered the binoculars. "No, I don't think so. I've seen that."

"Any anthrax reported this year?"

"Nothing so far this season. Twenty or thirty animals died last summer, but that was over in Red Deer." His knees went weak as he remembered. Twenty or thirty animals. The shape he was in right now, that'd be a hard hit.

"Have you lost any other animals?"

"Like this? No."

Lauren tugged on a pair of work gloves. "It wouldn't have to be exactly like this. An acute case can die within an hour without symptoms, while a subacute case can last days or weeks."

"No." He shook his head. "We lost a couple of calves in calving season, a few yearlings to a brush fire and some more to lightning strikes, but nothing like this."

"Would you necessarily know, with the cattle in pasture?"

"Yep. We move the herd to prevent over-grazing, and when we move 'em, we count 'em. My men would have detected any losses."

"What about other herbivores? Mule deer, white-tailed deer, that sort of thing? They're vulnerable because they churn the spores up, then ingest or inhale them while grazing."

"Don't think so. My men would report anything like that, too." He watched her chew her lip.

"Speaking of reporting, you'd better call the veterinary inspector."

The full gravity of the situation crushed down on him. This was more than a dead cow. More than the prospect of twenty dead cows.

"This'll ruin me, won't it?" He gripped the binoculars until his fingernails hurt. "I report this, it'll be in the *Globe and Mail* tomorrow. DEADLY ANTHRAX TOXIN SUS-

PECTED AT GUEST RANCH. Who'll want to spend their vacation here then?"

She blanched. "But, Cal, you have to report it." She laid a hand on his arm. "You have a statutory obligation. It's a federally reportable disease. . . ."

He pulled away. "Hell, Lauren, of course I'll call them. I know what my responsibilities are."

"I realize this could make it tough for you, but . . ."

"Tough?" He laughed harshly. "If this guest ranch revenue dries up, I'll lose everything."

Cal felt wound about as tight as he could get, but there was no need to take it out on Lauren. None of this was her fault. He passed a hand over his tired eyes. If only he'd slept last night, he might be able to think. He watched Spider pull a black tarp from the back of the truck. "Okay, what do we do now?"

"Why don't you go make that call while I secure the scene?"

"Secure the scene? Sounds like a crime novel."

"The carcass has to be wrapped to protect it from carrion-eating birds and insects."

Protect it? "What? You're worried about a few ravens dying?"

"Probably wouldn't even kill them. Birds and bugs aren't really very susceptible, but they can transmit it to other hosts. But that's not the real problem."

"It's not?" If the prospect of mosquitos loaded to the gills with anthrax wasn't the real problem, he wasn't sure he wanted to hear what was.

"The real problem is that they would open the carcass," she said. "Exposing this bacterium to oxygen induces sporulation."

Damn. "That doesn't sound good."

"It's not. The spores can persist for up to forty years.

But if we make sure the vegetative cells stay inside the carcass, they'll be killed in a few days from putrefaction."

"You're kidding?" He blinked. "They'll rot?"

"Yep. But some jurisdictions require you to incinerate the carcass whole or bury it with quicklime, though the latter can leave viable anthrax spores for future generations to dig up."

He could feel sweat on his upper lip, but resisted swiping it. "So we just have to tarp the carcass?"

"I'm concerned about the bloody smears all over the grass, too. If anthrax killed this animal, it could be sporulating like crazy everywhere you see blood or feces."

"What can we do about it?"

"I don't know."

Panic skittered along the edge of his control. "You don't know? You're a vet, dammit!"

She paled. "A vet with only a few months' experience with livestock."

"But you know all this other stuff . . ."

"You never forget the pathology of something like this, but the scene management aspects . . . I just don't know." She looked stricken. "I'm sorry, Cal."

Damn, get a grip, Taggart. "No, I'm sorry." He tipped her chin up. "Don't mind me. You've been a big help already."

Behind them, Spider cleared his throat. She stepped back.

"One tarp."

"Thanks, man." Cal took the black tarp before Lauren could.

"What we gonna do with it? Wrap the sucker?"

"I'm going to wrap it," Cal said. "Meanwhile, I need you to call the feds to report a suspected case of anthrax."

Spider drew his breath in on a hiss. "I 'spected as much, but it's still a shocker."

"I'll say. Oh, and use the cell phone in my Ford back at the ranch. It's unlocked. I don't want to alarm anyone."

"Gotcha. These lips are zipped soon as I make that call. But first I'll help you wrap that poor ol' whiteface."

"I can manage."

Spider blinked. "Beggin' your pardon, but how you gonna do that, boss? That steer's gotta be six or seven hun'ert pounds."

"It's my problem, Spider. I don't want to expose anyone." He shot a look at Lauren. "And that includes you."

"Oh, but it's not terribly dangerous," she said.

"I said it's my problem. I'll figure something out." Hell, did she think he'd just let her walk right into a toxic mess? Apparently she did, judging by the stubborn set of her chin.

"And how do you propose to do that?" she demanded.

How indeed? He looked around the pasture. "I could use a fence rail and a rock to leverage it. . . ."

"And risk perforating its hide?" Her eyebrows shot up into her hairline. "Give those spores a breath of fresh air? I don't think so. Not when we can help you roll it right onto the tarp."

Stubborn woman. Didn't she realize he was trying to protect her? Well, he was going to, whether she wanted him to or not.

"You may be a vet, but you're not *my* vet. You're just another *guest*," he said coolly. "With due respect, butt out."

She stepped back as though he'd slapped her, those pale blue eyes going wide. There. After the intimacies they'd shared, he'd relegated her to a mere guest. That should do it. Turning away from the hurt in her face, he started off toward the fallen steer. He felt like the worst kind of bastard, but it couldn't be helped. She wasn't putting herself in harm's way for him.

He didn't realize she'd fallen in beside him until she spoke. "Forget about doing this by yourself, Taggart. You need our help."

He stopped and faced her. Her chin was set at a determined angle. Worse, Spider stood behind her, looking equally resolute. Cal cursed. "Come on, Lauren, what about those spores you talked about? You think I'd let you touch them? Inhale them?"

"First of all, we don't know for sure that it's anthrax."

"But we have to treat it as though it is," he shot back.

"Agreed, but I don't think there's much of an inhalation risk. The spores are in fairly damp environments in the carcass, which means they can't get airborne easily. Even if a few spores got off the ground and we inhaled them, we still wouldn't get sick. Humans aren't nearly as dose-sensitive."

"What about contact?" he challenged. "I know there have been cases of people getting it from handling carcasses."

She returned his glare. "Yeah, people who work in slaughterhouses. There's a big difference between being awash in blood and guts and rolling an intact cow carcass over." Her eyes snapped with anger. "Besides, we'll use gloves. You've got gloves, right, Spider?" She didn't even look sideways at Spider, just held Cal's gaze with a steely gaze of her own.

"Yes, ma'am. We got gloves."

Cal shot Spider a dirty look, but it was clear his employee had already decided whom to take his orders from. He turned back to Lauren, torn by indecision. "You're sure about this? The risk really is minimal?"

"Very minimal. And if it'll make you feel any better, the public health officer will no doubt want to prescribe antibiotics as a preventative measure."

"You mean antibiotics will cure it?"

"Absolutely. We're not very susceptible to begin with, and even if we did contract it, penicillin would wipe it out."

Cal shoved a hand through his hair, stifling a groan. Talk about your good news/bad news. Good to know they weren't risking slow, hideous death. Not so good that he'd probably kissed his newfound sex life good-bye for no good reason by pissing her off.

Just then, she lunged past him, shouting and waving her hands. For a split second, he thought she was having another seizure. Either that or the toxin had already gotten to her. Then two glossy ravens rose into the air amid raucous cawing. Dammit. The birds had found the carcass.

"Okay, you win," he growled. "We all roll the damn steer."

It didn't take long. As an extra precaution, they tied kerchiefs around their faces. When the carcass was securely wrapped in the waterproof tarp, they shed their masks and gloves and left them for disposal.

"Guess I better go make that call," Spider said.

Call nodded. "Get them out here as soon as you can. Tell them we've tarped it, but we'll wait right here for them."

Spider pushed his hat back. "Will do. Anything else?"

"Anyone else tramp out to look at the steer besides you?"

"No. Dilly spotted it, but I was the one come for a look."

"Call Doc Hale and find out what to do. He might want to jam some antibiotics into you."

"I do believe I will."

"Spider?" called Lauren.

He turned back to her.

"When you get back, it might be a good idea to bag

your clothes and boots until we find out what to do with them."

"Yes, ma'am."

When Spider had left, Cal turned to Lauren. "What I said earlier, about you being just a guest . . ."

"I know."

He blinked. "You know? What do you mean, you know?"

"You were deliberately trying to piss me off to keep me away from the carcass, because you thought it posed a health hazard."

His knees weakened with relief. "Then you understand."

Her eyes flashed with temper. "I understand that you were trying to do it all by yourself, as usual."

"Damn right I was." Stubborn woman! Her refusal to appreciate his sacrifice galled him. Dammit, he'd been prepared to give up the pleasure he'd found in her arms— a pleasure he hadn't even begun to plumb the depths of— to keep her safe. "What's wrong with that?"

Lauren sighed. Really, the man was such a trial. "If you can't see it, there's no point my belaboring it, is there?"

"Humor me. I'm a little slow sometimes."

Well, she'd give him that. Along with a piece of her mind. "You're not God, Cal Taggart. You can't be responsible for every little thing. Have you ever considered how arrogant that is? '*It's my problem. I'll deal with it,*'" she mimicked.

"It *is* my problem," he thundered.

"Maybe so, but you don't have to face it alone. That's what friends are for."

His face hardened. "No, friends are for helping celebrate the high times, or maybe to drink your best bourbon. When the chips are down, you can't count on anyone but yourself. If you think different, you've never been dumped down the well."

With that, he turned and strode toward the road. Lauren gazed after him, dumbfounded. He really couldn't see it, the way Spider would go to the wall with him, if he but asked. The way Jim Mallory would lay down his life for him in a heartbeat.

For a moment, she allowed herself the luxury of fury at the cold father who'd taught his son the need for such complete self-reliance, and at Marlena for reinforcing the lessons.

Then she reined herself in. Yes, he had trust problems. Yes, he had intimacy problems. But they were no concern of hers. Their time would be too short to make that her focus. Already the nights were getting colder. Once the leaves began to change, Marlena should be safe for another year.

She shivered. Weeks. That's all she and Cal had.

He gave no sign that he heard her coming. Leaning on the gate rail, looking east, he looked as though he might summon the federal inspector's vehicle with the sheer force of his will. When she laid a hand on his arm, though, he didn't react at all, a pretty good indication he'd heard her approach.

"I'm sorry," she said, sliding her arms around him from behind. "What I said back there . . . it's none of my business. I just hate to see you taking so much on your own shoulders."

He didn't turn. "I've been all kinds of a fool in my time, Lauren, but the biggest fool is one who puts his fate in someone else's hands. So far, I've managed to avoid that."

Her heart clenched at his aloneness, but she pushed it aside. "You're a very honorable man, Callum Taggart."

He snorted, but she could feel the tension in him changing. "Lady, you don't know the half of it. If you had any idea of the things I've done . . ."

"I know enough. You're the most responsible man I've ever met. And quite possibly the best kisser."

He did turn in her arms at that, as she'd known he would. Whereas praise for his character fell on deaf ears, she knew he'd respond to compliments on the physical.

"Yeah?"

"Yeah."

"Think we can safely engage in a little necking, Dr. Townsend?" He settled urgent hands on her waist, and his silver-gray eyes had caught fire.

"I thought you'd never ask."

His mouth crushed hers almost brutally, but she welcomed it, knowing he put all his bottled-up fears into it. For a brief while, she escaped her own worries, too, in a blaze of sensation.

When the federal inspector arrived two hours later, he found them sitting on the unshaded edge of the road, slowly burning under the late August sun.

Lauren liked Bruce Dysan at first sight. The federal veterinarian was a tall man in his mid-forties. His face was partially obscured by a full blond beard and his hair was a little ragged, but his eyes were alight with intelligence.

"Got it covered already, I see. That's good," said Dr. Dysan. "Not many people know to do that. You're lucky you had a veterinarian on hand." He cast an appreciative glance toward Lauren as he donned disposable coveralls.

Cal agreed.

"I don't normally get here this early. Often the local vet would have been in already and tested for other possibilities. Anthrax isn't usually the first suspicion."

Cal frowned. "You think we jumped the gun on this?"

"Not at all. From the report your man gave me, you've got at least some of the cardinal symptoms. It was a good call. Sometimes the animal dies so fast, they don't present with any symptoms, in which case it doesn't get reported until cattle start dropping like flies."

"What now?" Cal asked.

"I've got to take some blood samples, which means we have to unwrap the carcass. Can you give me a hand?"

"If you can provide the gloves," Cal said. "We ditched ours after handling the animal."

"I can do better than that."

A minute later, outfitted in full biohazard gear, the three of them unwrapped the steer for Dr. Dysan's examination.

"What do you think?" Lauren asked him.

"I'd know better if I could examine its spleen, but that's out of the question for obvious reasons. Can't risk spores getting out of the carcass." His voice was muffled through his mask. "On physical exam, there's a wee bit more rigor mortis than I'd expect to see. Most cases have little or no rigor. Still, the rapid death and the watery discharge . . . it's possible."

Lauren's mind buzzed as she watched him aspirate peripheral blood from the dead animal's jugular vein. It looked like anthrax, yet it didn't. There'd been no previous outbreaks among cattle this season and no wild herbivores were turning up dead

What had Cal said about his run of bad luck? Brush fires and lightning strikes. And now anthrax? Could anyone's luck go so bad so fast without a little help?

Just then, a large truck pulled up with a hiss of air brakes. It carried an excavator behind it on a trailer.

Dr. Dysan looked up from swabbing discharge. "Excel-

lent. That's the backhoe I commissioned to dig our pit."
He glanced at Cal. "Would you mind getting the gate for
him?"

"That was quick," Cal said.

"Quick is our only defense. We can't do much to prevent these outbreaks, but we've got a very good record of
containing them, and one of the ways we do that is to act
expeditiously."

As soon as Cal left, Lauren turned to Dr. Dysan. "Do
you think you could take some extra blood?"

He glanced up, surprised. "Oh, I've got plenty here for
the tests we'll need."

"What if it turns out not to be anthrax?"

"I don't know . . . celebrate?"

Lauren didn't crack a smile as he aspirated more fluid,
this time from the animal's spleen. "You're going to destroy the carcass immediately, right?"

"Yes, ma'am. Unless you can afford to post a twenty-
four hour guard to keep the scavengers away. I assure you
it's quite safe. We'll dig a seven-foot pit and build a pyre
at the bottom, soak it with diesel fuel, topple the animal in
and incinerate it, along with contaminated soil and grass
and anything we've used to handle it. The high tempera-
tures will kill any spores. Even the heavy equipment gets
disinfected afterward with formaldehyde. We don't leave
any loose ends."

"I don't doubt that. But if it turns out not to be anthrax,
will you have enough blood to run other tox screens?"

He gave her a sharp look. "What are you getting at?"

"I don't know." Lauren chewed her lip. "Foul play,
maybe?"

His eyes widened. "You think someone destroyed this
steer?"

She felt foolish under his scrutiny. "I don't know what

to think. All I know is Cal's had a lot of natural disasters this summer. It would just make me feel better if you had a few extra blood samples to fall back on if this comes out negative. Once you destroy the carcass, the option will no longer be there."

He gave her an assessing look. "Okay," he said. "I guess I could take a few more vials."

Cal trudged back across the pasture in time to hear Lauren ask the fed about a quarantine order.

"Will you impose it now, or wait for the blood work?"

The big man stowed his samples carefully in a special transport container. "I haven't decided yet. If there'd been any cases reported this year, I'd slap an order on right away. Maybe I should anyway. Several cardinal signs are present. There's only one lab in the whole country does this particular analysis and that's the Animal Diseases Research Institute in Lethbridge. It'll take at least three days to get the results back, and three days is a long time to wait."

Cal's stomach clenched. An official quarantine order. That'd be no good for business, and there'd be no hope of keeping it out of the press.

"Do a Gram stain with some of that peripheral blood," Lauren urged the vet. "You could do that at the local vet's office before you leave town, couldn't you? What's that take? A microscope and a couple of simple reagents?"

"Could do." Dr. Dysan gave her a thoughtful look. "Actually, by the time I arrive on a scene, the local vet has usually already done that."

"If you get a positive Gram stain, then you can impose the quarantine."

"With a positive Gram stain, you bet your ass I would," he said sternly, "and that means closing the ranch to all traffic—human, animal or vehicle. But if the Gram stain is negative, we still can't rely on it to eliminate anthrax. We'd still need a blood culture and hemagglutination test."

"Okay, if it's negative, Cal will voluntarily quarantine his operations until the results come back from the lab. How's that?"

Cal's mouth fell open at Lauren's offer. "What the hell? Quarantine my ranch without knowing if it's anthrax or not?"

Lauren silenced him with a none-too-subtle jab to the abdomen. "What Cal means is, he runs a guest ranch here. It could spook a lot of people unnecessarily if this gets out to the media. He'll be more than happy to cooperate with you to make sure an official order isn't necessary. Isn't that right, Cal?"

Hell, she was negotiating him right out of a humongous PR mess. He'd fumbled the ball, but it wasn't too late to pick it up again. "Er, that's right. That's where I was going."

"A guest ranch, eh?" Dr. Dysan looked skeptical. "How do you plan to keep paying customers from riding out on the range?"

Good question. How could he keep a dozen guests down on the farm? Then inspiration struck. "I'll put on a rodeo."

"A rodeo?" Lauren said.

"Yeah, we'll make a big event of it."

"Taggart . . ." Dr. Dysan turned curious eyes on him. "Oh, hell, now I know where I've heard that name. Bull-riding, right?"

Cal wished he had his hat to tug down on his forehead. He felt naked without it. "Once upon a time."

"I saw you cover all five bulls at the World Championship." Admiration shone from his eyes. "You must have a bunch of gold buckles at home."

"A few," Cal said, trying to keep his voice relaxed.

"I gotta ask—what's it like climbing on the back of a Whitewater or a Yellow Jacket?"

"Just like they say." Cal gave him his best cowboy-to-cowboy grin. "Like stepping into an eight-second hurricane."

Dr. Dysan laughed. "Well, I guess you have the credentials to entertain folks for a few days. But don't be using any cattle from this particular pasture."

Cal was buoyed by the other man's implied acceptance. "We'll just use calves, which are pastured with their mamas on the other side of that ridge." He hooked a thumb eastward. "Don't have a corral big enough to rope steers anyway."

Dr. Dysan mulled it over a moment. "Okay," he said at last. Then, turning to Lauren: "I'll agree to no official order on a negative Gram stain—as long as I have your assurance that you'll live up to the spirit of a quarantine until the final results come back. It'll be my ass in a sling if this goes bad."

Lauren gave her commitment without hesitation, and Cal could have kissed her. One land mine sidestepped, at least for now.

The fed must have heard his sigh of relief, even over the roar of the approaching backhoe. "Don't call in the bullfighters just yet, Mr. Taggart. If this comes up positive, I'll slap that quarantine order on tonight."

Cal made no reply; the roar of the approaching machine would have drowned it anyway. He took Lauren's arm and drew her back from the din while the inspector conferred with the operator.

127

"Thanks for what you did back there," he shouted.

"Don't thank me, thank Dr. Dysan."

"Oh, I will, but you're the reason he cut me some slack."

She looked away. "I think you overestimate my influence."

"If you hadn't stepped in, he'd have shut me down."

"Not if you'd flashed one of your gold buckles."

He snorted. "Like I said, it's a good thing you were here."

She looked up at him. "You wouldn't have mentioned it, would you, if he hadn't recognized your name?"

Damn, why did it feel like she could look right into him with those pale blue eyes? He shrugged. "No, I wouldn't have mentioned it. Talking about my glory days makes me feel about as old as dirt. So it looks like I owe you one."

It was her turn to shrug. "It was no big deal."

"It's a big deal to me." He held her gaze intently. "You asked him for a professional favor, and he granted it. You put yourself on the line for me when you had nothing to gain by it." His voice grew gruff. "No one's ever done anything like that for me. I'll see that you won't regret it."

He turned and strode back toward the others before his voice could crack like a twelve-year-old's.

Lauren stared after Cal, her eyes stinging. Could it be that no one had ever stood up for him? Even though her own family practically thought her a changeling, she'd always known they'd be there for her if the going got rough. Every child needed to know that. What kind of a parent had Cal's father been to deny his own son that basic birthright?

Her anger melted as something more insidious curled around her heart. Merciful heaven, did he have any idea

128

how she ached to put her arms around him when his vulnerability peeked out from under those layers of tough cowboy? Did he do it on purpose?

No. There was no guile there. He wouldn't angle for sympathy. Basic honesty had forced the admission from his lips.

She watched him cross the pasture, noting the fine shape of his head without his Stetson, the cowlick on the right side of his nape. Oh, but she loved him.

Lauren sucked in a sharp breath. No, that was just careless thinking. It was lust, pure and simple. She loved his tough, wiry body. She loved his mobile mouth and the hard planes of his face. She loved the way he stood sometimes, one hand on his hip, the other thumbing his eyebrow in that way that was uniquely his. And she loved the way he made love to her.

Yes, that was it. Just a greed to possess—and be possessed by—his driving masculinity.

Heaven help her, she was going to miss him when she left.

Later that night, she lay nestled against him in the narrow bed in her cabin, their bodies cooling quickly in the aftermath of their lovemaking. As he stroked her back, his rough hands impossibly tender, she wondered how she was ever going to live without this. When this was over and she went back home, how was she going make her life work for her again?

That was when it hit her, the ominous prickling sensation crawling across her scalp. Oh, God, here it came again. The vision.

Cal lifted his head from the pillow. "You okay?"

She must have tensed, given herself away. "Migraine," she murmured. "I can feel it starting."

He raised himself up on one elbow, his grey eyes serious. "Migraine, or that other business?"

She didn't have to ask what *that other business* was.

"No, this is different."

The lie passed her lips easily, convincingly. If he thought she was going to be rendered helpless by paralysis, he'd never leave her to face it alone. And she couldn't bear for him to see her that way again. "But I'm going to need you to leave. If I turn off the lights, draw the blinds and remove all stimulation, it'll go away quickly."

"You want me to go?"

"Yes."

"I don't know, Lauren." A frown furrowed his brow. "I don't like the idea of leaving you alone, especially when you're in pain."

"Oh, but it doesn't hurt." She had no trouble infusing that statement with honesty. The tingling would tighten into a hot band of pressure, but that part would pass quickly. "It's more of an ocular disturbance." Which it was. Sort of. "If I can just get rid of all external stimulation for an hour or two, I'll bounce right back. Scout's honor."

His gaze pinned her. "You're sure it's not the seizure thing?"

She rolled her eyes. "Please. I've had this since puberty. I think I know what I'm dealing with."

His lips curved. "Okay. I should get some rest anyway. And I definitely should let you get some."

She grinned wickedly. "Oddly enough, I do feel a little drained. Maybe I got too much sun this afternoon. . . ."

He snorted. "Too much sun? Woman, you got too much lovin'."

Five minutes and a half-dozen kisses later, she closed

the door on him. She leaned against it a moment, her smile fading as she listened to him stride off. A perverse sense of abandonment rose in her chest.

Stupid. She'd sent him away, after all. He hadn't abandoned her. What she felt now was nothing more than the loneliness that always engulfed her when the visions came. No one could help her with that. They'd come and go as they pleased, dragging her off to some place she was destined to experience alone.

She walked back to the bedroom on trembling legs, made the bed and stretched out on the coverlet.

"Bring it on," she muttered through stiffened lips. "Just you bring it on. I'm gonna find you."

Ten minutes later, the vision exploded on her consciousness. This time, she was ready for it.

Marlena from behind, with the breathtaking pink and purple tableau of Sunset Ridge behind her. Marlena turning. Marlena smiling that sultry, inviting smile. Instead of wasting time on taking in those details, Lauren reached for the murderer, strained toward his mind. If he were in her head, showing her this, or if she were in his head, then dammit, surely she could feel something of him.

Marlena getting closer in the "camera" of her vision. Gloved hands coming up, seizing Marlena's throat. Marlena's surprise, shock, terror. The struggle.

No, no, no, don't look at that! Look inward. Look at *him.* Die!

The word came through as clear as though it had been spoken inside her head.

That's right, you stupid slut. I want you to die. That's the only thing I want from you. That piece of heaven between your legs won't help you now, you whore. Now give me what I want!

Marlena's struggles growing more feeble. Marlena sagging, collapsing. No life left, no breath.

The vision faded and there was nothing left in Lauren's head but her own scream. *Goddammit, who are you?*

Chapter Eight

Cal leaned on the fence of the makeshift arena as one of his men pelted through the tight cloverleaf pattern of the barrel race. A. J.'s last turn left a barrel wobbling, but it stayed upright as he sprinted out to appreciative applause.

"That was Foothills's own A. J. McKay," said Jim Mallory over the borrowed PA system. "Let's give the man a hand."

Since he'd gotten word late yesterday that the test was negative, Cal had put it in overdrive to get things ready. Though Jim, Spider and Brady knew the real reason for keeping everyone cooped up on the ranch, he'd kept it as quiet as possible. His men had had to be called in, but they hadn't minded leaving the sweaty job of putting up hay to strut their stuff on horseback. And so far his guests seemed to be enjoying the show.

The next rider was Marlena. Her mount, one of Cal's most promising young quarter horses, could turn on a dime. With a "Hiyah!", Marlena burst onto the course. Marlena's balance was perfect, and the compact sorrel beneath her chewed up the course, then hurtled back out the gate to enthusiastic cheers.

They weren't set up to measure split seconds, but that was fast. Serendipity was one fine animal. Hell, Marlena was a fine animal herself, he conceded. Amazing that he could look on her beauty now and be utterly unmoved.

"Wow, that was incredible."

Cal turned to find Lauren at his side, fresh and pretty in a flowered skirt and T-shirt. She'd taken to wearing skirts since they'd stopped the trail rides. As much as he liked her long legs outlined in jeans, he had to admit this was good, too. There was something about the way the soft material draped from her hips. . . .

"Incredible," he agreed. "Serendipity's her name and she's still got a few rough edges, but she's gonna be something else."

The explosion of another horse from the gate drew their attention back to the corral. This time it was Brady putting his paint through the course. When horse and rider surged back out of the gate, the crowd appreciatively erupted again.

"How's the head?" he asked.

"Much better. It was gone within the hour."

"Glad to hear it."

"What were you doing this morning with the other corral?" Lauren nodded in the direction of the east corral with its series of chutes normally used to work the cattle at branding time. "Getting it ready for another event?"

"Yep." He wasn't sure how she was going to like this. Hell, he wasn't sure *he* liked it that much. "Checking the tensile strength of the rails. Had to replace a few."

Her brow furrowed. "How come? Are you going to run steers after all? I thought you said the corrals were too small."

Just then, Spider hailed him. "Yo, boss. I think I found just the bull you're looking for. He's on his way this very minute." Belatedly, he tipped his hat to Lauren. "Ma'am."

Cal cut straight to the point. "You sure he'll buck?"

Spider looked insulted. "Wouldn't be much of a show if he didn't, now, would it?"

Lauren gasped. "You're going to have bullriding?"

"Yup," said Cal, regretting the leap of fear in her eyes.

"Cal, what if someone gets hurt? Think about liability."

"This'll be a one man show, and nobody's going to get hurt."

"You could get hurt."

The words seemed wrung from her.

"The only thing that might get hurt is my reputation," he assured her. "If this bull lets me ride him like a yard dog, I'll never hear the end of it."

"No fear there," said Spider. "I found you a bona fide professional. Leastways he used to be. Rancher over in the next county bought him with an eye to breeding bucking bulls."

"A pro?" Cal felt his pulse quicken. "Do I know him?"

"Boy, howdy, I'll say!" Spider's grin almost split his face. "It's your ol' one-horned pal from Vegas."

A jolt of respect straightened Cal's spine. "Misadventure?"

"Yep. Looks like you've got yourself a rematch, boss."

"Rematch?" Lauren's horrified gaze went from Cal to Spider. "What do you mean, his old pal?"

Spider was more than happy to fill in her information gaps. "Misadventure's the devil who ventilated Cal's innards for him."

The noise of the crowd seemed to soar, then recede, like waves breaking on the shore. Lauren's heart sank as she gripped the fence. Cal was going to ride a bull. Not just any bull, but one that tried to kill him, judging by the scars it left behind. Scars she'd traced with her own fingers. With her mouth.

Death by Misadventure. The phrase popped into her brain. Beside her, Cal and Spider continued to talk as though there were nothing wrong, but their voices, too, faded in and out.

"He'll go to the left out of the chute . . . remember Calgary that time . . . he looked left, but went right . . . getting a little stout these days . . . still got that nasty belly roll . . ."

"No!" Lauren found her voice at last. "You can't do this."

Both men turned to look at her. From their expressions, she might have shouted an obscenity. Spider's eyebrows were lost somewhere under his hat and Cal looked mildly astonished.

"Oh, but I think I can."

Lauren's pulse kicked again. "You don't have to do this, Cal. The barrel races, the calf roping, the roping clinics—"

"Will hold their attention for a full day, maybe a day and a half. And what do I do then, when people get restless?" He made an impatient noise. "This stuff," he gestured to the barrel racing course, "is about speed and skill, but rodeo is more than that. It's about risk. We can't give them steer wrestling or roping, so it has to be bull riding." He gave her his most lethal smile. "Besides, I happen to be pretty good at this, you know."

Fear and anger gnawed at her gut. She wanted to smack that grin off his face. Hands fisted at her sides, she forced her emotions down. She had to be clearheaded, appeal to his reason.

She took a breath. "I know you're good at it, but you've been retired a long time. What's it been? Four years? Five?"

"So has the bull," he countered. "Spider says he's gotten fat and lazy eating Alberta grass. It'll be a cakewalk."

His gray eyes blazed with an excitement he couldn't hide, and her heart sank. There'd be no changing his mind, she realized. He *wanted* to do this. "I wish I could believe that."

"Of course you can believe it. Hey, why do you think he's retired?" He tipped her chin up with a gloved hand. "Lauren, it'll be just like riding a rocking horse. You'll see."

He spoke with kindness, the way an adult might reassure a terrified child. She knew then that he saw just how scared to the bone she was. *Oh, hell why not just announce to him and Spider and whoever else cared to listen that she love . . .*

Lauren tried to jam the brakes on that thought, but it was too late. Awareness exploded in her mind, jolting her to her fingertips and pushing away even her fear for Cal.

Heaven help her, it wasn't just a case of raging lust. She'd gone and fallen in love with him. Her mind went numb.

"Hey, Lauren, you all right?"

"Yeah, sure, I'm fine." She forced a smile. "And you know what? You're right. You know exactly what you're doing. It'll be all right." With a vague wave of her hand, she turned and headed for the house before she could embarrass herself further.

Cal watched her go.

"You're welcome," Spider said.

"Huh?"

"For not laughing my ass off when you said 'fat and lazy' in the same breath as 'Misadventure.'"

"You did say he was stockier." Cal's gaze followed Lauren.

Spider snorted. "He is that, but you and I both know why that devil was pulled off the circuit."

Cal resisted the urge to finger the ridge of scar tissue that rode his ribcage. "Yeah, we know, but she doesn't have to."

"See, I know when to keep my mouth shut."

"Aw, hell."

"Well, strictly speakin', I guess I coulda stayed mum about Misadventure being the one that sliced and diced you, but . . ."

"No, not that. McLeod's here."

Harvey McLeod had stopped Lauren. She lifted a finger to point to where he and Spider stood, then disappeared into the house. Harvey started toward them. Behind Cal, another rider burst onto the barrel course, but he ignored the commotion.

"Great, just what I need," he muttered under his breath, but when the older man drew within earshot, he called a greeting. "'Afternoon, Harvey. What brings you to Foothills?"

"Heard you had a little shindig going on over here and I thought I'd come take a look. You don't mind, do you?"

Cal minded, all right, but he couldn't afford to show any weakness in front of the man who would have his ranch.

"Of course not," he said, pasting on a smile. Out of the corner of his eye, he saw Spider slip away. At least he wouldn't have to lay on the false hospitality in front of his cowhand. "You're welcome to watch, but it's pretty small-time stuff."

Harvey lifted his eyebrows. "If there's any truth to the rumor I heard, I wouldn't call it small-time."

Cal narrowed his eyes. "What'd you hear?"

"That you'd be riding your nemesis."

Geez, his neighbor must have known about the rematch with Misadventure before Cal himself got the news. Of course, there was no way he'd admit that to Harvey. Cal put on his poker face. "Well, for once, the grapevine's right," he confirmed. "Misadventure's on his way right now."

"When do you ride him?" Harvey's eyes gleamed with poorly concealed anticipation.

Cal almost snorted. Did Harvey imagine Misadventure would finish the job this time, leaving the ranch up for grabs?

"The first time, you mean?" The words were out before Cal could stop them, and Harvey's black eyebrows disappeared clean up into his snow-white hair.

"You're gonna try to ride that devil more than once?"

There was no backing down now. Cal shrugged casually. "Wouldn't be much of a rodeo if someone didn't cover three bulls. Since we have only one, I guess I'll have to cover it three times."

Harvey fairly licked his lips. "Starting when?"

"Tonight after supper." Cal sincerely hoped the bull would arrive in time to save him from a lie. "I'll go twice tomorrow."

Harvey looked at his watch. "Mind if I hang around for it?"

"Be my guest. Delia lays on a real nice spread for supper. Now if you'll excuse me, I've got some preparation to do."

With that, Cal strode toward the barn. If he was going to get up close and personal with Misadventure, not once but three times, he'd better find his lucky bull rope.

While he was at it, maybe he could find a zip for his lip.

Lauren tried to stay away, but she quickly discovered the only thing worse than watching the idiotic jerk of a man she loved risk his neck foolishly was *not* watching it. Consequently, six o'clock found her corral-side with Brady and Marlena as Cal tried to settle atop the bellowing yellow monster.

"Relax, honey," Marlena advised, not taking her eyes off Cal. She'd given no indication of wanting to spend time anywhere but the ranch since the makeshift rodeo had first been announced. "Our Callum's done this a thousand times."

Lauren shuddered, knowing it was true. No doubt Marlena had watched him with that same avid gleam in her green eyes.

Just then, Misadventure jumped, grinding against the chute.

"Look! Do you see what that bull's doing? He's going to crush his leg." Lauren shoved her hands into the pockets of her skirt to conceal their trembling.

Marlena laughed. "They're just jockeying. Cal won't nod for the gate until the bull lets him get a leg down, and the bull knows it. Misadventure wants this contest as much as Cal does."

Lauren swallowed. Marlena was right. Even from this distance, she sensed the keen edge of the beast's anticipation.

"What's Spider doing? Are you sure there's nothing wrong?"

Marlena cast her a scathing glance. "I'm guessing you've never watched bull riding before?"

Lauren resisted the urge to tell her just what she thought of bull riding and the people who watched it. "You'd be right."

"No, there's nothing wrong," Marlena said, returning

her attention to the activity in the chute. "He's helping Cal get the bull rope on there just right. A rider can only use the one hand to hang on. The other one he has to keep in the air. If his free hand slaps the bull before the eight seconds is up, the ride's no good. That rope'll be the only thing he'd got to hold onto once that gate swings open, so it's got to be secure."

Secure. Lauren let out a breath. Secure was a good word. And Cal was taking his time. That had to be good, right?

"Only thing is, he doesn't want to get tied down *too* good," said Brady. "If he can't free his hand when it's time to bail out, it can get ugly."

Lauren had a mental picture of Cal tethered to the monstrous animal, getting flung around like a rag doll.

"He's ready," cried Marlena. "See, he's nodding his head."

Lauren saw Cal's Stetson bob rapidly, almost as rapidly as her heart was beating, and the gate swung open.

The Brahman exploded out of the chute with incredible vertical loft, landed stiff-legged, then started spinning dizzyingly, all the while bucking and rolling.

Lauren's heart stopped. Beside her, Marlena ran a rapid-fire commentary. "He's going to the left! Atta boy, Cal. You read him like a book. No, wait! He's reversing the spin."

Lauren knew nothing about bullriding, but it was obvious even to her that the bull's move had thrown Cal off balance. He was leaning too far left. One more twist and he'd come flying off.

It didn't happen.

Somehow Cal pulled himself back to center, leaning dangerously far out over the bull's head. For the last few seconds, he looked in complete control, if a one-hundred-eighty-pound man could be said to control a ton of enraged bovine.

When the whistle sounded, it took Cal a second to free his hand, long enough for Lauren to think for one terrifying moment that he was stuck. But the next instant she saw daylight between bull and rider. Cal landed in a crouch, stumbled a few steps, then scrambled up on the fence. The crowd inhaled as Misadventure roared after him, but the rodeo clown, or bullfighter, as Marlena called him—successfully distracted the beast. Within seconds, the bull, still raking the air furiously with its single horn, was herded into a chute. Lauren released a shaky breath, along with the rest of the crowd.

"There you have it, folks." Jim Mallory's voice crackled over the PA. "Cowboy one, bull zero."

The small crowd went wild. Grinning, Cal retrieved his bull rope and his hat, which had come off in the unceremonious dismount. Dusting his hat off, he scanned the thin crowd of spectators, his gaze stopping on Lauren. He jammed the hat back on, stopped to shake hands with his bullfighter, whom Lauren now recognized under the frizzy, red clown hair as one of Cal's hands, then came straight toward her.

Lauren caught her breath again, this time for an entirely different reason. As he strode toward her, his tanned forearms caught the sun. The protective vest he wore hugged his torso, emphasizing the way broad shoulders tapered to a trim waist. *And man, oh man, the chaps*. Worn over his faded Wranglers, they seemed designed for the sole purpose of framing his masculinity.

Suddenly, as she stood there with desire unfurling in her belly, she had a clear picture what it must have been like for Cal all those years. Conquering the bulls, then having his pick of beautiful women, all eager to share his bed. A surge of raw jealousy singed her already ragged nerves. She stepped back from the fence as though to distance herself from the intensity of it all, but Marlena and Brady crowded closer.

"Pretty ride," Brady said, reaching through the fence to take the bull rope from Cal.

Cal scaled the fence and dropped lightly to the ground.

Marlena caught him around the neck and laid a kiss on his mouth.

"That was just like old times," she said when she finally let him breathe. "I don't know how you stuck on there. He had you bucked off for sure. I swear there was nothing holding you on but willpower."

To Lauren's relief, Cal pried Marlena's hands from around his neck and nudged her firmly away.

A layer of dust clung to him, but his eyes shone like burnished silver when he finally turned to Lauren. Lord, he was so beautiful. And such a reckless fool. She wanted to throw herself at him, kiss him hard, claw him. Instead, she smiled tightly, turned on her heel and left.

"Whoops, guess the lady doesn't have the stomach for rodeo."

Cal ignored Marlena's comment. Stripping his riding glove off, he handed it to Brady. "Stash that for me, would you?"

Without waiting for a reply, he strode off after Lauren. It took some doing to catch up to her long-legged stride.

"I guess I don't have to ask what you thought of the show," he said when he finally fell in beside her.

"We've been over this." Lauren let a couple of kids race across her path, then continued toward the house. "I just hate to see you risk your neck needlessly."

He bit back a sigh. "I had to do something to hold their

interest. Look how soon they tired of the barrel races." He placed a hand on her arm to slow her. "I had no choice."

She stopped abruptly, fixing him with a glare. "Don't give me that, Cal Taggart. You loved every minute of it. Don't deny it. I saw it in your eyes back there."

He looked away for a moment, watching Jim and three other hands transfer an irritable Misadventure back into his trailer.

He turned back to her. "Okay, I enjoyed it," he admitted. "It's what I did for a good part of my life. I'm *good* at it."

"Well, I didn't enjoy it," she snapped. "It's worse than stupid auto racing."

He lifted an eyebrow. "You think they're hoping to see a wreck?"

"Don't you?"

"Hell, no. I mean, sure, the risk factor plays into it, but they watch for the same reason I ride—they enjoy the contest."

Her eyes narrowed. "If you enjoy it so much, why'd you quit?"

"I already told you. Because I'm not a kid anymore. It was time to start thinking about something other than having fun."

She gave him a hard stare.

"And I was slowing down a little, I guess," he conceded. "I couldn't ride at the level I needed to ride to keep winning."

"Precisely. Which is why you have no business riding that . . . monster. Your reaction time—"

"My reactions are plenty fast enough for a retired bull."

"Retired bull! Don't humor me, Cal."

"I'm not—"

"I talked to Jim about that bull. He told me it was pulled

off the circuit because it was too dangerous."

Great. Thank you, Jim. "That was years ago. He's mellowed a lot since."

She grasped Cal's arm with surprising strength. "Don't ride him again. You beat him once, the crowd got its thrill. Please, Cal, let that be enough."

Cal looked down into blue eyes gone dark with worry, and wished with surprising vehemence that he could oblige her plea. No one had ever asked him not to ride a bull before. Well, except his father, maybe, but his father's distaste for the sport had nothing to do with concern for Cal's well-being. He'd just wanted his son to stop fooling around and settle to ranching.

But he'd already committed himself. An image of Harvey McLeod, a knowing smirk on his lips, sprang to mind. No, he couldn't back down. Not now.

"Sorry, that's the drill. Cowboy has to cover three bulls."

"Yeah, but Misadventure is a third-round bull. In real competition, the first two bulls would be a lot easier."

Cripes, he supposed he had Jim to thank, too, for her newly acquired rodeo savvy. "I wouldn't call any of them easy."

"But they get progressively harder with each round, right?"

"Right," he clipped.

"So why put yourself in the position of riding three third-round bulls? You'd never do that in competition."

He drew breath to protest that it wasn't the same, that Misadventure would be beaten down each time he was ridden, but he never got his answer out. A voice cut him off.

"Cal, there you are."

He glanced up to see a flushed Delia hurrying across

145

the grass. Oh, hell. What could possibly have gone wrong now?

"Trouble in the kitchen?"

"No, nothing like that." She aimed a quick "hi" at Lauren, then turned back to Cal. "I just wanted to warn you we've got an unexpected visitor and I'm not sure what to do with him."

"Oh, you mean Harvey McLeod?" Relief flooded his nerve endings, making him aware of how tense he was. "He's been here since four. I told him he could stay and take in the show."

"No, I'm not talking about Harvey freakin' McLeod!"

Cal looked at Delia then, really looked at her. The unflappable, indispensable Delia was practically wringing her hands. His anxiety leapt like a brush fire in May. "Who, then?"

Before Delia could reply, a voice boomed from Cal's left.

"Hello, Callum."

Wonderful. Just exactly what he needed. As if anthrax and Mis-goddamned-adventure weren't enough to fill his plate.

Slowly, keeping his face carefully blank, Cal turned to face the speaker.

"Hello, Dad."

Beside him, he heard Lauren draw a sharp breath, but Cal didn't take his eyes off his father.

Zane Taggart had aged shockingly. Somehow, when Cal had thought of his father over the years, he'd pictured the same man he'd left standing in the driveway—a blond-haired, vigorous man of less than forty years. He hadn't counted on time robbing the color from his hair or adding height to that forehead, which back then seemed permanently furrowed with disapproval. Nor had he mentally etched in the crow's feet that now surrounded his eyes or deepened the grooves around his mouth. Time had also lent his father's face a kind of softness, too, Cal noticed.

"Still riding bulls, I see. Thought you'd grown out of that."

Cal felt his face burn under his father's words. Softness? The old man might look different, but he hadn't changed.

"Special event, this weekend only," Cal said with an easy drawl. "A bit of a curtain call, I guess you'd call it."

"I see."

I see. Two tiny words, but they said it all. Cal wanted to tear off his protective vest and hurl it. He wanted to drag the stupid show chaps off, too. Instead, he said, "So, what are you doing here after all these years, Dad? Nothing wrong, I hope?"

"No, no," came his gruff reply. "Thought I'd just come down here for a spot of vacation, see how the other half lives."

Vacation? He was staying? "You might have called first."

"What? You're so busy you can't accommodate a last-minute reservation?" Zane Taggart clasped his hands behind his back and thrust his chin out in a gesture Cal used to think of as his drill sergeant mode. "That's not what I heard."

Cal felt the flush of anger reach his neck. "You're right; I do have vacancies, but that's not what I meant. You don't need a reservation. You'll stay in the house as my guest."

"Of course," said Delia. "I'll get the east bedroom ready." She turned to make her escape, clearly conscious of the tension.

"Wait, young lady," Zane called after Delia. "Don't bother with the room." He turned back to Cal. "I appreciate the offer, son, but one of the cabins will be just fine. I can pay my way."

Sonofabitch. He couldn't resist rubbing it in, could he? "Fine. You heard the man, Delia. Get him checked into a cabin." Cal had to force his words through a tightened jaw. "Now, if you'll excuse me, I've got a roping clinic in an hour."

Cal turned and strode off toward the barn.

Lauren couldn't take her gaze off what could have been an older version of Cal. He was stockier and his hair was shot with gray. His face, too, was more weathered by life and the prairie sun, but he had the same proud, almost arrogant bearing as Cal. Then, before her eyes, he seemed to deflate as he watched his son's retreating back. Quite suddenly he looked like an old man.

"Would you like to come with me, Mr. Taggart?" Delia said. "We'll get you settled in a cabin."

At Delia's words, he seemed to recall himself. He straightened his spine. "Of course." His right hand came up as though to remove a hat, but he wasn't wearing one. The absence seemed to disconcert him for a second. "Lead on, Miz Delia."

As Zane and Delia moved off, Lauren turned to scan for Cal. She caught sight of him just as he disappeared into the barn, his stiff-necked carriage telling her volumes about his state of mind. She took two steps in his direction, then stopped herself. *Wait a minute! Don't go after him. He's going to ride that bull again tomorrow and to hell with what you think. He'll probably break his stubborn neck.*

But despite her misgivings, Lauren knew she wasn't angry anymore. Cal really felt he had no choice. And now his father had landed on him, complete with literal and emotional baggage.

With a resigned sigh, she started toward the barn, picking her way carefully in her sandals. She found Cal in the tack room. Scowling, he looked up at her, then went back to rummaging through boxes of odd leather straps and mismatched work gloves.

She drew a slow breath, inhaling the clean scents of oiled leather and horse. Unbidden came the memory of the last time she'd shared space with Cal in this tiny room. She pushed the shuddery feeling down; now was not the time to think about sex.

"Cal, are you okay?"

"Where in hell are my gloves? I left them right here." He slammed the last box back on the shelf.

Lauren jumped at the force of his action. "Your riding gloves? You gave them to Brady."

"No, my work gloves."

"I don't know, but I'm sure you could borrow some—"

"I don't need to borrow any damned gloves." He yanked out another box, pulled out a brand new pair of work gloves and shoved the box back into place. "I just want my old gloves."

She bit her lip. "Are you sure you're all right?"

"I'm fine."

Granite-gray eyes warned her to leave it alone, but she ignored their message. "Your father dropping in like that without warning, after all these years. And on top of the anthrax threat and having to organize this rodeo . . ."

Her words trailed off as she saw his face change. In a heartbeat, his demeanor shifted. Cool eyes now raked her with an unmistakable sexual appraisal that bordered on the insulting.

She swallowed, ignoring the prickle of unease at the nape of her neck. "I mean, anyone would understand if you were upset. We could talk about it, if you—"

"I don't feel like talking." His glittering gaze fixed on her mouth.

"Okay, maybe we could go for a walk by the creek—"

"Don't feel like walking, either." His arm lashed out like a rattlesnake, capturing her wrist. "But since you're so damned anxious to accommodate, I'm sure you won't mind giving me a little of what I *do* want."

In a fluid movement, he crushed her against his chest with one arm. She tried to twist away, more from his offensive words than from the idea of his kiss, but he used his other arm to hold her head. Then he proceeded to plunder her mouth with such ferocity that she was shocked into stillness.

Lauren gasped. It felt as if he'd put a lifetime of anger and confusion into his kiss. His teeth ground against her lips, and the pressure of his hand at her back flattened her breasts against his chest. She slid her hands up as far as she could and pushed against his chest to buy a little room.

He let her go the moment she pushed back. Let her go so suddenly, in fact, that she almost stumbled. Chest heaving, eyes glittering dangerously, he dragged a hand across his mouth. "Better run for it, little girl."

Little girl, hell! She touched a trembling hand to her own mouth, but made no move to leave. "Dammit, Cal, what was that kiss about? That hurt."

He looked away. "Then you'd better get out of here while the gettin's good."

She studied his rigid demeanor, taking in his tight shoulders and averted head.

He was trying to drive her away. That was his intent.

The man who handled everything on his own didn't know how to lean on anyone. He'd rather run her off than have her witness what he clearly perceived as a moment of weakness.

The knowledge changed everything. He wouldn't hurt her, and she wasn't leaving. She couldn't make him share his burdens, but she had an idea how to ease the lid off the pressure cooker of his emotions. She stepped closer, laying a hand on the vest.

"Who's running away? I just wanted to get this thing off you." She couldn't feel his heartbeat through the vest, but a muscle leapt in his jaw. "I was glad to see you wearing it, mind you, but it's got to go now. I can't feel you through it."

He closed a hand over her roaming one. "Don't."

She used her free hand to skim his right hip. "Why not?"

"Aren't you afraid I'll hurt you?" he challenged.

She held his gaze. "Do you want to hurt me?"

"No," he said on an exhalation. "I don't want to hurt you."

"Good." She stood on tiptoe and pressed her lips to his, but he pulled his head back, evidently not ready to surrender yet. She groaned. "What is it now?"

"This might not be such a good idea." The words came out sandpaper-rough. "What I did before, grabbing you, was to scare you off. But I'm so messed up right now, I don't know if I can be careful enough. Do you know what I'm saying?"

The raggedness of his voice excited her. Clearly he wasn't as in command of himself as she'd thought. Suddenly she wanted to see him lose control completely. She wanted—needed—to drown her own fears and anxieties in the taste and smell of him.

"Careful wasn't what I had in mind, anyway." She freed her trapped hand to slide her arms around his neck.

His answer was to jerk her close, but this time his forceful kiss sent a jolt of excitement to her very core. Meeting his invasion of her mouth greedily, she dropped her hands to tug at his vest, needing to be rid of that piece of armor. As though sensing her need, he shrugged out of it, letting it fall to the floor with a thump. Flexing her fingers, she raked her nails over fabric-covered muscle.

Groaning, he wrenched his mouth away from hers. "Better slow this down," he said, his voice strangled.

"No. Don't hold back on me now," she protested.

"Lauren—"

"Please, Cal." Impossibly, desperately aroused, she surged against him, forgetting this was supposed to be for him. "Don't hold anything back."

His mouth crashed back down onto hers. She was drowning, dying for oxygen, yet she didn't want to breathe anything but Cal. Then she felt cool air on her legs as he rucked her skirt up to her waist. Bunching the material in his fist, he stepped back. Lauren could have screamed her regret at losing full body contact, but then she saw his face.

His skin seemed stretched more tautly over his bones, and dark patches of color rode his cheeks. For a moment, he just stared with hooded eyes at what he'd exposed.

Lauren knew what he'd see—bare, tanned legs and sensible white cotton briefs. She wished she'd worn some tiny scrap, some gossamer-thin thing, so he could rip it away with one strong tug. The thought made her knees wobble.

He caught her, lending the support of his chest even as he plunged a hand into her panties. Anticipating his touch, she moaned, spreading her legs, but he merely yanked the briefs down to her knees. Somehow, that was even more arousing.

She shimmied, and her panties fell. She barely stepped free of them before he backed her up against the wall. He kissed her, fiercely and at length, as though he would have her very breath.

From outside, she heard voices buzzing, laughter. *Someone could walk in at any moment.* Instead of horrifying her, the thought just made her hotter.

"Spread for me," he commanded.

Lauren obeyed instantly. When his hand found the wetness between her legs, she fairly climbed onto him.

Growling, he lifted her. Her heart leaping against her ribs, she wrapped her legs around him. As though she weighed nothing, he carried her across the room and deposited her on top of a tack trunk, the cool metal sending shivers up her back. She expected him to follow her down, crush her with his weight, but he hauled her closer to the edge of the trunk and swiftly lifted her hips. She hadn't even seen him free himself, let alone get the condom on But there was no arguing the evidence of the blunt, latexsheathed hardness nudging her opening.

Without preliminaries, he pushed into her, stretching her. She muffled a scream.

He froze. "Are you okay?"

Oh, don't let him stop. Not now. "Yes," she gritted.

"Don't let me hurt you," he rasped.

"Do it again," she begged. "Just like that."

Shuddering, he withdrew and plunged into her again. This time, she swallowed her sob. Shifting her legs, she opened wider, arched higher. He grasped her hips more tightly, anchoring her against his next thrust. She writhed against him. She couldn't be open enough, take him deep enough. He drove into her again. Like a flash flood, her climax came out of nowhere, taking her with sudden, shocking violence. *Too soon,* she mourned.

He rocked against her as she rode it out, but incredibly he didn't follow her. Her muscles still contracting around him, he lifted her, knocked a horse blanket to the floor and lowered her onto it. Propping himself on his arms, he plunged into her with ferocious, hammering thrusts, over and over and over again. Lauren cried out as the ever-tightening waves began to build again. She tried to spin it out, but his rhythm was too insistent. Again, she was cata-pulted over the edge into oblivion. This time, he followed.

Unbelievable, thought Cal. *Fantastic. Amazing, tooth-rattlingly thrilling sex.*

He rolled, pulling Lauren with him, letting her skirt drape them modestly. Her body felt like dead weight, her head heavy against his chest. Alarm jolted through him. Dammit, had he hurt her after all? He tipped her head up.

"Lauren, are you all right?"

She lifted her head, giving him a smug smile. "Are you kidding? If I felt any better, it'd be illegal."

He laughed, relieved. "I'm not sure it wasn't, consider-ing we could've been caught. Public lewdness, at the very least."

She blushed and buried her head against his chest again.

"Hey, we better get dressed and out of here," he mur-mured into her hair.

"Mmmmm, I wish we could stay here like this."

"Me too." He stroked her back through her shirt, know-ing if they stayed here much longer, they wouldn't stay quite like *this*. "But before long, someone's going to come through that door. They'll be looking for me soon to start the roping."

She tipped her head up and kissed his chin. "I guess I better get moving, then."

Despite the fact that he'd prodded her to get up, he felt like a piece of himself peeled away as she rolled off and got to her feet. Damn, didn't it seem like he handed her big chunks of himself every time they made love? A frown creased his brow.

Lauren scooped her underwear from the floor, pushing it into a pocket. By the time he'd dealt with his jeans, she'd tidied her own clothes. She slipped into his arms, and he brushed a piece of straw from her hair.

"I'll leave first so as not to raise any eyebrows."

He tried not to stiffen. His insecurity was not going to ruin this. "How very circumspect of you, Miz Townsend."

She grinned. "The least I can do after inciting you to public lewdness."

"Right." *And you still don't want anyone to know we're lovers*. Blank-faced, he bent to pick up the blanket.

"Cal?"

He looked up to see that she'd stopped with her hand on the doorknob. "What?"

"Sit with me at the bonfire tonight?"

He bared his teeth in a wolfish grin. "Try and stop me." Smiling, she stepped out into the fading sun.

Cal laughed as he folded the horse blanket. Whether Lauren knew it or not, sitting around the bonfire together would be like sending an engraved announcement. No way would they be able to keep their hands off each other. Not that anyone who saw her leaving here just now was going to need an announcement, anyway. With her delicate skin abraded by his beard and her lips swollen red from his kisses, she was a walking bulletin.

His smile faded as he remembered his earlier thought about losing himself to her piece by piece.

But that was a figurative deconstruction. He stuck the new gloves in his pocket and jammed his hat on his head.

Facing two more go-rounds with Misadventure, his more pressing concern was quite literally holding his pieces together.

Then there was the matter of his father. What the devil was he doing here after all these years?

Zane Taggart would have to tell him in his own time, Cal decided, grabbing his hat. No way would he give him the satisfaction of asking.

Chapter Nine

Cal pulled his riding glove on, carefully adjusting each seam on each finger. Well, here they were, set to go again under a blistering sun on day two. He scanned the crowd, stopping when he found Lauren's pinched white face. His heart squeezed.

They'd sat together last night during the bonfire, inhaling the smells of wood smoke and night. He'd draped his coat around her shoulders and pulled her close while the cowhands spun yarns. Then Jim had pulled out his mouth organ and Brady his guitar. Under cover of thin, lonesome music, they'd slipped away to her cabin. There he'd made sweet, languorous love to her to make up for the way he'd ravaged her in the barn.

In the morning, she'd made strong coffee and smiled brightly at him, and not once did she ask him not to ride the bull.

But he knew she'd wanted to.

And where was Zane this morning? He hadn't turned up at the bonfire. Not that Cal had expected him to. As Cal had so often heard as an adolescent, his father didn't hold with late nights.

His father didn't hold with vacations, either. So what the hell was he doing here?

Damn, he was wandering. He had to clear his mind, focus.

He rolled his shoulders, then climbed the fence. In the chute beneath him, the yellow Brahman stood deceptively docile, like one of his gentle, white-faced Herefords.

Spider joined him. "Looks tame as a tabby cat, don't he?"

"Umm."

Wordlessly, Spider helped Cal get the bull rope on below the Brahman's massive hump. The only sign Misadventure gave that he even noticed this activity was to twitch his ears, but Cal wasn't fooled. As he'd done a hundred times before, he took a deep breath and let the fear wash over him.

Fear was good. It kept the senses sharp, reactions honed.

He straddled the bull, feet planted on the rails. As Spider held the rope taut, Cal whipped his gloved hand up and down it to heat both glove and rope. Then he slid his hand into the grip, palm up, and gestured for Spider to tighten the rope.

Yeah, this rope was an old friend. He'd resined it lovingly and treated it with glycerin to get just the right shape and stickiness. And now he would commit his safety to it once again.

He cast another sideways look at the crowd. Still no sign of his father. Thank heavens.

But it wouldn't have killed him to watch, would it? It's not like he ever came out to see me.

With a stab of irritation, Cal shoved those thoughts aside. That was the disappointed kid talking, the kid

who'd won his first major event and hadn't a soul to celebrate it with.

A head of white hair caught Cal's attention from across
the corral. Harvey McLeod, come to cheer for the bull, no
doubt. Then Cal saw the man by McLeod's side—Brady.
Great. It was hard to tell, but he guessed they were talking, cowboy fashion, each looking out over the corral. Cal
sent a prayer skyward that they wouldn't come to blows
right here in front of his guests.

"How's that feel?"

"Give me a little more torque. There you go, I got it."
Cal stretched the taut rope over his upturned palm, closing
his fingers to trap it. Then he fed the rope back under his
arm. Opening his fingers, he crossed his palm with it a
second time, pulling the rope tight. Finally, he squeezed
his fingers closed, then pounded his grip a couple of times
with his free hand.

There, his rope was pulled as well as he could pull it.
Nothing more he could do but ride this bull.

Gingerly, he settled himself onto the bull, flexing his
rope arm. Leaning over the rope, he coiled and nodded for
the gate.

For all his quietness in the chute, Misadventure came
out like a firecracker, but this time, he didn't flatten into a
spin. Cal knew right off it was going to be bad, a hopping,
skipping, belly-rolling, ugly ride with no rhythm to help
him anticipate where he needed to be. Every second was
going to be an eternity.

Right away, his legs blew out, but he pulled up on the
rope for all he was worth and managed to right himself.
Then, trying to compensate, his free hand got whipped
back too far and he slipped back a few inches onto the
rumble seat.

He knew he was toast right then, knew he should bail

out. He could pick a spot over his shoulder and probably land there, maybe even on his feet, if he just let go now. But he didn't. Instead, he clung to the rope stubbornly, pulling himself back into a low center of gravity over the bull's neck. The next thing he knew, Misadventure gave a mighty twist and a roll.

Shit, he thought as he flew over the bull's head. *I'm a yard dart. Guess I shoulda let go.*

Then there was nothing.

Lauren screamed.

She'd watched it unfold, knew Cal wasn't going to defy the laws of physics this time, but she thought he'd come off like he had yesterday, bounced off the bull's rump. Then she'd seen him go headfirst over the bull's shoulder. Even so, she figured he'd roll to safety, but he hit the ground and didn't stir.

"Omigod, he's knocked out!" cried Marlena.

Everything seemed to slow down. The twisting action the bull had used to unseat Cal carried the beast away from Cal's inert body. For a few seconds, the bull bucked as though still trying to dislodge a rider. In that brief window, the bullfighter rushed to Cal's side. Gripping Cal under the arms, he started dragging him to safety, but in the next instant, Lauren knew he wasn't going to make it. She felt the animal's rage turn onto the garishly dressed bullfighter and his unconscious burden. It pawed the ground once, then charged.

Lauren went hot, then cold, as the bull bore down on the two men with inconceivable speed. Cal's men scrambled over the fence in a human wave, but to Lauren they seemed to be moving in molasses. There was no way they were going to reach him in time. Without thought, she slipped through the rails and streaked toward Cal. She wasn't going to get there either, she realized, a sob bursting from her throat.

Then, out of nowhere, a man sprang into the shrinking space between the bull and his target, arms waving wildly. Cal's father. And he was going to be trampled.

At the last moment, Zane Taggart stepped aside. The bull took the bait, veering after him. With amazing nimbleness, the old man dodged the bull's lowered head, stretching his arms out to protect himself. The bull clipped him with its shoulder as it shot past. The impact sent Zane sprawling. By now the corral was flooded with shouting men. Lauren felt the bull's rancor dilute now that it had lost a specific focus. In the end, the bull was herded easily into the chute, and she found herself trembling in the middle of the corral.

In no time, the bull was fenced in, Zane had dusted himself off and Cal had come around. Lauren felt like crumpling into a heap where she stood. Only the realization that she'd become the center of attention prevented her from doing just that.

She lifted her chin. "What?"

"Begging your pardon, ma'am, but we've never seen a woman charge a two-thousand-pound bull before." Spider struggled to keep a straight face, but failed when the others cracked up.

"Very funny." Except it wasn't very funny at all. The significance of what she'd done hit home. Knees wobbling, she made her way over to Cal, who was now sitting up.

Cal shook his head, then groaned. "What hit me?"

"The ground, partner" Jim was positively cheerful. "Misadventure slam-dunked you."

"Yeah, I remember now." He touched his head cautiously. "Did I connect with anything on the way down?"

"Nothing but air." Jim extended his hand. "Michael Jordan couldn't have done it any cleaner."

Cal grinned. "Well, there's a break." He grasped Jim's hand and got to his feet. "I'll be good to go again by tonight."

Lauren blanched. He was going to ride that killer again, after what had just happened?

"Might want to get that head of yours checked first," put in a grinning Trey Thomas, the man who'd dragged Cal to safety. "You hit so hard, I think I saw nickels fly out of your pockets."

What was wrong with these people? They were treating this as though it were some kind of lark.

Cal's father pushed himself through the ring of men. "Son, you're not riding that bull again. He's a killer."

Finally! A voice of reason. She could have kissed the man, regardless of what kind of a parent he'd been. Cal didn't share her enthusiasm, though, judging by the way his face tightened.

Cal pulled himself up straight. "The days are long gone when I had to listen to you, old man."

Zane snorted. "When did you ever take my counsel anyway?"

Spots of color stained Cal's cheeks, but he shrugged casually. "Maybe you should stop offering it."

"Ain't counsel I'm offering this time. You'll not ride that bull again, even if I have to put a bullet between his eyes."

Zane turned and limped away.

"Crazy old fool," Cal muttered, peeling his glove off.

"Crazy?" Shaking, Lauren stepped into the spot Cal's father had just vacated. "You think *he's* crazy? Let me tell you something, if your father doesn't disable that bull, I will."

Then she spun on her heel and ran after Zane Taggart.

* * *

Cal blinked as he watched Lauren disappear out of the corral with his father. *With his father.*

"What the hell was that about?" No answer. He searched the faces around him, but no one wanted to meet his gaze. "Jim?"

His trail boss sent a glance at Trey, then turned back to face Cal. He cleared his throat nervously. "Well, you see, Cal, the boys had a little trouble getting you clear."

"My fault," Trey said. "Tactical error. I should have taken the bull and let the other guys drag you out of there."

Cal's mouth went dry. "Tell me everything."

"After he dumped you, Misadventure just kept on bucking and spinning like a windup toy on Duracells. I thought I'd have plenty of time to drag you clear, but the devil came after us."

"It ain't Trey's fault," put in Spider soberly. "We were slow coming over the fence. We shoulda jumped in the second you hit the ground, but we thought Trey was gonna get you out okay. Time we realized he wasn't gonna make it, it was too late."

Cal's stomach clenched. "Then how'd you get me out?"

"The old man . . ." Spider took an elbow in the ribs from Jim. "I mean, your father jumped in there and deflected ol' Misadventure like a pro. You shoulda seen it, man. Looked like he'd been turning 'em away for years."

Cal wondered if his legs were going to fail him after all. "My father stepped in front of Misadventure?"

"Yep." Spider's eyes sparkled, but Cal felt only nausea. "That bull was in full dozer mode. Man, he was gonna take out the trash! Ol' man's lucky he didn't get more of a clip."

Cal sucked in a breath. "The bull hit him?"

Spider grinned. "Brushed him is all, but I reckon it's

enough to put a little hitch in his git-along for a day or two."

Goddammit, lose consciousness for one minute and the world goes to hell. "Thanks for telling me."

Trey cleared his throat. "Er, that's not quite all."

"What else?"

"It was kind of a footrace between your dad and Miz Townsend to see who'd get there first."

"Lauren?"

" 'Fraid so."

Cal's already churning stomach took a flip and black spots danced in front of his eyes. Gripping a metal rail of the chute, he squeezed hard, anchoring himself. "Spider?"

"Yeah?"

"Load that bull and take him back to his owner. Do it now."

A pause. "Yes, boss."

He turned to his trail boss. "Can you and Trey throw together a team roping demonstration by tonight?"

Jim looked at Trey and nodded. "No sweat."

"Then do it. That'll be tonight's entertainment."

Insides still shaking, Cal crossed the corral to pick his bull rope out of the dirt. Coiling it carefully, he headed to the barn to hang it up. For good.

Twenty minutes later, showered and changed, Cal stood outside the door of Cabin Six. All these nerves over talking to his own father. Ignoring the butterflies fluttering in his stomach—butterflies, hell, it felt more like a flock of blackbirds had taken up residence in there—he rapped on the door. A few seconds later, the door swung open, but it was Lauren who stood there, not his dad. The blackbirds gave up fluttering and went straight to pecking and scratching.

"Delia told me Dad'd be here," he said, averting the right side of his face, where his temple had taken on a purplish hue.

Lauren stepped back. "Come in."

Cal stepped inside, glancing around. "Where is he?"

"I convinced him to lie down."

"How's he doing?"

Cal caught a flash of anger in her eyes before she dropped her gaze. "Bruised. I was just going to make a cold compress."

She started to move toward the sink. He caught her arm. "Ice is what he'll need. Call the house and ask Delia to send down an ice pack."

"Better make that two ice packs." Cal turned to see his father in the doorway. "Looks like you need it more than I do."

Lauren gasped. "Cal, look at you!"

Damn. He'd given her a full view of his purpling temple when he turned his head. "It's nothing."

"Nothing? Cal Taggart, you can't ride that bull again in your condition," she said. "You might have a concussion."

"I don't."

"How do you know?"

"Because I've been bounced off bulls often enough to know the difference. And," he held up a hand when she started to protest, "one of our guests turns out to be a GP from Orillia. He looked me over pretty good." He turned back to his father. "I think we should have Dr. Reinhart look you over, too."

"Bah" Zane waved a dismissive hand. "I've taken worse lumps on the dance floor, so don't think I won't carry through on my promise. I'll kill that bull before I see you get on it again. Any fool can see it's got a taste for blood—"

"You're right."

"Someone should have put a bullet in him after what he did to you in Vegas that time. A couple of inches in any direction, he'd have killed you."

His father had seen the Vegas footage? The thought floored him for a moment. Though he shouldn't be surprised. That wreck was one they never tired of showing. But had he seen any of the victories? Had he watched his son win a gold buckle?

"Mark my words, Callum, that animal will run you through again if it gets a chance."

Cal shook off his reverie. "I know. I won't be riding him again. I shouldn't have ridden him in the first place without two solid bullfighters. He's on his way back home right now."

Lauren gripped his arm. "You sent him back, really?"

"Really."

"You're not riding him again?"

"Nope."

She pulled a chair out and sank down on it. "Thank heaven!"

His father hobbled to a chair and sat, too. " 'Bout time you saw the light, boy. You're too old for this tomfoolery, anyway."

Cal felt his pulse leap painfully in his bruised temple as that old anger lunged against its chains. Nothing had changed. "According to you, I was always too old for it."

"I never made any secret that I thought it was foolishness."

All the leashed resentments inside howled pure frustration. He had to get out of here.

"No, you sure didn't. And you're right about one thing—it's long past time to hang up my spurs when women and old folk have to do my bullfighting for me." He strode to the door and stopped with his hand on the knob. "I'll send someone with ice."

Cal didn't see Lauren again until supper.

She'd missed the kids' roping clinic, an event she'd been looking forward to, and it was his fault.

He'd gone to his father's cabin to thank Zane, and what'd happened? He'd lost his damn temper and all but accused Zane and Lauren of embarrassing him by coming to his rescue. What must Lauren think of him? His dad, well, Cal couldn't remember it ever being any different between them. But Lauren . . .

And where had she spent the afternoon? Had she gone back to her cabin to reflect on her poor judgment in hooking up with such a miserable SOB? Or worse, had she stayed with Zane to hear him recite a litany of his son's many transgressions? By the time she showed up, Cal figured she'd come to tell him off.

While he debated how best to approach her, she spotted him and made a beeline across the dining room.

He stood. "Lauren, I'm glad you're—"

"Have you seen Marlena?"

"Marlena?"

"You know, ex-wife." Her gaze roved the room. "Blonde, lots of curves, hard to miss in a crowd."

He grinned. "No, I haven't, but I'm not surprised. A kids' roping clinic wouldn't rate very high on her excitement meter."

Lauren released her lower lip, which she'd been worrying with her teeth. "No, I suppose not."

"She won't have ridden off, if that's what you're worried about. Brady knows about the anthrax threat so he'd make good and sure she doesn't saddle up. Not that she's likely to go anywhere just now anyway, what with all this testosterone swaggering around under her nose."

Lauren gave him a faint smile, but it didn't reach her eyes. Was it concern for Marlena he saw there, or disappointment in him? The thought depressed the hell out of him, but whatever it was, they had to talk about it.

"Hey, we've got forty minutes before the roping starts, and Jim's got everything in hand. Walk down to the creek with me?"

Her eyes darkened with indecision, and Cal prepared himself for a refusal.

"Okay," she said at last.

He let his breath out. There was a nice grassy spot overhung by trailing willows. He'd take her there, tell her how his heart had stopped with fear when they'd told him she'd tried to put her slender frame between him and Misadventure. How it still pounded when he thought of her in the corral with that beast. Taking her elbow, he guided her outside.

They didn't get far. A shiny black Pathfinder pulled up just as they passed the corral.

"That's McLeod, come to see the third bull ride, I imagine," Cal said. "Can we hang back a sec so I can tell him it's off?"

"Sure."

Harvey jumped out of the truck, but instead of heading toward Cal immediately, he circled the vehicle and opened the passenger door. Cal's stomach lurched. He couldn't see the passenger through the smoke-tinted windows, but he had a damn good suspicion. An instant later, like a Cinderella being helped from her carriage, Marlena emerged regally. Then Harvey stepped in close to her and kissed her full on the mouth with explicit possessiveness, and Marlena gave it right back to him.

"Great," Cal muttered. "Of all the men Marlena had to choose from this weekend, she had to go and pick Harvey McLeod."

"He's very charming," said Lauren in a half-hearted defense of Marlena, "and you told her yourself he's wealthy."

"Yeah, well, it's what I *didn't* tell her that worries me."

Lauren gripped his arm. "What do you mean? What should she know about Harvey McLeod?"

"Well, for starters, he's the kid's father."

"Whose father?"

"Brady's," Cal said.

"Harvey McLeod is Brady's father?"

Cal tugged Lauren up against his chest. "Geez, could you say it a little louder?" He glanced at the people milling around outside the corral. "I don't think everyone caught it."

"Why didn't you tell me that?" she hissed.

"I just did."

"Brady will be so hurt, so angry, if he sees."

"That ship sailed," he said. "Though why it matters so much to you, I can't imagine." For the benefit of any on-lookers, he dropped a kiss on her tightly closed mouth.

Her fingers dug into his ribs, hard, and he lifted his head. "Cal, stop it! What on earth are you doing?"

"What's it look like I'm doing? Making a spectacle of us so everybody doesn't gawk at Marlena. For Brady's sake."

She strained in his arms to turn and search for the younger man, but he held her still. "No, don't look. It'll only compound his humiliation."

169

"Oh, no. This changes everything."

"What do you mean?" Cal caught her chin in what he hoped looked like a lover-like grasp. "How does this change anything? Marlena couldn't have made her . . . admiration . . . for Harvey more plain the last time we crossed paths with him."

She pulled away. "But I didn't know that Harvey . . . that Brady . . ."

"Yeah, but Harvey and Brady knew." His eyes narrowed on her face as he let her go. "What does *your* knowing change?"

"It's so much more volatile than I thought." She chewed her lip a moment. "I take it there's no love lost between them?"

He shrugged. "Brady got Harvey's name from an old journal his mother left when she died a couple years ago. He tracked Harvey down, and Harvey denied paternity. Hell, he chased him off. Can you blame the kid for holding a grudge?"

"Of course not."

Cal fixed her with a hard look. "Oh, geez, you've still got a thing about Marlena, don't you?"

She colored, but held his gaze. "Am I worried that she's putting herself at risk with her behavior? Absolutely."

He laughed harshly. "Join the crowd. Marlena makes an art out of putting herself in these situations. Ain't nothing we can do about it. What we *can* do is deflect attention."

"But . . ."

"Trust me when I say I've had some experience in this," he gritted. "Come on, let's join the other guests."

Cal placed a possessive hand on Lauren's back, guiding her over to join the crowd gathered outside the corral. As he hoped, his uncharacteristic public display drew attention to himself and Lauren. Anything to get the focus off Marlena, Brady and Harvey.

"Afternoon, Cal."

Harvey's voice, right behind him. Damn the man. Couldn't he just get in his vehicle and go back home?

"Harvey." He cast his neighbor a casual glance, moving closer still to Lauren. She relaxed into him, playing the part. "Hope you're not back for an encore. I sent Misadventure home earlier after that last mishap. There won't be a repeat."

Harvey flashed a toothy grin. "Yeah, I heard you blinked."

Cal smiled a slow, fierce smile as he fought down the urge to knock a few of his neighbor's pearly whites down his throat.

"Yeah, that's right, McLeod. When it comes to other folks getting hurt, I guess I just don't have your stomach for it."

Harvey's smile widened, but his eyes turned hard. "You got the stomach for some other stuff, though, don't you, Taggart? A little garden-variety cover-up, for instance."

Conscious of their audience, Cal drew himself up, putting Lauren behind him. "You got something to say to me, McLeod?"

"Me? No, I got nothing to say. Not when this says it so much better." Harvey uncurled a newspaper he'd been clutching white-knuckled in his right hand and thrust it at him. "DEADLY ANTHRAX OUTBREAK SUSPECTED AT FOOTHILLS GUEST RANCH."

Cal froze, his heart sinking, as Harvey swivelled the paper around for all to see. Impossible. That veterinary inspector had given his word that he wouldn't go to the press. But there it was in black and white.

"What's wrong, Taggart? Didn't want your guests to know they're locked down here while this gets swept under the rug?"

Hell, how'd he know that? "Dammit, Harvey, nothing's being swept under the rug. There's no positive diagnosis yet."

Harvey snorted. "That supposed to make me feel better?" He curled the paper up and wagged it like an accusing finger. "The pasture where that dead steer was found is hard up against one of mine, and you didn't see fit to tell me?" Harvey waved the paper toward his audience. "You didn't see fit to tell these folks?"

Cal's fingers curled into fists, but before he could lay hands on McLeod, Lauren stepped quickly between them.

"Wait a minute, Mr. McLeod," she said. "Your herd is one thing; I understand your concern. But as far as Cal's guests go, there's no risk to them of contracting anthrax."

"Yeah, right." Harvey's handsome face had turned a mottled red. "It gives hardened soldiers nightmares, but these folks shouldn't worry about it?"

Cal shouldered his way past Lauren. "That biological warfare stuff is a different thing, and you know it."

"Excuse me if I don't feel reassured, especially after you kept it under wraps for two days."

"If you don't believe Cal, you can believe me," Lauren said calmly, though Cal noticed her own hands were fisted, too. "I'm a qualified veterinarian. I'm telling you the risk to humans is negligible, even if they were exposed, and no one was exposed."

"How can you be sure it's so negligible?" Harvey shot the question at Lauren, then turned back to Cal. "You said yourself, Taggart, that you don't know what you're dealing with yet."

Cal felt the anger in him howl for release, but managed to keep his voice flat and quiet. "I know what you're doing, McLeod. This isn't about a single animal that may or may not have gone down with anthrax. This is about opportunity, plain and simple. You want my land and you're not too particular about how you get it. Isn't that right?"

Cal stood his ground as Harvey thrust his now florid face closer. "This is about business, Taggart. I can't afford to be tainted by this."

"Bullshit!" Cal stood toe-to-toe with Harvey. "An episode like this wouldn't even put a crimp in your business. How many head you slaughter a day over there now? A thousand?"

"Not as many as I'll be butchering when your herd falls to me at auction. When the bank forecloses on this circus, I'll—"

Without thinking, Cal shot a hand out and grabbed Harvey's shirt front. "That's it, McLeod." He yanked the taller man close. "Get the hell off my land and stay off. You're not welcome here." He released Harvey with a shove that sent him staggering. "Go on! Git!"

Harvey stumbled a few steps, then recovered his balance, tugged his twisted shirt back down. "Enjoy it while you can," he spat, throwing the paper in the dust. "The tables'll be turned soon enough and it'll be me kicking *your* skinny ass off *my* land."

With that, he stormed over to his truck, reversed it in a hail of gravel, and sped off down the long driveway to the road.

Beside him, Lauren let out a shaky breath as they watched the truck disappear in a trail of dust.

"Well, that went well, don't you think?" she said.

Cal's laugh came out as a hollow bark. "Oh, yeah, real

173

well." He turned back toward his group of guests, many of whom looked shell-shocked. Some met his gaze with frank concern, but other gazes slid away. The sliders, he knew, would check out immediately; the others he might be able to keep.

He took a deep breath. "Okay, here's the situation. We *did* have a steer die forty-eight hours ago, way over yonder, past that ridge you can see in the distance." Heads swivelled to contemplate the horizon toward which he pointed. "Like I told Mr. McLeod, we don't have a diagnosis yet to say yea or nay whether it's anthrax. No more cattle have died, though, and that's a real good sign. We expect to hear for sure within the next twelve hours, but if you prefer not to stay under the circumstances, your money will be refunded."

Dr. Reinhart, the physician who'd checked Cal over earlier, stepped forward. "For what it's worth, I've never seen or even heard of a case of anthrax in my whole career. I suspect he's right that it's not a big risk for us."

The investment broker cleared his throat. "Excuse me, doc, but you're from back east, right? Couldn't it be that anthrax is just not endemic there like it is here?"

The doctor rubbed his chin. "I honestly don't know, Neil. You could be right," he conceded, giving Cal a shrug and a look as though to say *I tried*.

Another man spoke from Cal's left. "Well, we'll be leaving." He shrugged apologetically. "I've got a family to think about. We can't stay with this thing looming." Dale Travers, a lawyer, Cal recalled with a sinking sensation.

He scanned the group, saw the way other parents exchanged worried glances.

Cal nodded curtly, then turned to Jim. "Would you explain the situation to Delia? Tell her to refund Mr. Travers's money, and anyone else's who wants to leave." Jamming his hat down on his head, he strode toward the corral. "Spider, Brady," he called. "Let's get this show on the road."

Chapter Ten

A man's back could say so much.

Lauren's throat ached as she watched Cal. She'd seen the stiffness creep into that spot between his shoulder blades, noted the way he pulled his shoulders back, as the audience dwindled to four spectators—Dr. Reinhart, his wife, Marlena and Lauren.

Cal backed his horse behind the barrier for the last run, and the chestnut danced skittishly. Lauren could feel the mare's agitation. This time, Spider was heading and Cal was heeling. When the steer was released, Spider broke after it, roping it neatly around both horns. Cal's rope snaked out, but snagged only one of the animal's back hooves. Sienna danced backward to pull the rope taut and the steer went down, but it wasn't clean. Cal looked grim as Jim announced the time into the PA, complete with a five second penalty for failing to rope both back feet.

"That's our show, folks," said Jim. "Thanks for watching."

As the men cleared the steers out, Marlena turned abruptly and headed to the house. Lauren didn't know whether or not to be grateful that there'd be no confrontation between Marlena and Brady tonight, at least not in public. If it *were* public, she might be better able to gauge Brady's emotion. On the other hand, Cal didn't need another scene on top of everything else.

Lauren glanced at the horizon. At least she could relax on one score. Nothing was going to happen to Marlena tonight—the sun was already sinking, staining the sky a deep magenta. Another night approaching with Marlena still safe. Another day gone by with her no closer to unmasking Marlena's killer.

From the corner of her eye, she caught a movement and turned toward it. Cal. Shoving his stiff new gloves into his pocket, he strode toward her. Her lungs felt overfull as she watched him, and her chest grew tight. So this is what it's like to love someone, she realized. To feel his pain like your pain.

Cal stopped in front of them and removed his hat, exposing that close-cut hair that stood up in a most uncowboy-like way. "Thanks for staying, Doc, Mrs. Reinhart."

"Don't take any of this personally." Dr. Reinhart clapped a hand on Cal's back, and Cal tensed. "I've seen it before. One case of meningitis and folks won't let their kids go to school. Gut-level fear like that is hard to combat with mere reason."

"I understand." Cal shrugged out from under the doctor's sympathetic arm. "And I appreciate your staying. I really do. In fact, tonight's on me."

The older man looked surprised and a little taken aback at the suggestion. "We couldn't. You just lost all your guests—"

"I insist," said Cal, clamping his hat to his hip. "As a thank-you for your efforts to educate the others."

"But—"

"Really." He ground his hat against his hip. "I insist."

Lauren could read the signs even if Dr. Reinhart couldn't. "I think this is one argument you're destined to lose, Dr. Reinhart. Why not just say, 'Thank you, Cal,' and make him happy?"

"Okay. Thanks, Cal." Dr. Reinhart shifted uncertainly, and his wife looked even more uncomfortable. "Er, well, think we'll head back to the cabin now. I think there's a ball game on."

"What'd you do that for?" she asked when the Reinharts were out of earshot. "That's revenue you can ill afford to pass up."

Ignoring her comment, he lifted his right hand and dragged a thumb across his eyebrow from the inner edge to the temple. The gesture, so familiar now, caught at her heart.

"See how I blew that last steer? Greenhorn mistake." He dropped his arm to his side. "Fitting end to the sideshow, eh?"

"I'm so sorry, Cal."

Nervously, she twisted the newspaper she'd rescued from the dirt. The motion attracted his attention.

"Let me see that."

Wordlessly she handed him the paper. He unrolled it, his face hardening as he read Bruce Dysan's comments. He thrust the paper back at her. "If he wasn't going to keep his mouth shut, he should have said so. I'd have done things differently."

"Bruce Dysan didn't leak the story."

The tamped down anger she'd sensed in him flared. "You coulda fooled me. They seem to quote him pretty extensively."

"I slipped back to my cabin and called him, vet to vet.

178

He says the journalist who phoned him had all the details. In light of what they already knew, he didn't think it prudent to deny he was investigating a possible case."

Cal massaged his temple as though to quiet the pulse she could see beating there. He probably had the mother of all headaches. His anger seemed to ebb, leaving him looking bleak. She wanted to pull his head down, ease his pain.

"Then the leak had to have come from one of my men."

She met his gaze. "It might have been the backhoe operator, but that seems contrary to his best interest. An outbreak could mean repeat business, but not if he's feeding the press."

"One of my guys," he reiterated dully.

"I'm sorry. I wish I could think—"

"I saw Brady and Harvey talking just before that last ride."

Lauren inhaled. "You think Brady might have told his father? But why? I mean, if it's as bad between them as you say, why would Brady volunteer anything?" She tried to search Cal's eyes, but he appeared to be inspecting his hat.

"Maybe he thought he could barter information for approval." He shrugged. "The need to please a parent can be pretty powerful when you're young, and Brady's just a kid."

Pretty powerful at any age, she thought as she studied the shadow of his downswept lashes against his face. Then he looked up and she found herself looking into his eyes. She'd braced herself to see anger, hurt, dejection, but when he lifted his lids, she might as well have been gazing at the gray Atlantic.

"I see my father bailed out, too, with the rest of them. Guess seeing his son screw up so many things simultaneously must have made him rethink his little holiday."

She blinked in surprise. "Oh, I'm sure he hasn't left."

Cal smiled, a grim, self-deprecating twist of his lips. "He's gone, all right." He angled his head in the direction of the parking area. "His truck was the first one out."

"I'm sorry." Lauren didn't know what else to say.

"I'm not." His response was immediate and unequivocal. "I didn't ask him to come here and I'm not sorry to see him go."

Could he really shrug off his father's unexpected appearance and hasty departure? She tried to put herself in his shoes. Tried and failed. As society-conscious as her parents were, she knew they'd be there for her when the chips were down.

Cal didn't have that familial support. In fact, he didn't have a support network at all, she realized. At least, not in *his* mind. He would succeed or fail on his own. To cultivate a support network would imply that he had emotional needs, and Lauren knew he would die before admitting to any such thing.

"Cal, what are you going to do?"

"Have a shower, a belt of ten-year-old whiskey and a cigarette, in that order."

"But what then?"

His smile held a world of self-mockery. "Then I expect I'll repeat steps two and three, as often as necessary."

"No, I mean tomorrow and the next day."

His smile faded. "I don't know. If we have any more animals go down, that'll dictate what I do for the next weeks."

"And if you don't have an anthrax outbreak on your hands?"

"Bring in that second crop of hay, I guess, then gather the yearlings to sell them off. If I can find a buyer, that is."

Her gaze flew to his eyes. "You make it sound as though you'll be out there with your men."

"I will."

"What about your guests?"

"What guests?" He arched an eyebrow. "The Reinharts?" He grimaced. "I imagine my bookings are melting like hailstones on August asphalt. And since I can't run this kind of operation for so few guests, I'll have to refund their money and send them on their way. Put my back into some real work for a change."

Close the guest ranch? Lauren's face froze.

He talked on about pregnancy-checking cows, selling dry heifers and weaning calves, but Lauren didn't really process it. She was too busy realizing he was going to send *her* away, too.

Her heart cramped. Pack up and leave? She wasn't ready.

And what about Marlena? Lauren sucked in a breath. *How could she have forgotten Marlena?* That was her whole purpose for being here. If she left, who would prevent Marlena from getting her beautiful, reckless, self-absorbed neck wrung?

"You're evicting me?"

He looked up at her, then his gaze slid away. "Maybe it's for the best. You have to get back to your practice some time."

"No!" The word was wrenched out of her.

His head came up again, gray eyes really looking at her. Looking deep. She felt naked, vulnerable, especially after he'd as much as told her to leave.

She lifted her chin. "What I mean is, I'm not ready to go back yet. I paid for a ranch vacation, and that's what I want."

"Unfortunately, I don't think I can provide it. If the bottom falls out like I think it will, I'll have to cancel the liability insurance." He dipped his head again, angling his face away. "Without insurance, I can't run a guest program."

"So hire me."

That brought his head back around. *"What?"*

"I'm a vet," she reminded him. "I can help. You said you had to pregnancy-check cows, vaccinate, that sort of thing."

"Lauren, I can't afford liability insurance; I sure as hell can't afford to keep a veterinarian in the field."

"Who said you had to pay me? I'll work for my keep."

A flare of something that looked like hope blazed in his eyes for an instant, but he shuttered it quickly. Raising an eyebrow, he gave her a skeptical look.

"A busman's holiday?"

She lifted a shoulder. "Why not? Frankly, I was getting bored. There's only so much leisure a working girl can take."

He laughed. Relieved, she laughed with him.

"Okay, that'd work for me, if your practice can spare you."

Lauren's smile dimmed when she remembered her phone message earlier today. When she'd gone back to call Bruce, she'd learned that Peter Markham, the young vet covering her practice, was getting antsy. According to Heather, he'd talked about hanging out his own shingle. Not that Lauren blamed him. He wanted to build rapport with his own clients, not someone else's. God only knew how long she could hold onto him. If he left, she'd have to lay Heather off. She'd lose clients. Her practice would suffer.

Unless she went back herself.

No. The answer came as strong as it was instantaneous. She couldn't go back, not until Marlena was safe. She wouldn't be plunged into that hell again. She'd already failed too many times, too many victims. If she failed this time, she'd lose more than a few clients. She'd lose another piece of her soul.

And Cal? How could she go back if it meant losing him?

Shivering, she took a step closer to Cal and slid an arm around his waist. His arms came around her instantly.

"What were those steps again?" she asked him.

"I don't know. Shower, smoke and a drink, I think."

"Any chance of doing them at my cabin?"

"That depends."

She leaned back to look at him. "On what?"

"On whether or not you'll join me for step one."

The shower. Despite the sense of impending doom that hovered over her since Harvey had ridden up with Marlena, Lauren's blood heated. "Just try and stop me."

An hour later, Cal lay in Lauren's bed, chest to chest, knee to knee, stroking her damp skin while their racing hearts slowed.

After the shared shower, he'd skipped the whiskey and the smoke, fully intending to use their passion to work off his paralyzing fear of failure and the anger that was its companion. He'd thought to give vent to it in a vigorous physical joining, but their lovemaking had been different this time, edged with a new dimension. For once, the desperate physical hunger was supplanted by more tender emotions.

Not that he hadn't come at her with desperate hunger.

He'd sought to inhale her, devour her in his greed. But she'd met his desperation with such generosity, and with something else—some soft, almost sorrowful quality beyond his experience. It had been his undoing. And somehow, magically, he'd felt cleansed of some of his demons.

She sighed and settled herself against him, and he shifted to accommodate her long limbs. *Perfect,* he thought. She fit him perfectly, and had from the first.

He nuzzled the fine, smooth skin of her forehead, and she made an appreciative noise into his neck, which made him smile.

Damn, how could he feel this good? His world was falling apart. The guest ranch business was as good as dead, thanks to whomever leaked that article. Without guest revenues, it was just a matter of time before he lost the ranch itself.

He jammed the brakes on that thought. Tomorrow, and hard reality, would come soon enough. He'd worry about it all then.

Cal pulled the covers over their cooling bodies, trying to ignore the sudden suspicion that there might be worse things in life than failing to best his father or losing the ranch.

Like losing this.

His hand tightened on Lauren's hipbone. She turned her face up to his, pale eyes searching, and he lowered his lids quickly, catching her lips with his. An eternity later, he lifted his head again. This time, he didn't bother to veil his eyes. The exquisite delicacy of the kiss had given him away.

Reverence. That was it, the quality he'd felt in her soft hands and in the brush of her dark hair across his skin. And now he felt it in his own fingertips, right down to the bone. He traced her collarbone with hands that felt newly made and watched her pale skin flush with fresh arousal. When he used his mouth to follow the path his fingers had taken, she cried out.

"Cal?" Her voice held a question, and she tried to arch up.

"Shsssh," he hushed her, urging her down. "Just feel this, baby. Just feel for me, will you?"

A sob tore from her throat, but she subsided. He skimmed her rib cage lightly, fingers stroking, arousing, loving. With hands and mouth and body, he worshiped her, praising her responsiveness as he took her to the limits of her senses and beyond. When he finally joined with her, it was like a prayer, each thrust and slide carrying them closer to total communion.

Only when she'd found a deep, shuddering release did he allow himself to be hurled over the edge into a terrifying, thrilling freefall, the likes of which he'd never known.

When his world righted itself again, Lauren clung to him with a desperation he knew was echoed in his own fierce embrace.

It was the light that woke her, streaming in through the curtains. Way too much light. She sat up. Eight o'clock.

Cal was gone. The pillow next to her still bore the indentation of his head but the sheets were cold.

Lauren sucked in a disbelieving gasp. He'd left without her? And after agreeing last night to let her ride with them.

Last night. Her irritation at being left behind was pierced by a spurt of pure wonder as she remembered last night. They'd come together again and again, hands skimming faces as though they'd discovered some new kind of braille.

She threw off the covers and padded to the kitchen. That was where she found his note, anchored to the counter by a bag of freshly ground coffee beans.

Decided to hang around today after all and wait for Dysan's call, but I had to give the men their marching orders. Didn't have the heart to wake you. Meet me for breakfast? I'll come drag you out if you're not there by 8:30.

No, on second thought, I'll phone. If I come over there, we might starve to death.

She grinned foolishly at that. He'd signed it simply, *C.*

She studied the note while she waited for her caffeine fix. His handwriting surprised her. It was strong, as she'd known it would be, but she hadn't expected the elegance. She slipped the note into the pocket of her robe. He was full of surprises.

Like the way he'd made love to her last night . . .

The coffeemaker sputtered as it finished. Smiling, she filled her mug. Lord, how she loved the way he touched her—carnal and demanding one moment, soft and solemn the next.

Her smile faded. Who was she kidding? It wasn't his touch she loved; she was hopelessly in love with the man himself.

And if she even hinted at the way she felt, he'd drop her like something one of the barn cats dragged in. They'd made a bargain—just sex. What had Cal said? *No happily-ever-after.*

She bit her lip. Problem was, it *felt* like more than sex. Lauren knew that was her own emotion coloring her perception, not any sudden change in Cal. He wanted her, no doubt about it. She was pretty sure he respected her, even liked her. Maybe a lot. But he didn't love her. He'd never allow himself to love anyone.

Thank you, Zane Taggart. Thank you, Marlena.

She took a swallow of the coffee, gasping as the too-hot liquid burned its way down her esophagus.

Maybe she should pull back, try to inject some emotional distance back into the relationship. Despite the fact that her heart told her not to, she forced herself to consider the option.

She had no idea how much time they had left. She could be gone tomorrow, or in a week's time. What was the point of getting in any deeper? The smart thing would be to withdraw now.

Intellectually, she saw the sense of it, but knew with a sinking heart that she wouldn't. Couldn't. These few nights they'd had together weren't going to be nearly enough to sustain her. She needed much more. She loved him. And from now on, she'd memorize every look, every touch, every word.

As she dumped her coffee, she caught a glimpse of herself in the mirror over the sink. She looked like hell, all sad eyes and worried forehead. She'd better shower and pull herself together or Cal would take one look at her and head for the hills.

Lauren walked into the dining room and Cal's breath stalled. He put his mug down with a clunk. She looked the same, yet so much more. Her long-legged stride, which never failed to drive him crazy, was more confident. Sexier. Even her short hair looked carelessly sexy this morning. The kicker, though, was her face. She should have looked tired—he'd lost count of the number of times he'd reached for her in the night—but she was luminous, her bottomless blue eyes lit from the inside.

"Save any breakfast for me?"

With a start, he realized he'd risen to his feet. To cover his confusion, he smiled. "More than you can possibly handle." He gestured to the covered dishes on the table. "I guess it'll take a while for Delia to adjust to cooking small."

She slid into the chair on his left. He sat too, seizing the opportunity to pass off his standing as courtliness rather than the instinctive move toward her that it was. The moment she'd entered the room, he'd yearned toward her, wanting to claim her with his hands, brand her with his kiss. He'd wanted the whole world to know he'd put that swing in her hips.

"I thought you'd left without me this morning, until I found your note," she said as she filled her plate with fluffy scrambled eggs. "Want some?"

He nodded, and she proceeded to heap his plate. "I said you could ride out with us and I meant it, but I figured we'd better hang in for Dysan's call."

"Good idea." She lifted the dome from another plate and helped herself to crisp, thick bacon.

Cal gaped at the fatty slices she deposited on her plate. "What? No fruit cup and skimmed milk this morning?"

Her lips parted on a wicked smile that sent a jolt directly to his groin. "I've decided to live dangerously."

Suddenly, all he could think about was kissing that luscious mouth. "I think I need to have you again."

She sat there staring back at him, her breath going rapid and shallow, as she held the lid in midair, forgotten.

Then someone cleared his throat behind Cal and the

spell was broken. Lauren dropped the lid onto the plate with a small clatter, her attention riveted somewhere behind him. Cal turned to see Zane Taggart standing stiffly behind him.

Chapter Eleven

Cal's mind went blank. "What are you doing here?"

His father nodded at Lauren, then glanced around the room. "Thought I'd have breakfast. This *is* the dining room?"

"You left." There was no accusation in the words, just a statement of fact.

"I'm back." Zane's reply was equally laconic.

Cal pushed his chair back. "Forget something, did you?"

A flush stained the older man's face. "Dammit, Cal, is it so hard to believe I might have come back just to see you?"

"Yeah, it is hard to believe. Yesterday, when the crap hit the fan, you couldn't get out of here fast enough." Cal's heart thundered as it had when he was a kid, but his voice was calm. "And you know what? I wasn't even a little bit surprised."

"You're a mind reader now, are you?" His father's eyes flashed with anger and something Cal didn't recognize. "You know what's going on in my head?"

"No, I sure don't, though it's a skill that mighta come in handy once upon a time," he said tightly, suddenly dizzy with the ball of anger he'd thought was locked safely down in the back of his mind. He drew a deep breath, forced his hands to relax. "Look, Dad, the guest ranch is closing. Our last guests checked out today. But you're welcome to join us for breakfast."

"Hell, you're closing your doors over this little setback?"

Little setback? Cal prayed for control.

"Not much choice. All but two guests left yesterday, and we've had cancellations all morning." Cal was relieved to hear his voice emerge so matter-of-factly, without a trace of self-pity. Zane Taggart would abhor any trace of such weakness. "I expect all my bookings will go south after that article."

"Well." His father's face was blank as Cal knew his own was. "Guess you're gonna need this, then." He drew an envelope out of his breast pocket and dropped it on the table.

Cal eyed the envelope, which bore the imprint of a local bank, and he felt his pulse stumble. "What's that?"

"Certified check."

Cal picked it up. Beside him, Lauren leapt to her feet. "This sounds like family business. I'm just going to . . ."

He put a restraining hand on her arm. "Stay."

She looked as though she wanted to make a break for it. Cal reinforced the command with a silent request, his eyes pleading. He needed her to stay. If his father thought he could rub his nose in his failure by tossing him this bone, Cal wanted someone around to witness it when he threw it back at him. He'd rather drown slowly in red ink than accept help from Zane Taggart.

"Well, if your father doesn't mind . . . ," Lauren said.

"Just as Callum prefers," said Zane Taggart.

She subsided again as Cal picked up the envelope, tore off one end, and shook a certified check out onto the table.

Thirty thousand dollars. It took all the discipline learned at the poker table for Cal to keep his face blank. He picked the check up with fingers gone numb and held it out to his father. "I appreciate the thought, but I can't take it."

Zane's jaw went slack. "What do you mean, you can't take it? You're in trouble, son."

Cal lifted an eyebrow. "Says who?"

"Says me, and everyone around here."

Cal felt his face flush. "I suppose it's obvious enough. Why would I be running a dude ranch for nancy boys unless I was strapped for cash, right?"

Zane snorted. "Who said anything like that? Hell, there's nothing wrong with showing city folk a taste of ranch life."

"Yeah, sure." Cal laughed, a harsh sound. "It's such a hot idea, you're gonna run right home and open your own guest ranch on the Taggart homestead."

Zane's back stiffened again. "No, you're right there. I won't be doing that."

"See? If you can't do it and hold your head up, why am I supposed to be so damned thrilled about doing it?"

"Ain't got nothin' to do with pride. It's just too late."

Too late? Cal found himself on his feet, a surge of adrenaline zinging through him. "What do you mean, too late?"

Before Cal's eyes, Zane Taggart seemed to shrink. "Maybe if I'd had the smarts to do it, I might have saved it, but I'm not like you. Seems like I only know one way to do things." The grim slash of his mouth twisted wryly.

" 'Course, I expect you'd be the first to agree about that."

Cal squeezed his hands into fists again to keep them from shaking. "Might have saved *what?*"

"The ranch," Zane said without a trace of emotion. "I lost it almost two months ago. It's gone."

"Gone?" Cal was starting to feel like a parrot. "But how can that be?" He looked down at the check. "You've got money. You're on vacation."

"Yeah, a permanent one."

"What happened?" asked Cal, his need to shove the check back into his father's face momentarily forgotten.

"Same thing that's happening all over the country. Rising production costs, falling prices." His father shrugged. "It's been a long time coming. I just buried my head in the sand. You're in a much better position with the guest ranch."

Better position? Hadn't the old coot heard a word he'd said? "I'm closing the guest ranch, remember?"

"In the short term, maybe, until this blows over. That's what the money's for," he said, as though explaining to a child of limited intelligence. "To tide you over."

Cal was hardly listening. Hell, his father had lost the ranch, a property homesteaded by Taggarts generations ago. Which meant that even if the bank foreclosed tomorrow, Cal had won. He'd outlasted Zane Taggart at his own game. No matter what happened now, his father's failure would always be first.

So where was the sweet release of victory?

Zane's voice cut through Cal's daze

". . . turned out I wasn't the steward I thought I was. If Charlie hadn't offered for it . . ."

"Wait a minute, Charlie Horton?" Ouch. For as long as Cal could remember, Zane had prided himself on being a better cattleman than his neighbor, whom he considered too laid-back for his own good. Why didn't that poetic piece of justice gladden his heart?

"Yeah, Charlie Horton. Gave me a decent price, too, all things considered."

Unexpected guilt pricked Cal. Zane Taggart might not have been father-of-the-year material, but Cal had left him high and dry. If he'd stayed, maybe the ranch wouldn't have failed. . . . Cal gave himself a mental shake. Stupid to let these thoughts interfere with his triumph.

"Of course, there wasn't much left after everybody got paid," Zane continued, "but it's yours."

Cal's heart jumped. He narrowed his eyes. "No, it isn't."

"'Course it is. I just gave it to you, didn't I?"

Cal looked down at the check in his hands. Thirty thousand dollars. A queer feeling gripped his gut. The same figure that struck him as so large a moment ago suddenly seemed a pitifully small amount for the lifetime of sweat his father had put into it. "This is it, isn't it? The entire equity in the place?"

"Nah." Zane rubbed the back of his neck. "I kept enough to see me through for a while. Not that I have a lot of needs. I expect I'll find myself a job easy enough. After forty years, I can turn my hand to most anything that needs doing on a ranch."

The proud Zane Taggart toiling for someone else? *Wrangler's wages*. The words echoed in Cal's head. *Mark my words, you'll wind up broken in that rodeo you love so much, or busting your hump for wrangler's wages.*

Now the father had come to the very fate he'd predicted for his son. Instead of the swell of victory he expected, a terrible emptiness opened under him. Panicked, his heart slamming against his ribs, Cal thrust the check at his father. "I can't take it."

Zane's eyes turned flinty. "It's your birthright, dammit. If I'd been able to hang onto the ranch, it'd have been yours."

"No need to get melodramatic, Dad. I never planned to come back." Considering he had to force the words past a log jam in his throat, Cal was grateful for how impassive they sounded.

"You think I don't know that?" His father's already florid face darkened. He averted his head, pinched the bridge of his nose. When he spoke next, his voice was again controlled. "That doesn't change the fact it would have been yours. If I hadn't gotten so far in hock, you could have sold it, gotten away with an easy half-million, maybe more. Maybe a lot more."

Cal felt a tic leap to life in his left eye. He resisted the urge to thumb his eyebrow to soothe it and frowned fiercely instead. Inside, conflicting feelings tangled up on themselves. *Dammit, it wasn't supposed to be like this.*

This was supposed to be his moment of triumph.

Inside, the tumult of emotion coalesced into fury.

"Don't you get it?" he grated. "I don't want your money."

His father's face darkened. Lauren's chair scraped back, but Cal didn't take his eyes off his father's flushed face.

"Cal, no. That's enough," said Lauren urgently.

Cal felt Lauren's hands catch at one of his, but he shook her off. Nothing and no one could stop this release of vitriol now. "I don't need anything from you, you understand? *Nothing.*"

"Well, that's too damned bad, 'cause I'm not taking it back," his father roared. "I promised your mother I'd take care of you. Maybe I didn't do a very good job of it when you were young, but by God, I can and will do this much—"

Zane's angry words were clipped off as suddenly as if he'd been struck dumb. One of his big hands lurched to his chest.

Lauren was there with a shoulder under his arm before Cal could react. "Mr. Taggart, are you all right?"

"My chest . . ."

Cal felt a new, singular emotion pierce his angry confusion, one he had no difficulty identifying. *Terror*. "Your heart?"

Zane looked down at his chest and back up, surprise mingling with pain in his eyes. "Don't know. Never had it before."

"Help me lay him down," Lauren said.

Cal jumped to do her bidding. With hands gone clumsy, he helped her lower Zane to the floor. Lauren loosened his collar, which he customarily wore buttoned up like a general's. Zane, his face now ashen, his breathing labored, made no protest. His compliance only sharpened Cal's anxiety.

He'd given his father a heart attack.

Dazed, he watched Lauren take Zane's pulse with two fingers pressed to his neck. His father was flat on the floor, having a heart attack, being tended by a vet. A vet.

Then he remembered she knew first aid. She had ambulance training. Relief washed over him.

"What can I do?" he asked.

"Get me a tablecloth from one of those empty tables and roll it up like a tube so I can slide it under his neck."

Cal did as she asked. She looked so calm as she slid the makeshift support under Zane's head. Her hands were so competent. Zane would be all right. Lauren would know what to do.

"Now what?"

"Now we call an ambulance," she said.

* * *

The smell of the waiting room reminded Lauren of her clinic. It shared that same antiseptic odor and the more subtle smell of fear and misery.

Shifting her legs to ease a slight cramp in her calf, she cast a glance toward Cal. He slumped in the chair beside her, staring unblinkingly at his boots.

Zane had arrived via the ambulance bay, while Lauren and Cal, who'd followed in Cal's truck, had come in through the public entrance. Cal had been upset, not knowing whether or not his father was being seen to. With the triage nurse's help, Lauren persuaded him that Zane's chest pain would get top priority. He'd subsided into fretful silence then. She'd made a couple of attempts at conversation, but he was too worried to talk.

He blamed himself, of course, and wasn't ready to hear that he couldn't have known his father had a heart condition. That is, if it were in fact a heart condition. Zane had maintained loudly that his heart had never troubled him before.

Lauren let her gaze rest on Cal. He sat hunched in the chair in the classic waiting-room pose, hands clasped between his legs, elbows resting on his thighs.

Such a broad, strong back. And no wonder, the way he insisted on shouldering the weight of the world. She pressed her own hands together to keep from running them over the tightly stretched fabric of his shirt. As much as it would comfort her to touch him, she feared he was too tightly wound to accept it.

After what seemed like forever, a nurse approached, her rubber-soled shoes squeaking rhythmically. "Callum Taggart?" she said, mispronouncing it "Cawl-lum."

Cal shot to his feet. "Here."

Lauren watched the nurse's gaze slide over Cal. She

touched her hair in a gesture Lauren was sure was completely unconscious. "Your father is doing just fine, Mr. Taggart."

"Thank God."

"The doctor would like to talk to you, though."

"Can Lauren come too?"

The nurse glanced at Lauren. "You're family?"

Lauren thought she detected more than professional interest on the other woman's part in hearing her answer. "No."

"Dr. Townsend is a medical professional," he said without missing a beat. "I'd like her to be there."

"Of course." Lauren blushed when the nurse looked at her with new deference. "This way, Mr. Taggart, Dr. Townsend."

They followed her to a small examination room at the end of a long hallway, where they found Zane reclined on a bed. He looked much better despite the alarming number of electrodes and wires snaking out from under his hospital gown. Electrodes that a short, white-coated doctor was in the process of removing.

Zane's color was much improved, she noted, but his gray eyes flashed his displeasure at finding himself in such a vulnerable position. A smile curved her lips. *Like father, like son.*

It struck her again how much he looked like Cal. For an instant, she saw him not as Cal's father but as a man, splendidly virile despite the silver in his hair and the softening jaw.

What would happen if Cal ever saw his father as another man? Maybe their relationship was in a state of arrested development, Zane the disapproving parent and Cal the rebellious child.

Cal cleared his throat. "How's the ticker?"

"Embarrassingly sound," Zane growled, tugging the johnny more modestly around him.

The doctor looked up. "You must be the son. Cal, is it?"

"Yup."

"Dan Matchett." He pushed the portable monitor clear. "And this is your . . . ?"

"Friend," Cal supplied. "What's he mean, sound? His heart's okay?"

"Whoa, I'm still here." The elder Taggart's voice was testy. "My heart's fine, thank you, and so are my wits."

Cal studied his father with narrowed eyes, then turned back to the doctor. "That true?"

Zane made a strangled noise.

"Insofar as we can tell, yes, his heart's fine. Certainly, he hasn't had an infarction, and he slows no irregular rhythms."

"He means I ain't had no heart attack, and it's ticking over like a Timex."

"But?" Cal didn't take his eyes off the doctor. "There must be something. I saw him, doc. He was in serious pain."

"That's what we need to find out. It could be as simple as a hiatal hernia giving him some gastric reflux."

"Indigestion." Zane grunted in disgust. "You hear that? You stuffed me into an ambulance for heartburn."

Again, Cal ignored his father. "Or as serious as . . . ?"

"Could be an ulcer."

"Is that a big deal?"

"It can be. Which is why I'd like to do some tests. I could set something up as early as next week."

"Next week?" Zane sat up, suddenly cheerful. "Geez, doc, I'm afraid I'll be long gone by next week, but I'll get that looked into." He swung his legs over the edge of the bed.

"Set the tests up," Cal said. "He'll be here."

Zane spluttered. "I'm *still* here and I can speak for myself. And I say I'll be gone next week."

"Gone where?" Cal asked.

Zane bristled. "Wherever I please. I don't expect I'll have any trouble landing a job."

"I'm sure you won't. But you're not going anywhere until they check out your innards." Cal fixed his father with a glower. "I know how it is hiring yourself out. I did my share of that before the rodeo paid off. You wind up going from pillar to post, taking jobs when and where you can find them. You'd never stay put long enough to get tests done."

"So I'm supposed to hang around here and do exactly what?"

"You can work for me."

Lauren's eyes widened in surprise. Judging by Cal's expression, she'd bet he'd surprised himself, too.

Zane scowled. "I didn't come here looking for charity."

"Good, 'cause you'd be sucking on the wrong teat for that." Cal beetled his brows fiercely, and Lauren had to cough to cover a laugh. They were so alike. "You'll stay until you have a clean bill of health," he said. "That's the only condition on which I'll accept your fat little atonement check. You can work if you want to, or kick back and rest. Makes no difference."

Zane drew breath in through clenched teeth. "You're a mean-spirited man. Anybody ever tell you that?"

"Yeah, well, I learned from a master."

"Hell." The older man lifted his left hand and dragged the back of his thumb across his eyebrow. Lauren smiled at the familiar gesture. "Okay, you got a deal. I'm your flunky until Doc here can get the tests done."

"Good," said Cal.

"Good," said Zane.

· *Good,* thought Lauren.

"This one needs to see the farrier, I think."

Cal lowered the bay's hind foot he'd just finished dress-ing. Giving the filly a scratch on the rump, he stepped around her to peer into the next stall where Lauren crouched next to a wiry little mustang. "That left front hoof again?" Cal said.

"Vertical shear about an inch to the outside of the toe."

"Yeah, it's been a devil to fix. Said he'd try a composite repair next time, maybe cover it with Kevlar."

She released the gelding's foot and stood. "He might want to try drilling holes in the wall on either side and su-turing it first for more stability."

Cal nodded. "I'll suggest that."

They'd worked companionably for the past hour, checking each of the animals over and dressing hooves.

Cal knew he should be in his office. He really should be thinking about animal unit months and tinkering with the grazing plan. Unfortunately, he didn't have the headspace for it.

His life was a mess and to top it off, he'd just taken his father onto the payroll and sent Delia to town to deposit that $30,000 check. His brain froze up when he thought about that, which was why he was out here in the cool, dark barn, rubbing pine tar into horses' hooves.

The door from the tack room banged shut and he glanced up to see Marlena approaching. Great. Feeling hunted, he elbowed his way into the roan stallion's box. "Hide me, Blue," he muttered.

Marlena stopped unerringly outside the roan's stall. "Ugh, pine tar. You'd think they could come up with something better."

Cal didn't look up. "Hundred percent hydration rate to the hoof, and it's generic. Pretty hard to beat."

"I'm bored."

He bit back a sigh. Thank God he'd anticipated this and had deployed his men accordingly. "Go play with Brady. He's all by his lonesome in the low pasture, extending the windbreak."

She lifted the hair off her neck with a flip of her hand. "I can't. He's mad at me."

This time, he rolled her a sideways look. "Whatever for?"

She had the grace to color. "Lend me the Blazer."

"No." He bent to examine the roan's right front hoof.

"The old Ford, then."

"You're not going into Calgary."

A pause. "You can't keep me here, Cal."

He snorted. "Who says I want to?"

"Then give me a vehicle, dammit!"

He straightened, abandoning hope she would go away and leave him in peace. "Your little loan shark problem disappear overnight? Some benefactor paid him back for you, maybe?"

Her beautiful eyes flashed. "No."

"I see. Then you think he's forgiven your default in the whole three weeks you've been here?"

"No, but . . ."

"Then don't go showing your face in town. You want to hide out here, fine, but you're not going to run back and forth to Calgary. I've got enough to worry about without you leading some enforcer to my doorstep. If you leave now, you don't come back."

"You are such a bastard."

Cal disregarded the insult. The sheen in her eyes told

him she was very close to the edge, and he hadn't finished with her yet. "One more thing. You need to decide what you're going to do about Brady. If you're done with him, stay clear of him. And if you're not, for God's sake, go put him out of his misery."

Marlena drew her breath in a hiss. "You smug, superior sonofabitch! It must be nice being so damned perfect."

On that note, she marched out. Perfect? Him? That was rich. He couldn't remember the last time he'd put a foot *right*.

Lauren emerged from Sarge's stall to stand outside Blue's. He took one look at her and sighed. She had that look again.

"What?" he demanded.

"I'm not being critical."

He arched a brow, searching her face with narrowed eyes. "No? You look like you want to say something."

She held his gaze for just a split second before glancing down at her hands, but it was long enough for him to glimpse indecision. Not your garden variety should-I-tell-him-his-judgment-sucks-or-keep-my-mouth-shut indecision, either. This was great big indecision. Mixed, he thought, with a little fear.

"Okay, spill it."

The faintest blush touched her cheekbones, but she lifted her head and looked him straight in the eyes.

"I was thinking, maybe Marlena would be better off somewhere else. Maybe you should just give her a vehicle and some money and send her off somewhere."

"Send her away?" His mind staggered under the thought. "Geez, Marlena's not my favorite person either, but there are people out there with a vested interest in messing her up. She defaulted on a debt and they aren't about to turn the other cheek."

"I know. It's just—"

"Okay, they probably wouldn't whack her over ten grand, but they can't afford to let her go scot-free, either." Lauren really thought he should cut Marlena loose? "That's the deal—you pay one way or another."

"She could go somewhere quiet, stay low. . . ."

"What's wrong with right here?" He watched her face carefully. "It doesn't get much quieter than this, especially now, with the guests gone. If we try to put her into total cold storage, she'd be back in Calgary inside a week."

"There must be a safer place for her."

He snorted. "Yeah, it's called protective custody, but I don't think they grant that for loan defaulters. Not that she'd go along with it anyway." He let himself out of the stall to move closer to her. "I don't get why you think she's at special risk here. She used her maiden name for the loan, so they're not likely to track her down. And even if they did, they'd have to get through me and the boys first. We can protect her here."

She bit her lip. "I'm not sure we can."

A sudden thought struck him. Maybe she just wanted to get Marlena out of the way? But why? Could she be jealous of the idea of him and Marlena?

No. He shook his head to clear it. *No way.* Lauren probably understood better than anyone how utterly uninterested he was in resuming that relationship.

What other reason could she have for wanting Marlena out of the picture? Could Lauren be interested in Brady?

No. Again, the answer came with absolute certainty. Not that he had any illusions that she loved him, but there was no doubt she *wanted* the hell out of him. No one could make love like that while fantasizing about someone else.

"I don't understand why you think she'd be safer somewhere else. You know something I don't?"

She drew a deep breath, then let it out slowly. "It's not so much the thugs I'm worried about," she said at last. "It's the thing with Brady and Harvey that scares me."

Of course. Damn, he must really be tired. She'd talked about it before. "This is about that premonition, isn't it?"

She clasped her arms around her chest. "It's kind of a recurring thing."

This time when he looked into her eyes, it gave him a jolt. Damn, she really was scared.

"Cal, I have a bad, bad feeling about this."

Despite the anxiety in her eyes, he felt himself relax. Just a bad feeling, a sense of impending doom. Now that was familiar territory. Lord knew he'd had his share of bad feelings over Marlena. Lauren was scared now, but she'd shake it off.

"Well, that makes two of us, sweetheart. Anyone can see Marlena's a menace to herself." He brushed a strand of hair from her forehead, then cupped her face. "But don't you see? It really wouldn't matter where she went. She carries trouble with her. At least we can protect her here."

Lauren lowered her lashes. "You're right."

Her acquiescence should have pleased him, but he couldn't completely shake the unease that had taken root when he'd seen that fear in her face. He tipped her chin up with his finger and smiled into her eyes. "She'll be all right. You'll see. Hey, nothing came of it the last time you had a bad feeling, right?"

"Right."

She returned his smile, but it didn't come close to

reaching her worried eyes. As he watched her disappear into Sarge's stall again, he had the disquieting feeling he'd just been gauged. Gauged and found wanting.

For the next half hour, they made their way around the stalls. Lauren's emotions ping-ponged wildly.

She should have told Cal about the vision. It was criminal to withhold the information.

No, she'd done the right thing. She'd seen the way his face cleared the moment he made the connection with what he'd qualified as a premonition.

But if she just had the guts to spit it out, they could work together to ensure Marlena didn't ride off into any sunsets.

No, they couldn't, because he'd dismiss it as hokum, just as her former fiancé had. He'd look at her blankly and think, *My girlfriend receives 911 calls via her head.*

If she told him, there would be at least a small chance it would make a difference.

If she told him, there was an excellent chance he'd dump her faster than Garrett Robertson had.

A voice from the barn door distracted her from this back-and-forth self-torture. "Yo, anybody home?"

She dropped the mare's foot and turned toward the voice. Bruce Dysan. Her heart leapt with a new fear. He'd said he would call with the test results.

Cal stepped out of the adjacent stall. "Down here," he called. Under his breath, he muttered, "This isn't going to be good, is it? He'd have telephoned if it were good news."

Lauren stepped out to join Cal, touching his back briefly. "Let's wait to hear what he has to say."

"Dr. Dysan," Cal said when the other man pulled up.

"I'd offer to shake your hand, but we've been into the pine tar."

"Of course." Dr. Dysan smiled, a glimmer of white teeth in a full beard. "Look, I'm sorry about that newspaper article. I understand you've had some collateral damage already." The smile faded from his eyes. "As I told Dr. Townsend, the reporter who called me already had the details. I didn't think it was prudent to deny the investigation."

"I understand. The leak is my problem and I'll deal with it." Cal rolled his shoulders. "Right now, I'd just as soon you gave me my medicine straight up. I'm thinking it's bad news, you making a personal trip out here."

Dr. Dysan laughed. "Well, I wouldn't qualify it as good news, but I can guarantee you it's not what you're thinking."

"It's not anthrax?"

"Nope."

Lauren watched Cal sag with relief. "Not anthrax."

"Absolutely and unequivocally not anthrax."

Cal straightened again. "You said it was bad news—if it's not anthrax, what is it?"

"Not so much bad news as disturbing news." Dr. Dysan took a deep breath. "Mr. Taggart, your steer was poisoned."

"Poisoned?" Cal's eyebrows lifted, then swiftly drew together. "Well, I'll be damned. I'd have sworn there wasn't so much as a sprig of tall larkspur to worry about in that pasture."

"I'm sure you're right about the pasture being clean, but even if it isn't, that's not what killed your animal."

"Then what did?"

The big man's face looked grim. "Malice."

Lauren's pulse kicked. "Someone did this deliberately?"

207

"Unquestionably." He handed Lauren a sheaf of papers. "Take a look for yourself and tell me what you think."

She scanned the first page quickly, but stopped on the second. "Oh no."

"What?" Cal peered over her shoulder. "What is it?"

"Just a second." She flipped the page and scanned the rest of the document, then looked at Dr. Dysan. "Are you sure about this? The tests are accurate?"

"I'm sure. After the first tests, I got a second lab to run another tox screen with the extra blood. Same results."

Cal swore. "You're saying someone fed poison to my steer?"

"More like injected it, I'd say." Lauren looked up at Dr. Dysan for confirmation.

He nodded. "That'd be my guess."

"Injected it? Like with a needle? That's crazy," Cal said. "Why would a person do something like that? If they had it in for me, why wouldn't they just shoot the damned thing?"

The veterinary inspector shrugged. "Bullets tell tales. Maybe your guy didn't want to leave any evidence behind."

"Slit its throat, then. That would have sent me a definite message. But this . . ." He shook his head. "Hell, we might have missed it altogether. Where's the point in that?"

Lauren's ears rang with a tinny sound and the fine hairs on her arms and neck stood up. "I can tell you the point."

Both men turned toward her.

"I think whoever did this had something specific in mind. I think they wanted to make it look like anthrax."

"Wait just a minute," the veterinary inspector said. "You think someone custom-tailored a toxin to mimic anthrax?"

A quick look at Cal's frozen face told Lauren he'd followed her leap. She turned urgently back to Dr. Dysan. "It could be done, right?"

Bruce Dysan took his glasses off, rubbed the bridge of his nose. "I suppose so, but it would be hard. You'd have to know a lot about both the clinical manifestations of anthrax and—"

"Devious, black-hearted sonofabitch."

Cal's tone was flat, almost conversational, but Lauren heard the controlled fury beneath. Apparently Dr. Dysan sensed it too. He couldn't take his eyes off Cal's back as Cal strode toward the tack room. Lauren had to catch the doctor's arm to get his attention.

"Bruce, this is important. It's possible, right? I mean, how hard can it be to learn about anthrax? You could probably find everything you need to know about it on the Internet. And if you knew your chemicals, or knew someone who did, couldn't you design a poison to induce one or two cardinal symptoms?"

Dr. Dysan replaced his glasses and turned back toward Lauren. "Toxicology's not my area, but yeah, I suppose it could be done. I can see where this combination might cause the epistaxis and rapid death, maybe even inhibit rigor. But why would someone do that?"

"Easy," Cal called from the door of the tack room. He'd lost the work gloves and found his Stetson. He jammed it low on his forehead, shadowing his eyes, as he closed the distance between them. "To put me out of the guest ranch business."

Dr. Dysan's brow furrowed. "But who would want to do that?"

"Who?" Cal plucked the pages of the toxicology report from Lauren's unresisting fingers. "Give me twenty minutes, and I'll show you who. I'll bring his head back on a pike."

Wordlessly, Lauren watched him jump in the pickup and barrel down the driveway, kicking up a trail of dust behind him.

"Bruce?"

"Yeah?"

"I think I'm going to need a ride."

Chapter Twelve

"I'm sorry, I really can't allow you to go in there. Mr. McLeod is in conference."

Cal glowered at the young woman who barred the door to McLeod's office. "Look, I know you're just doing your job, lady, but you'll have to step aside. I have business with your boss."

"I can see that." She stood unflinching under a scowl that usually sent his men scattering. "Urgent business, too, by the look of it," she said soothingly. "Why don't you follow me back to my desk? I'll give you the earliest available appointment."

Briefly, he thought about simply picking her up and moving her. God, he had to get a grip. He'd never laid an unwelcome hand on a woman and he wasn't about to start now.

Cal closed his eyes before she could see them harden. He took a deep breath, exhaled slowly, then opened his eyes. "Okay, ma'am, we'll do it your way," he said, letting his posture relax.

She flushed prettily. "This way, please," she said, and turned to lead him back to the outer office.

Instead of following her as he'd led her to expect, Cal whirled and strode to the double oak doors, yanked them open and stepped into Harvey McLeod's conference room.

Three male faces swivelled toward him as he burst through the doors. The men sat around a gleaming table situated on an enormous Persian rug. Cigar smoke hung in the air: thick, pungent and expensive. Fat cats, city-bred and slow. *No threat.*

It took Cal all of a few seconds to size up the strangers before zeroing in on McLeod. Surprise flickered briefly in the other man's eyes, but otherwise he betrayed no perceptible alarm at having his inner sanctum invaded.

For an instant, no one moved. No one spoke. Then the secretary, her face stained with a less attractive flush now, skidded to a stop beside Cal. "I'm sorry, I couldn't stop him."

Harvey took a fat cigar out of his mouth. "It's all right, Lorna. I know how . . . forceful our Mr. Taggart can be."

Lorna eyed Cal with hostility. "Shall I call the police?"

"Heavens, no." Harvey smiled as though hugely amused by the suggestion, and Cal experienced a powerful urge to rearrange the perfect symmetry of his neighbor's face.

"I'd reserve judgment on that, McLeod," Cal growled, moving closer. "Think you can jerk me around and get away with it?"

"Charming." Harvey's smile broadened even as his eyes hardened. The two suits across the table edged their chairs backward on silent casters. Just inside the door, the secretary held her ground. "How exactly have I . . . jerked you around Mr. Taggart? All I've done is offer to take that ranch off your hands before the bank takes it. My offer still stands."

"Go to hell." Cal clenched his fists at his sides, mainly

to prevent using them on Harvey's face. "You knew I wouldn't sell, so you poisoned my steer to make it look like anthrax."

Harvey's smile died and his face went blank. "The tests are back? You can confirm you don't have anthrax?"

"I can do more than that." Cal brandished the report. "I can tell you what *did* kill that steer, and it ain't contagious."

Cal watched Harvey's eyes carefully, but they betrayed not a flicker of alarm. Maybe McLeod knew nothing about it after all.

Or maybe he was a damned good poker player.

The two suits shifted uncomfortably, but Harvey ignored them, leaning forward to stab his cigar out in a crystal ashtray.

"Forgive me, Taggart, but what exactly is your problem? Man tells me his herd's disease-free, seems to me he ought to be counting his blessings."

"What's my problem?" Cal felt his pulse hammering in his head. "My *problem* is somebody used a needle to jam that steer full of toxic sludge. My *problem* is that same somebody then fed the papers a story about anthrax." His anger built with every word. "My *problem* is my guest ranch cleared out faster than a motel room after a cockroach sighting, thanks to the national media picking up on that article."

Harvey tipped his head back and laughed. *Laughed.*

A surge of pure bloodlust fogged Cal's brain. He was not a man given to violence, but with stunning clarity, he visualized knocking McLeod to the floor. He imagined the satisfaction of battering the other man's face with his fists, anticipated the gratification of bone and sinew yielding to his righteous anger.

"That's rich. You think I simulated an anthrax outbreak, then leaked it to the press to kill your guest ranch business?"

"Now we're making some progress." Cal was vaguely surprised he could form actual words, let alone make them sound so cool.

"How wonderfully diabolical!" Harvey leaned back in his chair. Elbows resting on the padded arms, fingers linked loosely over a trim abdomen, he seemed unintimidated by Cal's position above him. "Tell me, when did I do this thing?"

Cal felt the smallest pinprick pierce his certitude. McLeod wasn't nearly as unnerved as he should have been.

"What was that, Taggart?" Harvey cupped a hand behind one ear. "I didn't hear you."

That's it. *McLeod was going down.* An instant before Cal laid hands on Harvey's shirt, however, a female voice cut in.

"Thursday night or Friday morning."

All heads turned to see Lauren framed in the doorway.

The secretary made a sound of disbelief. "What, it's suddenly Grand Central Station around here?"

"I'm sorry, the door was open," Lauren said.

"Never mind," she huffed. "What's one more intruder?"

"Now, Lorna, mustn't be rude to our guests." Harvey turned back to Cal. "So, what was that? Thursday or Friday?"

Cal eased back marginally, more a shifting of weight than an actual retreat. "If that's what Dr. Townsend says."

McLeod, kept his gaze locked on Cal's. "Well, this should be easy to clear up. Lorna, tell Mr. Taggart where I was Wednesday night through Friday noon."

"The same place I was," she said, clearly relieved to

come to her boss's aid after failing so abysmally as threshold guardian. "In Calgary for McLeod Industries' annual meeting."

Cal snorted. "That's convenient."

"Hey, don't take my word for it. Here." McLeod leaned forward, extracted something from the neat pile of papers in front of him and nudged it toward Cal. "Our annual report."

Leaning back, Harvey picked up the unlit stogie. "I believe it mentions the date and location for the annual shareholders' meeting. I should think forty or fifty of our shareholders could vouch for the fact that I addressed them Friday morning."

Cal picked up the glossy document with nerveless fingers. "You were in Calgary."

"For three days running. I'm sure Lorna could produce the business cards of the people I met with over that period, if you like." Harvey clamped the cigar between white teeth again.

Cal flipped the report open and skimmed it. There it was in black and white. Last Friday, McLeod Industries' annual meeting at the Calgary Ramada. Cal lifted his gaze to McLeod's.

"My offer still stands," said Harvey. "Your land and your herd, same deal I gave your friend Hinchey."

"No, thanks." Cal tossed the report back on the table. "I've got other plans."

For the first time since bursting into the room, Cal thought he glimpsed a flash of genuine emotion in the other man's eyes, but it was gone instantly. What was it? Anger? Frustration?

"I didn't realize you were so flush, neighbor." Harvey picked up the report and offered it back to Cal. "Maybe

215

you should consider McLeod Industries. Ask your broker about it."

My broker? As if he'd ever turn enough of a profit in this market to play stocks. Cal smiled even as he fought down another uncharacteristic urge toward violence. "Another time, maybe." *When hell freezes over.* "I'll be talking to you again."

McLeod bared his own teeth. "I'll look forward to it."

Lauren had to jog to keep up with Cal as he strode back to the truck. He waited for her to climb in before he fired the engine, but she was still fumbling with her seatbelt when he popped the clutch. The truck shot forward, spraying gravel.

"We sure made a friend of Harvey's secretary, didn't we?"

As an attempt to cut the tension, her observation fell short. He just glanced at her and turned back to the road.

"How'd you get here?" he asked.

"I had Bruce drop me." Seatbelt secured, she glanced over at him. In profile, his lean face looked carved from granite, his jaw outthrust, mouth drawn down at the corners.

"Guess you reached the same conclusion I did about Harvey?"

Lauren adjusted her seatbelt. Truthfully, she didn't really think Harvey McLeod would stoop to this, but she'd known Cal would jump to that conclusion. Of course, there was no point saying any of that to Cal, not when his mouth was set like that.

Instead, she said, "Looks like we were wrong, huh?"

He turned out onto the highway and accelerated away. "It was McLeod, all right. I don't care what he says."

She chewed the inside of her lip a moment. "Do you really think he'd have offered you all those contacts if they couldn't corroborate his presence in Calgary for the critical dates?"

"Oh, I'm sure they'd pan out, all right. But who's to say he didn't hire someone to do it?"

Lauren suppressed a sigh. Far be it from her to defend Harvey McLeod. She'd revised her opinion of him since learning of his relationship to Brady. Now she was convinced Harvey would be the agent of Marlena's death. Oh, the hands that choked Marlena's life away might not be Harvey's, but the blame would ultimately be his. He was the one who knowingly, maliciously, created this explosive triangle by bedding his son's lover. He tried to humiliate the illegitimate son whom he denied in front of this community

But as repugnant as Harvey's conduct was toward his own son, Lauren had no reason to believe he'd go to the trouble of killing cattle, even by proxy. He had no need to.

She took a deep breath. "Yes, he could have hired someone to do it," she conceded, "but think about it, Cal. Why would he? From what you've said, he already owns more ranch land than he can possibly graze, even with his enormous operation. Why would he go to criminal lengths to get something he doesn't need?"

Cal kept his eyes on the road. "If McLeod was the kind of guy to settle for what he needed, he wouldn't be sitting on top of an empire, would he?"

"True, but having that empire, he must be confident he can wait you out. That's what he did with the others, isn't it?"

"But my situation's different. The income from the guest

ranch would've carried me through. That's why he sabotaged it."

"Carried you for how long?" she asked gently. "Spider says you're getting ready to sell the six-month-old calves as well as the yearlings. He also says you didn't keep any replacement heifers last year, and won't again this year." The hard lines of his profile grew harsher with every word she spoke, but she had to say it. "How long can you sustain your herd that way?"

She felt the truck, which was already pushing the speed limit, surge forward. "Spider's got a big mouth."

"He's concerned about you."

"He's concerned about his job. For good reason, after spouting off like that."

"Cal, Spider's your friend. *I'm* your friend. We were just talking shop." He kept his face averted, but she saw his lips compress. "Dammit, forget about Spider. The point is, if I know that much about your operations after only a few weeks, you can bet McLeod knows it. Which means he knows he can wait you out."

She felt him ease up on the accelerator.

"But the cash Dad gave me . . ."

"Will buy you some breathing room. But McLeod doesn't know that. As far as he knows, you probably won't last the winter."

Silence. The speedometer needle drifted downward again.

"Okay, so he knows I'm in a tight spot," Cal conceded a moment later. "But he also knows that even if the ranch fails, I wouldn't sell to him. I'd let the damned bank take it first."

"And then he'd buy it at auction for less than he's prepared to offer you." Lauren hated to have to say it, but she knew she was right. *He* knew she was right.

"I could find another buyer." Cal swung into his driveway.

"From whom Harvey could buy it, with a suitable markup," she pointed out. "Which brings me back to my original question. Why would he risk doing something like poisoning your steer when he's holding so many cards? Cal, he'd have to be crazy."

"Maybe he is crazy. Ever think of that? Maybe he's certifiable." Cal stopped the truck and killed the engine with a savage twist of the ignition key. A cloud of dust drifted past them. "For all we know, maybe he picks up messages from alien spacecrafts with his fillings. Maybe he sees Technicolor movies in his head. Maybe he hears Charlton-goddamned-Heston's voice telling him to do screwed-up stuff like this!"

Lauren stopped breathing. Cal sat there, hands clenched on the steering wheel, knuckles showing white. In the silence, she could hear the ticking of the engine cooling.

Maybe he sees Technicolor movies in his head. . . .

"Or maybe he's just crazy like a fox." Cal turned to look at her then, his gray eyes as bleak as winter. "But even if Harvey McLeod did kill that steer, we'll never be able to prove it. And that's not even the worst part."

"What?" She pushed the pain back to ask the question, but the word emerged as little more than a whisper. She licked her lips and tried again. "What's the worst part?"

"The worst part," he said, "is it won't even matter that we don't really have anthrax. The damage is done. We won't see a front page retraction in the *Globe and Mail.*" He laughed harshly. "Hell, even if they printed one, it wouldn't make an impression. People will read *Foothills Guest Ranch* and think *anthrax.*"

With that, he jumped out of the truck, slammed the door and strode toward the house.

Lauren pushed the button on her seatbelt. The restraint retracted energetically, but she made no move to get out. She sat there for long moments, hearing Cal's voice.

Maybe he sees Technicolor movies in his head. . . .

She fumbled for the door release and slid out of the truck.

Looks like you made the right call, keeping your mouth shut.

Closing the door with a quiet click, she turned toward her cabin.

Cal tossed the Southern Comfort back, grimacing as the amber liquid burned its way down his throat. Then he poured another small measure into the shot glass. Briefly, he considered topping it up a little more, then sighed. Recapping the bottle, he leaned back in the chair and kicked his feet up onto his desk. Despite talking a good line of trash, he knew better than to try to drown his troubles with booze. Besides, he doubted he could drink enough to escape the mess his life had become.

Cradling the whiskey in his lap, he closed his eyes. Then snapped them open again.

Dammit. Every time he shut his eyes, the afternoon from hell replayed itself. The laughable thing was, it wasn't knowing his guest ranch had been deliberately deep-sixed that galled him most, though it incensed him every time he thought of it. Nor was it McLeod's mocking smile, though that maddened him, too.

What really ate at his gut was Lauren's knowing the extent of his financial straits. The knowledge that her opinion of him should be the least of his concerns didn't seem to help.

He raked a hand through his wet hair. Yeah, yeah, stupid male pride. He knew it. But dammit, he'd wanted her to think he could do this one thing well. He couldn't ride bulls anymore and he'd been a half-assed host to his guest ranch customers, but he knew ranching. Did she think he'd made those decisions lightly? Did she imagine he didn't know what pressure he was putting on his herd? Hell, he'd had no choice in the matter. Of course, with the cash infusion, he could avoid both those measures. . . .

"Huh. Mighta known."

At the sound of his father's voice from the doorway, Cal's first instinct was to snatch his feet off the desk, but he controlled it. Instead, he tossed back the whiskey, which until this moment he'd had every intention of nursing. This time, he didn't grimace as it scorched its way to his belly. Only then did he drop his feet and sit up in his chair.

"Might have known what, Dad?" For effect, he uncapped the Southern Comfort, though he'd lost his desire for it.

"That you'd crawl into a bottle soon as the going got hard."

Cal chinked the neck of the whiskey bottle against the rim of his glass, barely managing not to slosh it onto his desk. Huh! Showed how little his father knew. Sure, he'd misbehaved plenty in his youth, but he'd grown up since then.

"Yeah, that's right." He gestured to the near empty bottle. "I was gonna get stinking on what's left of that."

"There's no need for sarcasm." Zane Taggart looked around, taking in the computer equipment. His gaze lingered on the monitor, which displayed colored graphs. Suddenly, his eyebrows drew together. "Well, I'll be damned! Are those growth charts?"

Cal flushed. "Yeah, well, some of us don't have a direct line to God almighty. Some of us have to rely on computers."

His father made a sound of disgust. "Dammit, Cal, I never said my way was better. I went by guess and by God because it was the only way I knew. Lord knows I was wrong often enough."

Cal dragged a hand over his face. Why were their exchanges always like this? Why couldn't they talk like normal men? "Sorry. I had no call to jump down your throat like that. It's been a long day."

Zane took a seat, then gestured to the whiskey bottle. "If you're not planning on drowning yourself in that after all, how about pouring your old man a drink?"

Share a drink with his father? Now there was a first. In his youth, Cal had done his drinking with his rowdy crowd of friends, carousing on Saturday nights just to spite the old man. The police had carted him home more than once.

"A drink? That's not against doctor's orders?"

Zane's face darkened thunderously. "There's nothing wrong with me that I can't handle that little drop of whiskey."

Cal bared his teeth in a smile. "Relax, I was baiting you."

Zane swore, then closed his eyes and sighed heavily. "I know you were. That's the worst of it, that I still rise to it."

Cal dug another glass out of the bottom drawer of his desk. Thumping it down, he poured the last finger of Southern Comfort into it and pushed it toward his father.

"And you still open every conversation with a criticism. I just lash back out of habit. That's why I got defensive over the bar charts." Cal nodded toward the computer

222

screen, which had winked out. "I just assumed you were going to dump on it."

His father picked up the glass, swirling the amber liquid but not drinking it. Cal picked up his own glass and took a sip. His old leather chair creaked as he settled back in it, then the room fell silent but for the white noise of the computer. It took about ten seconds for the silence to become uncomfortable.

"Do I really do that?" Zane asked.

At his father's words, Cal glanced up, only to find his father staring into his own glass.

"Do what?"

"Open every conversation with a criticism?"

Cripes, and here he'd thought the *silence* was uncomfortable. If he wasn't careful, this could turn into a real conversation, another one of those things he didn't know how to share with his father. Best to skate quickly over it, then change the subject.

"Oh, I wouldn't worry about it, Dad. It's like the chicken and the egg thing, hard to tell which came first. Did you disapprove of me because I acted up, or did I act up because you disapproved of me? I guess it doesn't really matter."

Zane's head came up. "I never disapproved of you."

Cal's fingers tightened on the glass in his hands. When he noticed his knuckles turn white, he consciously relaxed his grip. He opened his mouth to say, "Whatever you say, Dad," but what emerged was a disbelieving snort. "I was there, Dad, remember? You disapproved of me plenty."

Zane took a swallow of the liquor and grimaced. "I may have disapproved of your choices sometimes but I always knew you were a good kid. When you weren't doing your darndest to get my goat, I was proud of you. I may not have said it often enough—"

Or at all. Cal clamped down hard on the thought. *Don't think, don't think, don't feel.*

"I know I wasn't the best parent, but I did worry about you. Those kids you hung around with were bad news. Two of 'em, the Cookson boys, went on to prison. Did you know that? I wanted better'n that for you."

Cal felt the barrier behind which he kept the anger bulge. He couldn't hear this. Not now. Not twenty years too late.

"And the rodeo . . . I know you loved it, but I thought it would break your heart, if not your body."

"Don't say another word."

"Why not?" Zane growled. "I guess it needs to be said, if you think you were such an all-around disappointment to me."

Cal slammed his glass down on the table, sloshing the contents on his sleeve. "I said, shut up, old man."

Zane ignored the warning. "You've got a good heart, son, just like your mother. I always knew you'd make a good man."

The barrier snapped then, letting the pent-up anger escape. Cal lurched to his feet, sweeping his drink to the floor. The shattering of glass did nothing to soothe the beast inside him.

"Not . . . another . . . word! You hear me?" Even in his rage, Cal knew enough to keep the desk between himself and his father.

"Cal, what's the matter—"

"If you don't shut up, I swear I'll hit you."

Zane surged to his feet. "Then I guess you'll have to hit me, 'cause I won't shut up about this."

Cal rounded the big desk. His father held his ground but

braced for a blow. That subtle stiffening infuriated Cal even more. To think the old man actually thought he'd hit him . . .

Then he noticed his own right fist cocked at his side, knuckles gleaming white, the muscles of his arm coiled to strike.

Jesus.

With a muffled oath, Cal turned and stalked out.

Chapter Thirteen

Lauren had just slid into her bath when a knock came at her cabin door. Cal. That peremptory rap couldn't be anyone else's.

A thrill arrowed straight to her core, raising goosebumps on her skin. On its heels came a surge of resentment. How could she respond like this to the mere thought of him after he talked so scathingly about crazy people who saw "movies in their heads"?

But he didn't mean you. He doesn't know about your visions. Stupid to punish him when he doesn't even know.

Clutching the facecloth to her chest, she chewed the inside of her lip. She did want him rather desperately. . . .

Two more short, sharp raps followed. "It's me, Lauren. Let me in."

What had she vowed just this morning? *To grab every minute, savor every sensation, memorize each look and touch.* She stepped out of the tub, sloshing water in her eagerness. "I'm coming."

A moment later, she opened the door. As he brushed past, she tried to catch the tang of aftershave and night air and Cal that she knew he'd bring in with him, but this time it was overlaid with the smell of alcohol. That, along with the set of his shoulders, sent a small jolt of alarm through her.

"Cal, are you all right?"

He turned to face her, and she sucked in a breath. His face looked like a stranger's. His eyes burned with an intensity she'd never seen in them before.

"Come here."

She wanted to, but something stopped her. Again, she caught a whiff of alcohol. "Have you been drinking?"

"Not nearly enough."

She'd never known Cal to take more than a few drinks, but maybe this afternoon's run-in with Harvey McLeod . . .

"You haven't had more trouble with Harvey, have you?"

"No,"

Marlena! Fear jolted her, leaving an acrid taste in her mouth. "Has something happened to Marlena? Is she okay?"

His lips thinned. "See, now there you go again. I'm used to my men obsessing over Marlena, but I gotta say this is kinky."

She ignored the taunt. "Cal, just tell me, is she okay?"

"I imagine she's in her room, but I expect I could get her over here, if you like." He lowered his voice as though imparting a confidence. "Strictly speaking, I don't think she's into women, but if anyone could change her mind, you could."

"Stop it!" Who was this man?

"Honey, I'm just getting started." He took a step closer, surveying her through narrowed eyes. "I think what you need is a man in the middle," he advised at last. "She might go for that. Hell, I could even give you some tips about what gets her hot."

Nausea roiled in her stomach. "Why are you doing this?"

He stepped closer still, close enough for her to get another whiff of alcohol. Close enough to trace her collarbone with a callused finger, sending an involuntary shiver down her spine.

"So, what'll it be?" His voice dropped, warm, gravelly, sexy. "Shall I call Marlena for you? Would you like that?"

His breath fanned her face. Surprisingly, it didn't reek of whiskey. It was *on* him, not *in* him, she realized with a start. But her stomach revolted nonetheless. It was his words that made her sick. Just at this instant, she knew what it was to hate a man even as her pulse leapt despairingly under his fingers.

Knew it and despised herself for it.

She lifted her chin. "I take it you're volunteering?"

He dropped his hand abruptly. "Hell, no. I'm not the man for that job. I'd get her to bring young Brady, if I were you—"

Crack!

The sound of her open hand making contact with his jaw shocked Lauren, but it didn't seem to rattle Cal. If anything, he seemed gratified by it, baring his teeth in a fierce smile.

"Oh, dear, what am I saying? Two women and one man—how politically incorrect of me. No doubt the modern woman's fantasies lean more toward enjoying two men?"

Her hands fisted at her sides. For the first time in her life, she truly understood the lust to draw blood. Yet another insight into herself she could have lived quite happily never . . .

Then it struck her—he'd wanted her to lash out at him.

"What's the matter? I'd have thought a little three-way fun would be a pretty common theme in your line of work."

228

Was that what this was about? Her stupid lie that first day about writing erotica? She searched his face. No, it was something else, something more. Still, she'd have to confess her lie. Maybe she couldn't reveal herself to him the way she longed to, but she could give him that much truth. But it would have to wait. Right now, she needed to know why he was goading her.

She took a deep breath and uncurled her clenched fingers. "Okay, you had me going pretty good there, but I'm done now."

Something flickered in his eyes, but his only comment was to raise one skeptical eyebrow.

She met his gaze calmly. "So are you ready to tell me why you picked this fight?"

Again, something stirred, but it was quickly masked. "Pick a fight? I thought I was being quite agreeable about the whole thing, apart from refusing to stand in for the threesome. But maybe if you asked me nicely." He dropped his tone again. "With a little warming up—"

"Forget it, Cal," she interrupted. "I won't hit you again, no matter what you say, so you might as well just give it up."

"Clearly, you have no idea how low I can go." He bared his teeth again in that wolfish smile, but a muscle leapt in his jaw.

Her lips curved ruefully. "Oh, I think you've already been there, but it won't work again. We both know I'm not sexually interested in Marlena or Brady or anyone else." She shrugged helplessly. "I just want you."

I just want you.

Cal spun away from her to stand in front of the window, but he couldn't get away from the words. As they resonated in his head, the last of the anger he'd been clinging to slipped away, leaving a terrifying black hole yawning beneath him. He clutched for the fury again, but it was gone. Then Lauren closed the distance again. She was so close he could feel her warmth on his back. There was no escaping her either, it seemed.

"I just had a fight with my father," he said, staring out into the floodlit yard. Some disconnected part of his brain observed that since there was no guest traffic from the cabins to the house, he could probably stop lighting the area after dark.

"I'm sorry. Was it bad?"

"I nearly hit him." He lifted a hand to massage his neck.

Lauren caught his hand as he dropped it. "He must have said something to provoke you," she said softly.

His body angled toward hers of its own volition. She smelled like heaven. "You sound pretty sure of that."

"I *am* sure of it. You wouldn't attack your father—wouldn't attack anyone—without provocation."

Damp tendrils of hair clung to her forehead and moisture dewed her skin. If he could just bury his head against her breasts, if she would just hold him . . .

But he didn't deserve that kind of solace, he reminded himself.

He laughed harshly. "I just attacked *you,* didn't I?"

She shrugged it off. "I can take care of myself. Zane may not be so well equipped right now, and you knew that." She lifted a hand to his smooth his hair. "You did the right thing. Though next time, feel free just to tell me what happened."

He made no reply, but he brought his own hand up to trap hers against his face.

"Tell me about it," she said.

To his embarrassment, Cal felt tears prick his eyes. He turned his mouth into her hand, murmured the words into her fragrant palm. "I tried to make him shut up, but he wouldn't."

Lauren cupped the other side of his face. "Go on."

Cal's hand tightened on hers. "He said he was proud of me, had always been proud of me. He said I was a good kid and he always knew I'd make a good man. He said . . . he said—"

"He said what, Cal?"

He swallowed to ease his throat. "He said I had a good heart, like my mother."

Silence. He waited for her to say, "And your point is?" or, "So, what's the problem?" Instead, she drew his head down to her shoulder. He closed his arms around her fiercely.

"He's right. You *are* a good man, Cal Taggart, and your father will have to answer for not telling you that sooner, for not showing you that every day."

Her words laid his heart open as surely as a surgeon could have. She understood.

Then the fear set in. Sweet Jesus, she saw right through to the frightened core of him. Might as well crack his ribs and spread them, because it felt as if his heart were pumping right out there, vulnerable and exposed, where anything could happen to it.

He tried to pull back, but she held him easily, shushing him. Then suddenly, somehow, he just let go of it. All that mattered was the heat of her and the comfort she offered.

He lifted his head from the satin of her shoulder and found her mouth clumsily. The kiss was short on technique but long on passion, and she returned it with equal fervor.

When he lifted his head, she moaned and followed his mouth as though reluctant to relinquish it. She licked his upper lip, then nibbled at the corners of his mouth before finally drawing his lower lip between her teeth and biting gently.

"Love me," he groaned. "Oh, Lauren, love me right now."

"Yes."

A shudder went through her, or was it him? Then she was tugging him toward the bedroom, their lips still locked, hands fumbling. When the backs of her knees hit the bed, she sank down on it. He would have followed her, but again she stopped him, her fingers at the buckle of his belt.

"Let me, Cal."

"Just a sec." He tore off his shirt and fished a condom from his jeans before letting her resume her attentions. With delicate fingers, she slipped his belt free and undid the button on his jeans. Cal gritted his teeth, holding himself still as she eased his zipper down. Then she fisted her fingers in the material at his hips and started inching his jeans and briefs down. So slow. It was killing him. Finally his sex sprang free, heavy and eager. He needed to be inside her.

Urgently, he shoved his jeans down and kicked them free, while he tore at the condom packet with clumsy fingers.

She closed her hand over his fingers, taking the condom from him. "Not yet," she breathed.

Not yet? What did she mean, *not yet?*

Then she showed him. Leaning forward, she caught his shaft in her hand and guided the tip of it into her mouth.

His heart stopped. He squeezed his eyes shut.

Hot silk, wet suction, the tentative flick of a tongue . . . Not *a* tongue. *Lauren's* tongue. *Lauren's* mouth.

He opened his eyes. The sight of her, eyes closed, so intent on exploring him, gave him a jolt he feared might leave his nerve endings permanently singed. Then she released him.

He groaned, part relief, part regret, but she wasn't finished with him. She closed her lips around him again, but this time, she opened her eyes. Their gazes locked as she took as much of him as she could into her mouth.

"Lauren." He gripped her head with both hands, torn between the desire to stop her and the need to hold her there, imposing on her the rhythm his body cried out for. Somehow, he managed to do the former, pushing her away.

Her eyes, dilated with arousal, were clouded. "What's the matter?"

Yeah, Taggart, what was the matter? Why'd he stop her when he burned to feel her mouth on him? His chest heaved with the effort of control. "You don't have to do this."

"I want to, Cal. I can't believe how much I want to." He watched a shiver pass through her as she gazed up at him.

He groaned. "Lauren, sweetheart . . ."

"Was I doing it wrong? Tell me what to do and I'll do it."

His heart gave a jerk in his chest. Could it be she'd never gone . . . never given . . . never performed . . . Oh, hell! "Lauren, honey, are you saying you've never . . . loved a man with your mouth like this?"

She lifted her chin. "I never wanted to before, but I'd like to try again, if you'd just tell me what I did wrong."

He gave a shaky laugh. "You didn't do anything wrong."

"But you didn't like it?"

"Oh, yeah, I liked it. Too much."

Her lips curved in a slow, smoldering smile. "Me too."

This time, when she took him into the warm wetness of her mouth, he surrendered to it, telling her in broken words how much he loved what she was doing, begging her not to stop.

Too soon, he could stand no more, and he pushed her down on the bed. Her bathrobe came off with one sweep, exposing her silky skin, fragrant from the bath. *Perfect*, he marveled. *Mine!* On that fierce thought, he branded her with his mouth. Her neck, her breasts, the indentation of her waist. Then he started again at her feet, kissing his way up toned calves, past sensitive knees to the silk of her trembling thighs. She allowed it, welcomed it if her ragged breathing was any indication, but when he parted her with questing fingers, she squeezed her thighs together to prevent the ultimate intimacy, trapping him in a vise-like grip.

Another first?

His rational mind told him it couldn't be, but the maidenly clasp of her thighs told another story. A primitive elation seized him at the thought that he'd be the first to love her so intimately. But first she had to be persuaded.

"Sweetheart, you've got me in a leg lock here. Do you think you could relax 'em a little?"

"I'm sorry." Her tone was mortified, but she relaxed her grip on him only slightly.

He stroked the outsides of her thighs. "Don't you want me to love you the way you loved me?"

Her legs positively vibrated with tension. "I don't know," came her strangled reply.

He buried his grin against her warm thigh. "Did you like having me at your mercy, pushing me higher, making me crazy?"

"Yes!"

"Did it excite you?"

"Oh, God, yes." Her voice was high and thin.

"Then how can you deny me the same pleasure? You'll like it. I'll make sure you do." He felt her legs slacken another few millimeters. "Do you trust me?"

"Of course."

Her instant, unqualified response roughened his voice. "Then relax for me, baby. I'll go slow."

And so he did. By the time he'd worked his way down to the soles of her feet and back up to the apex of her thighs, she was whimpering with need. This time, when he honed in on her sex, she clutched the bedclothes but offered no resistance. Her hips jerked when he closed his mouth over her, but he knew she wasn't trying to elude him. It was involuntary, as was her choked half-scream. Then she was moving against him, her cries of delight echoing around him as his fingers joined the dance of lips and tongue. Within minutes, she found her release, bucking and straining beneath him, her breath a harsh sobbing in the otherwise silent cabin.

Cal told himself a gentleman would have held her then and soothed her, but unappeased desire had burned him clean down to pure need. Even as the aftershocks rippled through her, he searched the bed frantically and found the condom. Sheathing himself, he moved between her legs again, poised himself over her, nudged into her. God, she was so tight, her muscles still clenching. Could she take him?

"Cal?"

Oh, please, don't ask me to stop. "What?"

"Make it hard. Make it wild."

As her words sank in, he relinquished thought. With a rasping cry, he buried himself in her blazing, impossible tightness. She cried out at the invasion, but lifted her hips to meet him thrust for thrust. Mindlessly, he pounded himself into her—all that he'd been, all that he was, all that he might be—and she took it willingly, greedily, until her long, rolling climax triggered his, sending them both into oblivion.

Lauren rolled over, dragging a hand through her hair as her heartbeat slowly returned to normal. She was still tingling in places she barely knew she had, and she'd probably be sore tomorrow, but she was also happy. "That was the most . . . incredible sex I have ever had."

"Hmmmm, me too." Cal rolled onto his side, supporting his head with one hand while tenderly tracing patterns on her rib cage with his free hand.

"Really?" She lifted her own fingers to stroke his arm, so brown against her white flesh.

"Really," he said, his callused fingers circling her belly button. She sucked her breath in. "But I'm guessing it means something different to you than it does to me."

The words stilled her fingers. It was true. No doubt it was different for her. Unlike him, she'd probably still be taking these memories out years from now. She rolled away swiftly. Sitting on the edge of the bed, she struggled into her bathrobe. "I wouldn't be too sure about that, cowboy. Women don't confuse sex and love nearly as often as men imagine."

"That's not what I meant."

He'd crawled to the edge of the bed and she turned to face him with cool eyes. She wasn't prepared for the heat in his eyes. She looked away again. "Then what did you mean?"

"I meant the term 'best sex ever' is relative," he retorted. "Your experience base seems a little—no, make that a *lot*—thinner than I imagined. Particularly for an erotica writer."

Oh, hell! She'd just made a complete fool of herself. Well, it couldn't be helped now.

Besides, this was the opening she'd wanted, wasn't it?

"I'm afraid I lied about that. I don't write erotica."

His face went slack, surprise erasing the anger. "You're joking, right?"

She shook her head no.

"You really don't write erotica?"

"No."

"Do you write *at all?*"

"No. Well, actually, I wrote an article once for a veterinary magazine. . . ."

"Why'd you lie about it?"

"Because I wanted you to be interested in me." She felt her face flushing but couldn't stop it. It wasn't the whole truth, of course. She'd needed a cover for her inquisitiveness about the comings and goings on the guest ranch. But in retrospect there was more truth to it than she would have allowed back then.

He blinked. "Five foot nine with legs that go on forever . . . you thought you had to embellish on *that* to get my attention?"

"How was I to know?" Lauren's flush deepened, but she squared her shoulders. "Excluding you, I've had exactly two lovers. *Two.*" She held up two fingers to underscore her point.

"Okay, that's not even funny."

She smiled—a quick, nervous grin. "You're telling me. I'm thirty years old."

He snorted. "Thanks for the gesture, but I don't require the illusion of near-virginity in my women."

Lauren forgave the snort. After all, she'd tried hard to create a certain image. "Thank you for your open-mindedness, but the fact remains, you're number three."

"No."

"Yes." She tried hard not to let his denial irk her. "The

first was a fellow student in my first year of premed. I kept up the farce of a relationship with that man for a whole month so I wouldn't have to admit I'd done it out of sheer curiosity." She grimaced at the memory. "And the second . . . well, that was different. I was engaged to him for eighteen months."

"Eighteen months is a long time," Cal said gruffly. "Long enough to learn all there is to learn, I'd have thought."

It was Lauren's turn to snort. "I've learned more in the last eighteen days than I learned in that eighteen months."

"How can that possibly be?"

She shrugged self-consciously. "I don't know. Garrett was an uncomplicated man, I guess."

"Huh! I'd say Garrett wasn't a man at all."

Unexpectedly, she laughed. "That may be."

He scowled. "I'd have left you alone, you know, if I'd had any idea. . . ."

"I know."

"I let this go so far because I thought you'd be able to take a hot summer fling in stride."

She bristled at the note of panic in his voice. "Who says I can't? Are you afraid I'll fall in love with you? Is that it?"

Dark spots of color flagged his hard cheekbones. "No, not at all, but I do have a healthy respect for the power of sex."

Belatedly, Lauren remembered Marlena's sexual addiction and the agonies he must have suffered over it. She groaned. "Cal, let's not argue." She placed a hand on his bare chest and felt a tiny bit of the tension go out of him. "I'll keep a cool head about this, I promise. Scout's honor. I can handle myself."

"I don't want anyone to get hurt."

Lauren was afraid it was too late for that, but she smiled

confidently. "No one's going to get hurt. We both know the rules. Now, could we have a quick shower before we hit the hay? You'll want to be rested when you make peace with Zane tomorrow."

His gaze sharpened. "What makes you think I'm going to make peace with that old buzzard?"

Lauren's smile was real this time. "Because you're a good man, Cal Taggart."

Chapter Fourteen

How did I come to be here?

Cal slumped in a worn chair in the waiting room of the outpatient department, reflecting on how much his nice, ordered life had changed in a matter of weeks. Marlena had turned up on his doorstep like a bad penny; his father had materialized out of the blue; his guest ranch business had been scuttled by an unseen enemy and he had no idea how to fight back.

And then there was Lauren.

He didn't know how it happened, but somehow she'd wormed her way right into his heart. He'd lain in bed last night with her body cradled against his and faced the truth. He loved her. She was smart and generous and wise, but most of all, she'd seen him at his absolute worst—time and again—and hadn't turned away.

Of course, the realization was bittersweet. She'd made it painfully clear that this was nothing more than a walk on the wild side for her, a long-overdue sexual education.

A door opened and Zane walked out. Street clothes replaced the blue johnny he'd been wearing most of the morning.

Cal stood. "You ready?"

"Damned right I am," he growled.

"Any word on the tests?"

Zane waved a hand. "Bah! They won't tell me nothin'. Seems to me, somebody sticks a camera down your throat, or up some other orifice, they oughta tell you what they saw."

"They probably want to go over it up, down and sideways before they commit themselves."

"Well, I can tell you there's nothing wrong with me."

"I'd agree with you if I hadn't seen you flopping around on my floor like a fish," Cal said pleasantly.

"Insolent pup!"

"Crusty old man."

For the first time, the words were exchanged with a kind of affection. Cal smiled as they navigated the shining corridors.

Cal had searched his father out first thing that morning and slowly, haltingly, awkwardly, they'd started to talk about the past.

They'd both grieved the loss of one woman—Cal's mother, Zane's wife—but each had responded differently. Zane withdrew into himself, seeking oblivion in the endless grind of ranching which left him physically and mentally exhausted. Feeling twice abandoned, Cal acted out. Only the most flagrant misbehavior stirred the older Taggart from his numbness. Consequently, the only attention Cal got was negative attention.

Cal never thought the day would come when he'd forgive his father, but in the end, it was easy. All he'd had to do was imagine how he might cope if Lauren were snatched from him today. It wasn't the same; he and Lauren weren't man and wife, committed to each other for a lifetime, hadn't conceived a child together, but still, Cal could see how a man might shut down.

It helped that Zane recognized his failure. His regret was genuine and palpable. Cal had already granted his absolution, but he knew the old man would carry his remorse to his grave.

They exited the hospital, crossed the burning asphalt to Cal's truck. As Cal pulled out of the parking lot, he flicked on the radio, filling the cab of the truck with the latest Matchbox Twenty song. Zane fidgeted for about five seconds, then grabbed the tuner knob. A couple of twists, and he'd tuned in a country station. Cal just grinned and accelerated away.

"So, you gonna ask that Townsend girl to marry you?"

Cal ground the gears, found second, and popped the clutch. The truck shot forward. "Where'd you get an idea like that?"

"She's a smart one."

"She is that." *Too smart to get serious about a floundering rancher sinking in a sea of red ink.*

"Sits a horse good, too."

"Yup."

"Mind you, she could use some proper Western footwear."

"Un-huh."

"Veterinarian training would come in handy, too."

Cal slanted Zane a look. "She's a small animal vet, Dad."

Zane ignored him. "A looker, too."

"I *had* noticed," said Cal dryly.

"And she must find you passably handsome, judging by how many nights you spend away from the house."

"Dad!"

"I'm old, son, but I'm not stupid."

"Would you just drop it? She's not going to marry me."

He snorted. "'Course she's not, 'cause fool that you are, you've just said you're not going to ask her."

"That's right. I'm not going to ask her." Cal gripped the steering wheel so hard his knuckles turned white, but kept his face bland under his father's searching gaze.

"Okay." Zane sighed, lifting a thumb to scratch his eyebrow. "Just don't go breaking her heart, son."

That's it. Cal stepped on the brake and pulled the truck over onto the dusty shoulder.

"What?" Zane looked around. "Why are we stopping?"

"So I can straighten you out." Garth Brooks's voice filled the cab, and Cal gave the knob a twist to kill the radio. "Things are different between men and women these days, Dad. Women are just as capable of enjoying sex for the sake of sex as we are. They've leveled the playing field."

Zane lifted his eyebrows. "That so?"

Hadn't Lauren told him so last night? "Hell, Dad, she's got her own life, friends, a practice back east."

"I see."

He turned to glare at Zane. "I don't think you do see. She . . . doesn't . . . want . . . to . . . marry . . . me, okay?" He enunciated every word carefully.

Zane looked back at him with the same gray eyes Cal had seen in his own mirror for the last thirty-seven years, and they were filled with compassion. "Ah, son, I really do think I see."

Cal looked away. He was very afraid his father did see. Cal made a show of checking his mirrors. Throat tight, he gunned the motor, put the truck in gear and pulled back onto the road. For good measure, he flicked the radio back

243

on, tuned in the rock station again and turned it up good and loud.

Cal wasn't home ten minutes before Lauren tracked him down in his office. He'd have taken her in his arms and kissed her, but one look at her face dissuaded him. "What's wrong?"

"I guess we should have checked Marlena's bed last night after all."

"She's gone?"

"She was, but she's back now."

He slumped on his desk. "Where?"

"Harvey McLeod's."

Cal blew out a breath. "All night?"

Lauren nodded. "Harvey dropped her off this morning."

"I don't suppose this escaped Brady's notice?"

She bit her lip. "I don't think it was meant to."

"Damn that woman." Cal shoved a hand through his hair. "Were there fireworks?"

"Oh, yeah, between Brady and Marlena."

He massaged the back of his neck. "What about Harvey?"

She shook her head. "He didn't stay long, just dropped her off. The show was only getting started when he left."

"Quite the gentleman," he muttered. "What time was that?"

"Around eleven o'clock."

"And all has been quiet since?"

She nodded. "Brady rode out to the fields, and Marlena is locked in her room."

He crossed to her. She looked so worried, he couldn't help but lift a finger to trace the frown on her forehead. "I'm sorry you had to be here for that. It must have been tense." He dropped his hands to her shoulders to massage

244

them. "Look, it's almost suppertime. Why don't we go see what Delia's fixed?"

She backed away from him as though he'd suggested walking barefoot through rattlesnake country. "That's it? You're not going to do anything?"

He stiffened. "What do you expect me to do? Physically restrain Marlena?" He turned away from Lauren's accusing eyes. "Hey, I couldn't stop her when she was my wife, remember?"

"But Cal . . ."

"But nothing." He cut her off bluntly, his irritation from the talk with his father carrying over. "We've talked about this, and there's nothing I can do short of sending her packing, and I won't do that with this loan shark thing hanging over her."

Lauren's lips thinned. "Fine," she clipped, then left.

Cal rolled his eyes as he listened to her booted feet clomp through the house, followed by the bang of the screen door.

"Has everyone in this household gone insane?"

There was no one to hear his question but the walls, and they made no reply. Didn't matter, he decided. It was rhetorical anyway. They were all nuts.

Scowling, he sat, punching the computer's power button. Since he was in a foul mood anyway, he'd have a go at the books.

Two hours later, Lauren found Cal still in his office. She had news for him, and he'd just better listen this time.

"She's gone."

Cal rubbed a hand over his face and made an exasperated sound. "I told you, I can't keep her away from Harvey McLeod."

245

"Listen to me," she said. "Marlena got a call maybe twenty minutes ago. Then she ran out to the barn, saddled Tango and rode like hell in a westerly direction."

He shrugged. "So she was in a hurry."

"Yeah, but a few minutes later, Brady rode out after her. Spider says he's out of his mind, Cal. He's been talking wild since Harvey dropped Marlena off. What if he set her up? What if he lured her out with that phone call so he could punish her?"

Cal swore softly.

"Something bad is going to happen if we don't stop it. I just know it."

"I hate to agree with you, but you might be right," he conceded. "The kid's volatile enough." He surged to his feet. "I'll saddle up Sienna and fetch Marlena back."

"Sienna's ready to go. Buck, too. I had Jim saddle them." Cal lifted an eyebrow and she blushed. "You didn't think I'd stay behind, did you?"

"Not really," he said dryly.

They'd been riding ten minutes when they were hailed by one of Cal's men. Lauren recognized him as Trey Thomas, the man who'd acted as Cal's bullfighter during the rodeo.

"What is it?" called Cal. His horse danced sideways, but he reined the mare in. "We're in kind of a hurry."

"You saved me a few minutes," Trey said. "I was riding in to give you a message from Harvey McLeod."

Cal groaned. "I might have known he'd be involved in this."

"Huh?"

"Never mind. What'd he say?"

"Well, he was on his way to the MaKenny place when he heard some ruckus in one of them coulees over yonder." Trey pointed in a northwesterly direction. "Next thing you know, man on a paint comes up over the lip of it and he's got a woman on board, 'cept she don't seem to be willing. McLeod thinks the woman was—"

"Marlena," finished Cal. "And the paint has to be Brady's."

Lauren inhaled sharply. "Why didn't Harvey ride after him?"

"He tried to, ma'am," Trey said. "Pretty palomino pulled up lame. It was hobbling something bad when I came across him."

"Why didn't *you* ride after them?" asked Cal.

The older man looked insulted. "Burkett was with me, boss. I sent him after them. 'Tween us, he's the better tracker."

Cal nodded. Burkett was a good tracker, though he was almost as arthritic as Jim. "Sorry, man. I'm just edgy." The cowboy accepted Cal's apology with a grunt. "Could you ride in and call the cops? Give them the story and get them out here."

"I'm on it, boss." With a, "Hiyah!", Trey was off.

"Let's go," Cal said, spurring Sienna.

"Wait!" Lauren grabbed at his reins.

"What is it?"

Sienna tossed her head and danced anxiously.

"I know where they're going."

Lauren looked at the sun. It would set in half an hour, maybe less. Dear Lord, she was going to have to tell him. "There's no use riding north. He didn't take her there."

"Of course he did. We've got an eyewitness."

"He may have faked a start in that direction, but he's got another destination in mind."

He looked at her sharply. "What are you saying?"

"He'll take her to Sunset Ridge."

His eyes narrowed. "How do you know this? Another hunch?"

"More than a hunch," she said, watching him struggle for patience.

"Tell you what. If this doesn't pan out, we'll come back this way. Okay? But right now, daylight's burning. Come on." He wheeled his horse again.

"It's not a hunch, it's a fact." she shouted. "I *know* it."

He brought Sienna back around. "How exactly do you know this?" All attempts at humoring her evaporated. Now he just sounded angry. "Huh? You got a telepathic link with Brady?"

"Actually, it *is* something rather like that."

"Oh, hell."

"No, just listen, Cal. Eight weeks ago, on the other side of this continent, I had a vision. I saw Marlena strangled to death through the eyes of her murderer. It'll happen on that ridge." She pointed southwest. "And it'll happen as the sun sets, so we don't have much time."

"You're kidding, right?"

He looked positively sick. "No, I'm not kidding. I'm very sure. I've had the same vision four times—two times back east and twice here."

"No. That's impossible."

Cal's mount was backing away. Whether he was conscious of it or not, he'd commanded the mare to reverse. Lauren's heart faltered. Garrett had backed away, too.

"Four times," she reiterated. "And you were with me the third time. Remember the night you thought I'd had the seizure?"

"You told me it was a seizure."

"That's what the doctors call it, but I don't tell them the

things I see." She rolled her shoulders. "Technically, maybe they are seizures, but it doesn't change the fact that what I see is going to happen. I know it will, because it always does. And that night I said I had the migraine and sent you away? I had the vision again that night."

"This is—" He shook his head. "No, I can't believe it."

"Believe it." The words came out brittle. "That night, as we lay in my cabin, I watched Marlena's life choked out of her as though I were inside the murderer's head looking out."

"That's insane!"

Lauren's eyes burned. It was just as it had been with Garrett. Cal wasn't buying any of it either. She should stop right now, but somehow she couldn't. She had to get it all out.

"I was helpless to do anything. You see, I couldn't be sure it was Brady because I couldn't see him, I could see everything *but* him. You understand? It was like actually seeing out of his eyes. It felt like—"

She sucked in a breath and exhaled shakily. Beneath her, Buck jittered and trembled with the vibes he was getting off her. Cal stared at her as though she'd grown a second head.

"It felt like I was doing it myself, squeezing Marlena's throat with my own hands. . . ."

"Stop it. Just stop." Immediately, he seemed to regret his words. Urging Sienna closer, he grabbed the nervous Buck's reins and leaned toward her. "Look, I'm sorry, honey," he said soothingly. "That must have been horrible for you. I think you should talk to someone about it. The visions, I mean."

Okay, it was official. He thought she was certifiable. Pain seared her throat. *It shouldn't hurt this much,* she told herself. *You knew it was coming.*

But it did. It hurt like hell. She smiled grimly. "I know you don't believe me. I know you think I'm crazy, but I'm right. And I could use your help, Cal. I'm riding over to that ridge."

Cal straightened in the saddle, his face twisted with the conflict she knew must be flaying him. Marlena's life was on the line. Though he no longer loved Marlena, Lauren knew he'd feel responsible for her, for the fact she was here at all, for the fact that Brady's life would be ruined if he weren't stopped.

Not to mention Cal's reluctance to substitute anyone's judgment for his own. He was used to relying on himself, on what he could hear and see and feel.

"I'm sorry, Lauren. I've gotta ride in the direction they were seen going. I don't have any choice."

"Of course." Unshed tears burned the backs of her eyes. She wheeled Buck around and spurred him to a gallop. When the tears spilled a moment later, she blamed them on the wind.

Cal watched her for a few precious moments. *Dammit, dammit, dammit!* He had a bad feeling about this. He should have kept her with him, or sent her home.

Maybe he should ride after her?

No, he'd lost too much time already. She'd be all right. Sunset Ridge would be deserted because Brady had dragged Marlena into the coulees to the north. McLeod had seen them.

Feeling as though he were being torn in two, he turned Sienna to the north and urged her into a dead gallop.

Five minutes later, he reined his mare in and cursed. He couldn't ride away from Lauren. What if she was right?

Okay, it was a stretch. More than a stretch. But what if these visions were for real? What if he'd let her go riding into the scene she'd described to him? Would she try to stop Brady? Would she become an incidental casualty of the disastrous triangle Marlena had created?

But what if she were merely confused? Mistaken? Oh, hell, what if she was plain crazy? Could he live with himself if he turned back to hold Lauren's hand, leaving Marlena to face the consequences of her own folly?

Dammit, he was going to ride back to Lauren. Marlena would have to take her chances that old Burkett could talk Brady down.

Suddenly he was shivering in the eighty degree evening as a chill coursed through him.

Then he remembered—he'd felt this bone-deep chill in bed that night when Lauren had her seizure, or what she now claimed had been a vision.

"Sweet mother of God."

With a jerk of the reins, he turned Sienna again and streaked back toward the ridge.

That was when he saw McLeod. Maybe a mile away, he was heading toward Sunset Ridge, too, approaching on a tangent that would get him there a lot sooner. And his distinctive palomino was definitely not lame. It was flying like the wind itself.

How could that be? Unless he faked a lame mount? But why would he do that?

Then the other shoe fell. It wasn't Brady they needed to catch up with: it was Harvey. Harvey must have made the call to lure Marlena out here. But why would he want to kill her? He didn't care about her. Cal would stake his life on it. He was only toying with her to try to bait Cal.

251

Oh, hell, none of it made sense. But it didn't change the sick conviction in his gut. Harvey was riding to the ridge to commit murder, and Cal had sent Lauren right into it, alone.

Chapter Fifteen

Lauren spotted Marlena the moment she topped the ridge. She was alone, standing exactly where Lauren had seen her in the vision, a few yards from the lookout where Cal's guests had watched the sun set so many times. Marlena's mount, a sorrel gelding, was tethered to a nearby sapling.

A radiant Marlena turned expectantly toward the sound of approaching hoofbeats, but her expression turned ugly when she recognized the rider. Lauren pulled up beside her, vaulting out of the saddle even before Buck had stopped.

"What are you doing here?" Marlena's voice was incredulous as she took in Buck's lathered coat and heaving sides. "And what have you done to this animal? You've run him into the ground."

"You have to get out of here."

"I don't think so. I'm meeting someone." Marlena laid a hand on Buck's sweat-soaked neck, lifting his mane. "Poor baby."

"Look, I don't have time to explain, but he's coming here to kill you."

"What?" The word was an ugly squawk. "You're crazy. Why would Harvey McLeod want to kill me?"

Harvey? Her date was with Harvey? Lauren's mind reeled. It must have been Harvey who'd called. Harvey, not Brady!

"You're the one who has to get out of here, sugar. I've got business to transact."

"Business?"

"Harvey's going to pay off my little debt so he can take me back to Calgary without worrying about my safety."

Anxiously, Lauren scanned the eastern edge of the plateau. No rider yet. "It's a trap. He won't give you anything. He only said that to lure you out here so he could kill you."

Marlena narrowed her eyes. "You *are* crazy. Does Cal know you're out here?"

"Listen to me. I don't know why he wants to kill you, but he does. He's planning to strangle you. And he'll be here any minute. You have to leave now."

Marlena laughed harshly. "Stand him up? Kiss off ten thousand dollars? I don't think so."

"He's not bringing any money." Lauren fairly shouted the words. Then, more calmly, "Is the prospect of ten thousand dollars really worth dying for?"

"Why should I buy this story?" demanded Marlena. "And if I leave now, how do I know he was planning to kill me? How will I know I didn't miss the chance of a lifetime?"

She had a point. If Harvey was foiled in this attempt, what would stop him from setting up another assignation? Lauren had to go home sometime. She couldn't baby-sit Marlena indefinitely.

No, he had to be made to show his hand. He had to

make the attempt. Then he could be locked up where he belonged. But how?

The answer came to her. "We'll switch places."

"What?"

"Come on, take off your shirt. We'll swap, trade hats and boots. I'll pose as you."

Marlena looked down at her ample cleavage beneath the shirt that she'd tied at her midriff, then looked pointedly at Lauren's breasts. "Honey, no way is Harvey going to believe you're me."

"He will if I keep my back turned," she argued. "We're the same height, and I can hide my hair under your hat. He'll see what he expects to see."

"This is crazy," Marlena said, but Lauren could see that a small seed of fear had crept into her eyes.

"What have you got to lose?" Lauren tore off her shirt. "You can take Tango and hide in that stand of poplars and I'll stand here." She toed her left boot loose, then bent to drag it off. "If Harvey doesn't make a move, you can amble out and say you were relieving yourself or something. I'll be happy to leave you to your business." She tore off the second boot, her eyes searching the top of the ridge. "Come on, get your things off."

"Okay, okay."

Marlena peeled off her shirt, kicked off her elaborately stitched western boots and black Stetson. Lauren grabbed the shirt, shoved her arms into the sleeves and buttoned it with shaking fingers. What was she doing, baiting a murderer?

"Tie the tails up under your boobs, sweetie. Show some skin. That's what he'd expect."

Lauren took her advice, then shoved her feet into Marlena's boots, which pinched. Lastly, she tucked her short dark hair up under the hat and retrieved Marlena's gelding.

"Hey, these boots are kind of sexy."

"You can keep them if you'll just go." Lauren shoved the sorrel's reins at her. "Please, get into those poplars, *now.*"

Something in her tone must have reached Marlena. She looked shaken for the first time. "What if he does try to, you know . . . ?"

"If he tries anything, get back to the ranch as fast as you can and send the police."

"What about you? I'm supposed to leave you?"

"I can take care of myself, and I have the advantage of knowing what he's going to do."

"But if he overpowers you . . ."

"Listen carefully. If he makes a move, don't come back here. He probably carries a gun, and if his hand is forced he might make quick work of the both of us. I'm doing this to save your neck. If you die anyway, it will have been in vain. You understand? Just get back as quick as you can and send help."

Marlena stared at her, wide-eyed. "Why are you doing this?"

Lauren's throat threatened to close with emotion. "It's what I came here to do. Now, get going!" She gave the gelding a slap on the rump.

With one last look over her shoulder, Marlena urged Tango to a gallop. It seemed to take an eternity, but finally the other woman made the cover of the poplars, disappearing into the copse. Only then did Lauren move into the position Marlena had vacated, some fifteen or twenty feet from the lip of the ravine.

She stood looking out over the exquisite tableau of the

sun setting over the foothills, but in her mind's eye saw only gloved hands closing around her neck. She shivered, running a hand over her nape to make the hairs lie down again. Any minute now, she'd hear the approach of hoofbeats.

Her stomach churned. This was crazy. What was she doing here? She should have told her story to the police.

No, they wouldn't have done anything. Couldn't have done anything. Harvey had yet to commit a crime.

Maybe she should have let Marlena die, whispered a voice in her mind. The world wouldn't be any the worse for it. Look what she did to Cal. Look what she was doing to Brady. There's still time. Just ride away. Go on home. He'll get her next time.

Her stomach lurched again, this time in self-disgust. Was she really such a coward?

Yes.

If only Cal had come with her . . .

Cal. Her heart squeezed. The way he'd looked at her, backed away from her. He'd acted just like Garrett. She'd known it would be like that, so why this crushing disappointment?

Because somehow, sometime during the past weeks, she'd recklessly, stupidly come to hope that he loved her. But how could he when he didn't know who she was? The visions were an integral part of her, a part she'd never be able to share.

Snap out of it, she scolded herself. *If you're going to do this, you better keep your wits about you.*

She noticed then that the sun had finally dipped beneath the horizon, turning the sky a delicate magenta. Any minute now . . .

A weapon! She should arm herself.

That was when she heard the rider approaching. Was it him? She longed to turn and confirm it with her own eyes, but dared not. And she still had no weapon.

There! A sizeable piece of granite at her feet. Casually, she bent to pick it up, along with a smaller rock. The large one she slid into the waistband of her jeans. The smaller one she flipped over the cliff's edge as though amusing herself by listening to it clatter and tumble to the canyon floor.

Her nerves thrummed as the rider drew closer, the cadence of the hoofbeats slowing. Then they stopped. Her heart hammered against her ribs so hard she thought they might crack. With a creak of leather, she heard him dismount.

"You made good time."

It was Harvey, all right, the voice deep, well modulated. She tried not to hold herself too rigidly.

"You came alone, like I asked?"

She nodded, terrified. She had to stop these questions. She'd never be able to emulate Marlena's husky voice. She'd just have to make sure he didn't ask any more.

Inclining her head, she extended one arm in what she hoped was a sufficiently imperious yet provocative summons.

He laughed. "Ever the sex kitten, eh, Marlena?" She heard him step closer, felt his warmth at her back. Her heart thundered. Could he hear it?

"Such perfect skin."

Through her peripheral vision, she saw his gloved hands come up, saw that he would grasp her arms above the elbow. She steeled herself not to jump, knowing it would ruin everything. She had to let him make his move. At last, she felt the abrasive slide of his gloved hands. She quaked, but hoped he would interpret her tremor as a shiver of awareness.

"Such remarkable beauty." His hands slid up to rest lightly on her shoulders. "I'm really going to feel bad about this."

With shocking speed and strength, he whirled her around and closed his hands around her neck, squeezing hard. The pressure was unbelievable, choking off the scream that rose in her throat.

"What the hell?" Momentarily, the pressure slackened as her hat fell off and Harvey realized his mistake. She screamed then, an ungodly sound she didn't recognize as her own.

"Shut up." His hands tightened viciously on her throat.

His dark face swam in her vision as he continued to squeeze. She pulled at his hands, frantically trying to loosen his grip, but her arms felt like lead. Was she going to die here?

The rock! She fumbled in the waistband of her jeans, found the rock. Then, with desperation fueling her oxygen-starved muscles, she slammed the chunk of granite against his temple.

He let go, reeled backwards, fell to his knees.

Dragging in great, searing breaths, she staggered toward Buck, who reared his head back nervously, ears folded. If she could just get to him, she could get away. She'd run Harvey's palomino off so he couldn't overtake her on the exhausted Buck.

Wham! He tackled her from behind. She went down, but quickly rolled free. Then she was scrambling on hands and knees, blood pounding in her ears. If she could just reach Buck . . .

A hand closed on her ankle, dragging her backward.

She screamed again, kicking wildly. A blow landed and he cursed, but he didn't let go. Then he was on his feet. The next instant he grabbed a handful of her hair and dragged her up to her knees.

"Bitch! I'll kill you for that."

Lauren grasped his wrist, trying to ease his savage grip on her hair.

"You know, this is almost better," he said conversationally, regaining his composure quickly. "Kill you instead of Marlena, and still frame Cal."

She gasped, but he twisted his fist harder in her hair. "Frame Cal?" She managed to get the words out around her nausea.

"Yeah, that's the plan. And since you tried to crack my damned skull, I'm going to tell you all about it so you can die knowing he'll spend the rest of his life behind bars for your murder."

"No!"

"Yes." Harvey held up his free hand. "His gloves will leave distinct ligature marks, I think, not to mention reek with your DNA on the outside and his on the inside. I'll just drop one in my hurry to flee the scene."

"But your DNA will be in them, too."

He smiled. "I took the precaution of wearing latex gloves."

She was going to die and Cal would take the fall for it. *Keep him talking.* "But why? Why set Cal up?"

He scowled. "Because he's in the way."

"What do you mean?"

"It didn't have to be like this, you know. If he had just accepted my offer. It was very reasonable. I couldn't offer anything too extravagant. That would have made him suspicious."

"What was he in the way of?"

"Progress." Harvey's teeth glinted. "Look around, Miss Townsend. From horizon to horizon, as far as you can see, I own it all. Or rather, my agents do. Wouldn't have done to tip my hand."

"All but this piece?"

"All but this piece," he acknowledged.

"But it's so small. . . . Why do you need it?"

"I don't. I just need Cal Taggart off it. I'm about to launch a development project and I couldn't afford to have him squawking about environmental concerns. Stubborn sonofabitch would have mobilized the ranchers. Then the politicians, who are already antsy, would start talking tougher legislation." He smiled. "It's nothing personal, Miz Townsend. I just couldn't let the window of opportunity close on a billion dollars."

He still held her head tilted at a difficult angle. Her throat ached, but with the relentless pressure on her scalp, she couldn't shift to ease it. "What kind of development?"

"The lucrative kind. Do you have any idea how much a Hollywood actor or a *Fortune* 500 CEO would pay for a mini-ranch of his own right here in the shadow of the foothills? This is one of the most beautiful spots on earth."

"You'd carve it up."

"That's the idea."

"But you're a rancher. How can you do this?"

He laughed. "A rancher? My dear, that operation will close its doors as soon as this deal is done."

Cal had been wrong. He wasn't crazy, just greedy. Murder had been done for a lot less than a billion dollars.

She had to keep him talking. The longer he talked, the further away Marlena would get. "What about your horse? Trey said it pulled up lame. How'd you accomplish that?"

"I wedged a rock in the frog of his hoof. Soon as Cal's man rode off, I pried it out."

Her heart sank. "So everyone would know exactly where you were, miles from the scene with no means of transportation."

"Precisely. I'll put the rock back in, of course, so everyone sees us come limping in."

He seemed to relish his own cleverness. Could she feed that to keep him talking? "But the story about Brady abducting Marlena? Why did you make that up?"

"I wasn't sure anyone would give a damn if that slut Marlena disappeared, besides the fool kid, of course. And I didn't want them to assume she'd run back to the city. I needed someone to look for her, find her body while the evidence was fresh."

"But Brady will contradict your story."

"He'll do nothing of the sort. He got an anonymous telephone call that'll take him out to that old cabin Cal uses, where he'll expect to surprise me and Marlena. When he fails to find either of us, he'll ride back. Unfortunately, he'll meet with an accident on the trail."

"But he's your son!"

Something flickered in Harvey's eyes. "Couldn't be helped," he said gruffly. "He's also the man banging Marlena regularly, and therefore the only one I could manipulate."

Dear Lord, that sweet boy Brady, too. "You'll set Cal up for that murder, too, I suppose?"

Harvey raised an eyebrow. "You catch on quickly. Man kills his ex-wife and her current lover turns up dead? I think they'll draw some conclusions. Of course, we'll have to add you to the body count Cal is racking up. I'm not sure how they'll explain that. I guess he just snapped."

Lauren's mind wanted to shut down in the face of all this horror, but she couldn't let it. *Think. Keep him talking.*

"The telephone calls! The police will surely check the phone records, won't they?"

"I certainly hope so. You see, I took the liberty of lifting the cell phone from Cal's truck. Terrible habit, that, leaving your vehicle unlocked."

Lauren's heart sank still further. "You poisoned Cal's steer, too, didn't you?"

"Guilty, although the record will show I was in Calgary."

"Of course. So when the anthrax scare failed to spur Cal to accept your offer, you decided to do this?"

"Yes, ma'am. You know, I thought about doing you in the first place, since you and Cal are going so hot and heavy, but I couldn't figure how to lure you out. That slut Marlena was so much easier. Although how you figured out . . ." Suddenly, he looked up, scanning the area, and swore. His hand, which had relaxed in her hair while they talked, tightened again. "Okay, where is she?"

"Who?"

He shook her head, bringing tears to her eyes.

"Where's Marlena? She must have come. She's too greedy to have turned down the bait."

"I sent her back to the ranch to call the police!"

Harvey gave Lauren's head a vicious wrench. "I wouldn't play games with me, if I were you. There's only one approach to this bluff. I had a clear view of it for the last few miles, and I didn't take my eyes off it. No one rode out of it. Now, where is she?"

"She hid in the trees until you came through the pass, then slipped out behind you."

His face hardened. "Then I'll have to kill you quick so I can catch her, won't I?"

"You won't get away with this."

"Watch me." Once more, he closed his hands on her throat. Again, she clutched at them to try to dislodge his grip, but to no avail. In what seemed like an impossibly short time, she felt the blackness closing in.

No! If she was going to die, there was no way she was going to let Cal be framed for it. She had to do something.

Lifting her hands from Harvey's, she raked her nails down his face as hard as she could.

He howled with rage, lifting one hand to his face. It came away bloody.

"Explain that," she croaked.

Searing pain exploded in her head and she fell sideways. *He hit me. He actually punched me.* For some reason, the thought stunned her, in spite of the fact that he'd just tried to choke her to death. Then he was on top of her, straddling her. Before his hands could throttle her again, she said, "You're bleeding on me from that lovely head wound. Your skin under my nails, your blood on my clothes. Could be hard to explain."

A roar, followed by another smash. Pain blossomed anew.

That's it! she thought, her head ringing. He could choke her to death in minutes, but if she could keep him angry, keep him hitting her, it would take longer. Maybe much longer. Maybe long enough for Marlena to get away. Harvey's plan to frame Cal would fall apart if Marlena could just get back safely.

And if Harvey got Marlena, too? What then?

Maybe the forensic evidence would implicate Harvey, if it got messy enough. Which came back to keeping him angry.

"What's the matter?" She tried to laugh but it came out more like a spluttering cough. "Is that the best you can do?"

"Shut up!" Another smash, this time to the right side of her head.

Oh, God, it hurt. She closed her eyes, desperately wanting to curl in on herself, escape into some dark closet in her mind. She couldn't let him hit her again. She couldn't.

But she had to make him.

Remembering the line Zane Taggart had used after getting roughed up by the bull, she forced her eyes open. "Hell, Harvey, I've had worse knocks than that on the dance floor."

Crack!

Harvey still straddled her, his chest heaving. *Don't hit me. Don't hurt me. Please, I don't want to die.* She wanted so badly to cry out her fear. Instead, she touched her broken lip with her tongue, and said, "Ooh, Harvey, what a man."

Another roar. She closed her eyes, bracing for the blow, but it never fell. Suddenly, miraculously, Harvey's weight was gone. She rolled over, ears ringing. She should make another attempt to get to Buck but she didn't know if she could crawl. She felt so groggy. If she could rest a minute . . .

Then the noises of combat—scuffling, grunting, the sickening sound of fists hitting flesh—penetrated the ringing in her ears. She pushed herself up and squinted toward the commotion.

Cal. He'd come. And he was wrestling on the ground with Harvey. As she watched through eyes that still refused to focus, it seemed to her that Cal landed blow after blow. But Harvey was so much bigger. Cal needed her help.

Shakily, she got to her feet and stumbled toward Cal's mount. He always carried a rope. Maybe she could help restrain Harvey with it. *Or maybe she'd just strangle him.*

Sienna shied away from her but Lauren managed to catch the coil of rope and pull it free. When she turned back to the men, however, they'd sprung apart and were circling each other warily. Even in the fading light, she had no trouble discerning the dull gleam in Harvey's hand. A knife.

"Hell, I guess it'll have to be a murder-suicide." Harvey wiped his bloody mouth on his sleeve. "This is turning out to be damned hard work, but I've come too far to turn back now."

"Cal!" It was a cry of fear, anguish.

Cal didn't take his eyes off the knife. "Lauren, get on that horse and ride. Don't stop until you're home."

"Cal . . ."

"Just do it," Cal commanded.

Harvey spat what appeared to be a tooth into his hand and swore. "Fine with me. Let her make a run for it. I'll catch her before she gets far. Right after I stick you."

In a blur of motion, he lashed out at Cal, who ducked and rolled. Harvey dove after him. Then the two of them were rolling on the ground, grappling for possession of the knife, their struggles bringing them closer to the brink of the cliff.

Lauren watched, frozen in horror, but the next lurch brought them back from the precipice. Harvey still had the knife. Cal fought hard, but eventually Harvey, with his greater bulk, wound up on top, a heavy arm jammed across Cal's windpipe.

"Say goodbye, Taggart," Harvey panted. Lifting the knife high, he thrust it toward Cal's heart in a deadly arc.

Only then did Lauren's paralysis break. Sobbing, she staggered toward them.

In what seemed like slow motion, Lauren saw Cal twist violently, but the blade still bit into his chest. He grunted, but with a massive heave of his wiry body, he somehow dislodged Harvey and the knife went flying.

Whimpering her relief, Lauren lurched toward the spot where the weapon had fallen. She dropped to her hands and knees and searched the grass frantically. If she could just find the knife, she'd happily bury it in Harvey McLeod's back, and she'd aim for his black heart. At last, her fingers found the warm handle of the blade.

With a small cry of triumph, she turned back toward the fight only to see both men disappear over the cliff's edge.

Chapter Sixteen

One second he was free-falling and the next he was getting whipped by branches. Out of sheer, dumb luck, Cal managed to close his hands around a branch. But the tree, a scrawny poplar clinging to the cliff, was too slender. It tore away under his weight. *This is it,* he thought. *I'm gonna die.*

Then he slammed against the cliff face with a force that drove all the air from his lungs. Instinct alone kept his hands locked on the branch.

Don't let me black out.

Fighting back pain and dizziness, he looked up. *Shit.* The tree now hung upside down, anchored by a few skinny roots that hadn't sprung free. Just then, another root snapped and the tree sagged a few more inches. Gravel rained on him as he scrabbled to find a toehold. With the pointed toe of his right boot, he found a small outcropping that helped bear a little of his weight, easing the burden on his arms. Not to mention the tree.

Okay, Cal, buddy, you're not going anywhere for a minute. Get this breathing thing under control, he told himself. But his lungs wouldn't cooperate. If anything, each breath came harder than the last one. Dammit, he musta ruptured a lung. He knew the sensation well from losing contests with bulls.

Vaguely, he wondered if the damage had been done by Harvey's knife or by the body slam against the cliff face. Didn't much matter. He wouldn't be able to hang here long.

He looked down to the canyon floor below. Harvey lay sprawled against some boulders, his neck turned at an impossible angle. *Sonofabitch.* He'd gotten off easy. Cal wanted to beat the life out of him personally for what he'd done to Lauren.

Lauren. He closed his eyes. She must have taken Sienna. Just before Harvey pulled the knife, he'd caught a glimpse of her stumbling toward the mare, grappling for the saddle. Then he hadn't dared take his eyes off the knife. How long would it take her to get help? With a fresh horse, maybe twenty minutes to reach the ranch. With a tired one?

Fresh or tired, it didn't matter. It would take too long. Already he felt as though he were beginning to drown. Even if his arm strength held out, he'd lose consciousness and let his grip go.

At least Lauren would be all right. A wave of profound relief washed over him, followed by remembered fear. To think he'd almost left her to face that madman alone . . .

"Cal!"

He looked up to see the dim outline of Lauren's face in the twilight. She hadn't left.

"Hang on, Cal, I've got a rope," she called, then disappeared again.

Dear Lord, he was saved.

Well, maybe, he amended with a grimace. At least he wouldn't join Harvey at the foot of the canyon.

A moment later, Cal's own rope came snaking down to him. It dangled a little too far to the left, but Lauren materialized again, shifting it for him. He watched the rope swing past his face a few times, then he let go of the branch with one hand and grabbed for it. *Got it.*

He wrapped the rope around his arm several times so he wouldn't lose his grip.

"Are you secured?"

He looked up at Lauren. "I'm good." It would have to be good. He didn't have enough of a toehold to use both hands to tie the rope around him.

"Sienna is going to pull you up," she called. "The face of the cliff looks pretty rough. I'll try to take it slow so you don't get banged around too badly."

Her face swam impossibly far above him.

"Better make it fast."

He had no idea if she'd heard him or not, but she disappeared again. Seconds later, the rope tautened, then he was zipping up the cliff. *Guess she heard me.*

The cliff face abraded his arms, and roots and branches whipped his face. Dirt and rocks showered down on him, forcing him to close his eyes. Then he was up and over the ledge, lying on sweet, blessed ground that still held the day's warmth, the smell of crushed grass strong in his nostrils.

"Cal." Lauren's hands were on him, turning him over. "Are you all right?"

"Don't know."

She tore his shirt open, bending close to examine the knife wound. He flinched when her fingers probed it.

"Thank God! It didn't go through the chest wall."

Cal tried to drag in another breath. "You sure?"

For the first time, she seemed to tune into his breathing difficulty. "Cal, what's the matter?"

"Breath . . . gettin' short."

With a sob, she pressed her head to his chest. Cal's head spun. Geez, was she mourning him already? He closed his arms around her. "'S'okay," he slurred. "Be okay."

"Ssshhh," she commanded. "Don't talk."

Ah, of course—she was administering first aid, not enfolding him in a loving embrace. Despite his injuries, he smiled wryly up at the reddening sky as she listened, her ear pressed to his chest, to his struggle for breath.

She pulled away abruptly. A chill skated over his skin. Then he felt her fingers tapping his chest sharply. One side, then the other. Finally she sat back and met his gaze.

I must be a goner.

"I think you've got air collecting in your chest cavity, but the knife didn't do it, or air would be bubbling out. You must have had some blunt trauma to rupture the lung tissue." She smiled bravely. "Of course, I could be wrong. The last patient I percussed was a Great Dane."

Poor Lauren, trying so hard not to let her terror show. He tried to reward her attempt at humor with a laugh, but wound up making a coughing sound which only alarmed her more.

"We have to get you into a sitting position. It'll be easier to breathe."

"Closed pneumo," he rasped.

Her eyes widened. "Of course. You've probably had pneumothorax lots of times from your rodeo days. Once you've had it, the tissue is more prone to rupture. It wouldn't take much."

Damn, her face looked awful. Both eyes would be black later, and her lower lip was split. Her beautiful lips. Again, he wished passionately that he could resurrect Harvey McLeod and kill him all over again, this time with slow, deadly purpose.

And Lauren . . . she hadn't ridden to safety as he'd instructed. His heart stuttered as he allowed himself to think about the implications of that. If Harvey had managed to plant that blade a few inches to the right, he'd be dead now. And so would she.

"Told you . . . to ride away . . ."

"Ssshhh, don't talk." Kneeling behind him, she drew him up into a semi-sitting position, using her own body to support him.

"He'd been better . . . with a knife . . . both be dead."

"Please don't talk." Her voice rumbled against his back.

"Almost . . . didn't get here . . . in time . . ."

"Ssshhh."

"Vision . . . didn't believe."

"It's okay, Cal."

"'S'why you came . . . right? Save Marlena?"

She was crying now. A hot tear fell on his chest.

"Yes, that's why I came. But please, save your breath."

And why she stayed on after he closed the guest ranch. Not for him. Not for what they shared together. For Marlena, to save her from Harvey . . .

His torpid mind came back to the puzzle. Why would Harvey want to kill Marlena? Why'd he try to kill Lauren? If he weren't feeling so stoned, so dizzy, he might be able to put it together.

Then the dizziness broadened, deepened, widened. It was a black void sucking at him.

"So sorry."

He wanted to say more, but he had no breath left. He was sorry he hadn't believed her. Sorry he couldn't stay with her now. Sorry she didn't love him the way he loved her.

Then he let the blackness claim him.

* * *

Lauren's heart stopped. She felt for his pulse. It was there, but thready. Then she noticed his color, which had taken on a bluish hue. Crushing down panic, she tipped his head to one side and gasped. The veins of his neck were grossly distended.

Mediastinal shift.

Two words, but they ripped the lid off her panic.

The pressure of the air inside his chest was forcing all the structures—heart, blood vessels, trachea—to one side. With sickening certainty, she knew his lungs were collapsing. She imagined the great blood vessels kinking, cutting off the blood supply to his heart.

Minutes. That's all he had. If she couldn't relieve the pressure within a few minutes, he'd be dead.

What he needed was a trauma team to get a chest tube into him. What he had was her, and she had nothing to work with. *Nothing.* Dear Lord, her life for a large gauge needle!

Think.

She was going to lose him and she hadn't even told him she loved him.

The knife. She could use it to pierce the chest wall to let the air escape. She could use her fingers as a valve. . . .

The knife—where had she dropped it? She eased Cal back onto the ground and raced to where she'd found the knife, the spot where she'd been standing when she'd seen Cal go over the cliff. The sun had sunk so low that she had to search the grass on hands and knees. Ragged sobs tore at her throat.

In her panic, she didn't hear the helicopter approaching. Only when the downdraft tore at her hair did she look up.

Air ambulance, she realized. But how? Could Marlena have gotten back to the ranch to summon them this quickly?

As soon as the thought formed, she let it fall away. *Paramedics. Medical equipment.* They were here, and that was all that mattered. She began to cry.

Leaping to her feet, she waved wildly.

Chapter Seventeen

Cal opened his eyes and knew just where he was. *Recovery room. His old home away from home.* He moved experimentally and winced. *Bull musta stomped me good this time.* Funny, he didn't remember losing his seat, hitting the ground. Then memory surged back.

He tried to sit up. A nurse appeared immediately, her hands cool as she urged him back down.

"Welcome back, Mr. Taggart."

"Lauren," he croaked through a parched throat.

"She's waiting for you up on the ward."

"Is she all right?"

"Cuts and bruises only. She was very lucky."

Lucky, all right. Lucky she wasn't dead because he'd doubted her. Lucky his intuition had overruled his reason.

"How'd I get here?"

"You were airlifted off the mountain." The nurse checked his vitals. "How are you feeling? The anesthetist was a little alarmed. That sedative they gave you for the chest tube was supposed to just mellow you out, not send you to dreamland."

"No head for it," he muttered, trying again to sit up. "Take me to Lauren."

"Patience, Mr. Taggart." The nurse eased him back down. "You've got another fifteen minutes before we move you anywhere."

Fifteen minutes? He couldn't possibly wait that long.

A split second later, an orderly came to move him. Hell, he must have drifted off. He might have dozed off again on the way to the room, but with the bed rolling, he had to keep his eyes open to combat nausea. Pain he could handle. He'd walked on a broken leg and ridden bulls with his jaw wired up, but give him a little sedative and he was out of it. If he'd been halfway aware, he'd have told them to stick to just the local.

As soon as his bed emerged from the elevator, Lauren appeared beside him.

"Hey," she said, walking along.

"Hey yourself." Cal thought he was ready to see the bruising, but he wasn't. Her lip was split, and both sides of her face were bruised and swollen. It made him weak to see the blood trapped beneath her smooth skin. Remembered fear gripped his gut. "You look like hell."

She laughed. "Thanks. So do you. How do you feel?"

"A lot better than I did the last time I saw you. If it weren't for the damn sedative, I'd be good as new."

That wasn't quite true. He still couldn't say more than a few words without drawing a breath, but that would come soon.

"You're lucky you got a sedative at all." They were rolling through the corridor now. "If that chopper had been any longer getting there, I was going in with Harvey's bowie knife."

Her tone was teasing, but her voice broke on the last words.

"Guess I musta scared you back there."

"Scared doesn't even touch it."

"You scared me, too. I could have died when I saw that bastard whaling on you. . . ."

"You almost *did* die, Cal. If you had . . ."

They'd reached a bright private room. To his frustration, Lauren let go of the bed rail and backed off to allow the orderly to position the bed. Then a new nurse, this one younger and prettier, moved in on him to take his vitals.

"You've got a chest tube, Mr. Taggart, but they didn't have to operate. No bleeders or big lacerations. Your lungs should reexpand and heal nicely on their own," she said.

"Thanks."

"The doctor will be up to see you later today, and you'll be seeing me regularly for the next few hours."

"I'll look forward to it." He gave her what he hoped was a killer smile. "But could I have a word with my friend now?"

The nurse gave him a look that said he was in no condition to flirt, but she was smiling when she turned to Lauren. "Keep it short, would you? He needs his rest."

"Of course."

"So where were we?" he asked when the nurse had left. "Oh yeah, the part where you put yourself in Marlena's clothes and waited for Harvey to come and get you." He couldn't project his voice as loudly as he'd have liked, but the fear in his gut added bite to the words.

"I had to do it, but if you'd died trying to save me, I would never have forgiven myself."

"Forget me for a minute. Let's get back to 'I had to.' " Cal wished he had the breath for a proper tongue-lashing. "You knew exactly what McLeod was coming for. Why didn't you run? Hide? Drag Marlena with you?"

"I thought about running and-or hiding, believe me."

Her voice wavered. "But if Harvey'd missed his chance this time, he'd have just tried again. Unless he made a move on me, Marlena would never have believed me. No one would have believed me. He could have lured her out again at will."

A sudden dizzy nausea swept over Cal, and he gripped the raised bed rail to try to combat it. "*I* believed you."

She shot him a disbelieving look.

"Okay, so it took me a while, but I came around. That's why I turned back." Damn, he was tired, and it was getting harder to focus with the room spinning like that.

"You turned Sienna around on the *possibility* I was right," she corrected. "But what if Marlena and I had fled or hidden? What if Harvey had come and gone? What if you got there and found nothing? Would you still have believed me?"

Cal fought the desire to tell a flat-out lie. "Probably not."

"See? I had to make him show his hand. Until he did, no one would truly believe me, which means Marlena would never be out of danger. What was I to do? Stay forever to baby-sit her?"

Stay forever? No, not that. He felt a twinge in his chest that had nothing to do with his chest tube. She had a life to go back to. Mission accomplished. She probably wanted to leave right now. In her mind, she was probably already there, taking up the reins of her practice again.

The thought made him want to weep. His throat tightened warningly. Mortified at his weakness, he squeezed his eyes shut. "You know, I think I might be too tired for this after all."

He didn't have to open his eyes; he heard the consternation in her voice. "Oh, Cal, I'm so sorry. I said I wouldn't keep you long. I didn't think. I'll go now."

"Wait." He opened his eyes to find his request had stopped her at the door.

Let her go, man. Do the decent thing.

Are you crazy? Don't let her leave!

"Don't leave without coming back to see me, okay?"

She seemed suddenly tired herself, her shoulders drooping. Even from across the room, even groggy from the sedative, he could see that her beautiful eyes were troubled. The moment stretched out until he wondered if she was going to answer him at all. Was she in that much of a hurry to be shot of him? Or worse, could she see how badly he needed her to stay? Was she wondering how to keep it from getting awkward?

"Yeah," she said at last, smiling gently. "Yeah, I'll come back before I go. Now get some rest."

Rest. He watched the door swing shut behind her, then closed his eyes again. He might sleep, but there would be no rest. *She* was his rest, his heart, and she was leaving.

Lauren's eyes burned as she pushed blindly into the hall. Blinking, she glanced around, then strode toward the elevators.

He expected her to leave.

She pushed the button to call for the elevator, and a pair of doors slid open. Brushing wetness from her swollen cheek, she stepped into the empty car and hit the button for the lobby.

He expected her to leave. Not next week or next month, *now*.

Serious tears threatened, but she blinked them back. *Don't think about it.*

The doors slid open on a handful of people waiting to board the elevator. Several of them stared openly at her as she moved past them. For a moment, she thought it was because she was near tears, then she remembered her face. She must look a fright.

In the lobby, she stopped at the gift shop, bought a large pair of dark sunglasses and slid them on her face. *Better,* she thought, regarding her reflection. Couldn't be scaring her fellow passengers on the flight home.

Home. She thought about her friends and family whom she missed. Her really great house. The practice that sustained her. Instead of the satisfaction that usually filled her when she thought of these things, a deep desolation swelled in her chest. Oh, it would get better with time. She knew that. If only the parting weren't so abrupt, so wrenching . . .

No, this way was for the best. No point dragging it out. Much better to do it quickly, like ripping adhesive off a wound.

Except this wound was on her heart, and it might just tear it right out.

"Miss Townsend? You okay?"

She glanced up to find Spider looking at her, concern furrowing his leathery forehead.

"I'm fine. But I wonder if you could do me a favor? I need to arrange a ride back to the ranch."

"That's what I'm here for, ma'am. Mr. Taggart sent me to fetch you whenever you were ready."

Here's your hat, what's your hurry, eh? She tried to laugh, but it stuck in her throat.

"Ma'am?"

"Thank you, Spider. I think I'm ready right now."

Eight hours later, Cal glared at the tubes running in and out of him. He felt fine. His stomach was a bit iffy, but otherwise he was fine. His breath was coming easier, too.

There was no reason why he should still be tethered to this bed.

Not that he wasn't grateful to be alive. He thought he'd breathed his last on top of that ridge. But now he had to get out of here. He had to find Lauren, talk to her.

He'd been in no shape to say what needed saying when she'd been here earlier. Hell, he wasn't sure he even remembered all of what he *had* said, but he did remember extracting a promise from her to come back when he felt better. That had been hours ago, and the need to talk to her was eating him alive. If it weren't for the damned chest tube, he'd tear his IV out and go after her.

Hell with it. He'd make them get a doctor up here to remove the chest tube. He'd never needed one for the full forty-eight with a pneumo.

He'd just squeezed the call button when a knock came at his open door. He glanced up to see Lauren framed there. At last.

"Lauren, come in."

She stepped into the room, letting the door fall shut behind her. His relief changed to panic as he really looked at her. She wore the same black dress she'd worn the day she landed at the ranch, but she'd added a scarf around her bruised neck and a wide-brimmed straw hat. Her travel outfit.

"You're leaving?"

She patted her bag. "Got my ticket right here. Spider's going to drive me to the airport when we're through."

The words he'd planned to say died in his throat. Dammit, how could she do this? "That was quick," he said.

Her gaze slid away from his even as she came to stand close to his bed. "It's better this way, isn't it?" When he made no reply, she lifted her gaze to meet his, her blue eyes empty. "I mean, that's what we agreed, right? No strings, no regrets?"

His very words. "But I thought . . ." What had he thought? That she'd hang around so he could woo her properly? Yes, he guessed he had. "I thought you'd stay until you recovered."

"Oh, that. I'm fine. Just a little bruising. The doctor cleared me to travel, though I think I'll keep my hat on so I don't scare my fellow passengers." She said it jokingly, but her voice sounded brittle to his ears. "I have sunglasses, too. See?" She slid them on. "You can hardly tell."

That was an overstatement, but with makeup, she did look almost normal. As though none of this nightmare had happened.

"I'm sorry," he blurted.

"What for?" She removed the sunglasses.

For everything. "I'm sorry I didn't believe you right away. If I had, you wouldn't have those bruises."

She smiled ruefully. "Don't worry about it. In your shoes, I don't think *I* would have believed me."

"You could have tried me sooner." Despite his efforts to keep his words neutral, they carried an accusatory note.

Some emotion stirred in her eyes, then they went flat again. "I've been there before, Cal. That's what ended my engagement. When I told Garrett about my visions, it took him ten seconds to decide I was crazy. And this after eighteen months. Why should I have expected anything different from you?"

Why, indeed? It hurt, but he forced himself to face the truth. He wasn't her boyfriend. He wasn't her fiancé. He wasn't even her lover in the real sense of that word. He just happened to own the body she'd wanted to get sweaty with while she'd waited for a killer to make his move.

He thought of everything he wanted to say and his stomach hurt. "Anyway, I'm sorry. That's really what I wanted to say. That, and thanks for looking out for Marlena." He fiddled with the hospital bracelet on his wrist.

"No problem."

"So." He shifted his arm, rearranged the blankets. "You must be really anxious to get home after all this time."

A pause. "Yeah, I guess I should be going."

It wasn't until his throat closed that he realized he'd been hoping she'd refute his suggestion. She captured his hand with her own. Cal wanted to grip it tightly and not let go. Instead, he clasped it loosely, casually.

"We had fun, didn't we?" she said, her eyes glinting. "Well, apart from the last bit."

Fun? He remembered burying himself inside her and thinking he'd finally come home. He remembered pillowing his head on her breasts and coming apart in her arms. *Fun?*

She took a step closer, her body language shouting that she was going to lean over the bed rail and kiss him. A long, bittersweet good-bye kiss, no doubt. Jesus, he couldn't bear it.

"Yeah, it was fun," he said quickly. "Maybe you even learned a trick or two to take back east with you." His voice was harsh and far too loud for how close they were, but that seemed to be the only way he could make it come out. "Think of me when you dust those moves off with the next guy, won't you?"

She jerked back, as he'd intended her to, but recovered her composure quickly. Drawing herself up, she looked every inch the lady opting to ignore his crude lapse of manners.

"Goodbye, Callum," she said, giving his hand a last squeeze.

" 'Bye, Lauren."

He watched her go, his heart slamming painfully in his chest. *No score, cowboy. You lose.*

A dark head popped around the door. For a moment, he thought it was Lauren, but to his crushing disappointment, it was only the nurse. He remembered then—he'd summoned her to insist she get the doctor in to yank the chest tube.

"Did you need help with something, Mr. Taggart?"

No, he didn't need help. It didn't matter how long he lay here now. "Sorry, no. Musta pushed the buzzer by mistake."

"You sure?" She looked skeptical, as though he were harboring some pain he wouldn't admit to. "It's been six hours. You can have another shot of Demerol if you need it."

"No, I'm good."

Cal closed his eyes. The nurse fussed around him a moment, checking things, then went to leave.

His eyes sprang open. "Nurse?"

She turned back to him. "Yes?"

"I'm awfully tired. Maybe something to help me sleep?"

She smiled understandingly. "Of course. I'll see to it."

Morning found Cal mean as a bear with a sore head. Bad enough he'd taken the coward's way out with the sleeping pills, but the dreamless sleep they'd induced left him feeling lousy.

So had the lecture he'd gotten this morning from his father for letting Lauren go. No matter what Cal said, the old fool wouldn't believe it'd been Lauren's choice to leave. "Of course she left, you ass! You didn't ask her to stay," Zane had roared loud enough to bring the nurse.

What he needed was to get out of this damned hospital bed and get back to the ranch. There was always so much to do, a man could work himself into exhausted numbness.

Just like Dad, a voice whispered in his head.

"Oh, shut up, would you," he muttered.

"Mr. Taggart?"

Cal glanced up to see an RCMP officer standing just inside his door. Of course. The debriefing. "Come in."

The Mountie, a tall, graying man with a lean build, took his hat off and moved soundlessly into the room. "You're looking better than the last time I saw you."

"I can't say I remember the occasion, Officer . . . ?"

"Corporal Beldan, and don't feel bad; you were out cold." He held out his hand and Cal shook it. "Is this a good time?"

"Good as any."

The interview took an hour. Cal told his story, answered the man's questions as best he could, and then they went over it again. Cal hadn't been able to tell him much beyond what happened after he got to the ridge. When he finished, the detective, his eyes serious, had a lot to tell Cal. It seemed that in the last thirty-six hours, he'd interviewed Lauren, Marlena and Brady at length, as well as half of Cal's staff and all of Harvey's, to put the pieces together. And what a picture it was.

According to Beldan, if Lauren hadn't intervened, not only would Marlena be dead, but Brady as well, and the world—and the courts—would have believed their deaths were Cal's handiwork.

Harvey had stolen Cal's work gloves—the Mountie produced them in a sealed bag and Cal confirmed they were the ones he'd lost—intending to commit murder with them and plant them as evidence. The cop showed him other personal items Harvey'd been carrying which they suspected he intended to plant near the scene, including a cigarette butt, a book of matches, and some other stuff, but Cal couldn't identify any of it as his.

"No matter," Beldan said, "Lab'll be able to tell us."

Beldan's pen scratched over his notepad for a minute, giving Cal a chance to think about what he'd heard. His heart thudded heavily against his ribs as the full import of it struck him—without Lauren's intervention, he'd have been on his way to prison and Harvey would be launching his development project.

But she *had* intervened. She'd made herself Harvey's target.

Cal broke out in a sweat. If he hadn't turned Sienna around, Lauren would be dead now. As it was, he'd almost left it too late. . . . Suddenly, Cal was grateful for the support of the hospital bed he'd been so ready to abandon.

He'd have gone to jail for that murder, too, he realized with a jolt. But if Lauren had died, he'd have deserved prison and worse. Her blood would have been on his hands.

Finally, the Mountie flipped his notebook shut. "Miss Townsend is one remarkable woman."

"I know," Cal said, but he was listening with only half an ear, still grappling with the what-ifs.

"Do you really?"

Something about the Mountie's tone pulled at Cal. He looked at the detective sharply. "Why do I have the feeling you have something more you'd like to say?

The detective's gaze was steady. "I first spoke to Miss Townsend while they were working on you. She was very upset."

What was he getting at? "It was an upsetting experience."

"I understand she baited Mr. McLeod mercilessly to provoke that beating," the detective continued.

Cal paled, recalling her jibes. "I know. It's the only thing that kept her alive long enough for me to reach her."

"She did it to give your former wife a chance to get away."

Geez, what was the matter with this guy? It was Cal's chest that had been injured, not his brain. "I know. That's what it was all about. After having that vision—" He still felt strange saying that word, but it was getting easier. He cleared his throat. "Seeing that vision is what brought her here in the first place, for the sole purpose of saving Marlena."

Detective Beldan tucked his notebook into a pocket. "As I understand it, Miss Townsend had an extra incentive for wanting to keep Mrs. Taggart alive."

"Ex–Mrs. Taggart. And what do you mean, extra incentive?"

"Mr. McLeod explained to Miss Townsend in some considerable detail his plan to frame you, Mr. Taggart. That's how we unraveled it so quickly. She got it from the horse's mouth."

Cal opened his mouth, closed it, opened it again, without once making a sound. Beldan ignored his imitation of a fish.

"Miss Townsend didn't know your ex-wife was carrying a cell phone. She had no idea help was on the way, no expectation of rescue. Her only thought was that if she had to die, she would make sure you didn't take the fall for it."

"No." The denial was reflexive.

"Yes. Her first priority was to delay Mr. McLeod from pursuing your ex-wife, thereby allowing her to escape and tell the real tale. Plan B, in case Marlena didn't make it back, was to generate enough forensic evidence to refute the frame job."

Cal's stomach churned violently. The thought of Lauren out there, despairing of rescue, prepared to die hard . . .

The Mountie carried on, oblivious of Cal's nausea. "She scratched his face to mark him as the assailant, not to mention capture evidence under her nails. She'd clubbed him with a rock in a failed escape attempt, and the wound bled pretty freely. By inducing that beating, she ensured his blood wound up on her."

Cal swallowed. *Steady, man.* "Why are you telling me this?"

Beldan fingered his hat. "After that first interview, she closed up about that angle. Her statement says she was only trying to buy a few more minutes." Beldan stood, replacing his hat. "I had a hunch she wouldn't mention it. But I figure if a woman does something like that for a man, he oughta know."

The Mountie left the room as soundlessly as he'd come.

Cal sat there motionless. Why hadn't she told him? He owed her so much more than he thought. Not just for dragging him back up that cliff. Not just for the lives of Marlena and Brady. He owed her his ranch, his reputation, his freedom, his very life.

He felt something tear away in his psyche like a piece of burlap being rent. He'd needed her. Cal Taggart, the man who needed no one, had needed Lauren Townsend. She'd saved them all, never mind that none of them deserved it, except maybe Brady.

The really scary thing was he needed her still.

He needed someone he could trust his heart to.

He needed someone who could look on his impoverished soul and not turn away.

He needed Lauren.

He groaned. Once upon a time, he'd thought she might be beginning to love him, at least in a vacation-fling kind of way, before he'd let his insecurities run wild. And now . . .

Well, she *must* feel something for him, to have done what she did. Maybe it wasn't too late to fan that spark into something that would last in the real, everyday world.

You don't deserve her, cowboy.

The thought whispered in his head, subtle and persuasive as ever, but this time he silenced it. *Not yet, maybe, but eventually I will.* If she valued him enough to do what she'd done, he was just going to have to learn to deserve her.

First, he had to go after her.

Chapter Eighteen

"Lauren, I think you better come see this."

Heather's voice pulled Lauren out of her daze. She was supposed to be researching new treatments for hyper-adrenalcorticism, but she'd been staring blankly at the computer screen. Again. She'd hoped that coming back to work this week would snap her out of these funks. Sighing, she went off-line. "Coming."

She joined Heather in the reception area. "Okay, what is it?" she asked, striving for good humor. "The snake owner with the bifurcated tongue? The rat girl with the body piercings?"

"Even weirder." Heather gestured toward the window. "A *cowboy* in our parking lot."

Lauren blanched. "Where? Show me."

"Last car. He's helping Mrs. Foster unload her poodles."

For a moment, Lauren saw no one, but she could see that the door on the passenger side of the sleek sedan stood ajar. Then a man backed away from the car and stood. It was Cal.

Gesturing for Mrs. Foster to precede him, he stepped

around the car, a small cage in each hand, and strode toward the clinic.

Lauren drank him in. He wore a straw Stetson, what looked like brand new jeans and boots, and one of those soft blue shirts she'd come to love, although this time he wore a leather vest over it. Heather emitted a wolf whistle.

A fierce longing blocked Lauren's throat. "Cal."

Heather looked at her sharply. "You know this guy?" Lauren made no reply, but her assistant's eyes widened. "He followed you here, didn't he? Followed you all the way from Alberta!"

The reality of his being here hit her and she started to shake. Just in time for the front door to open.

Mrs. Foster entered first. "Thank you so much, young man."

"My pleasure, ma'am."

He placed the cages where Mrs. Foster indicated, but his gaze had already found Lauren's. He straightened, removing his hat. "Lauren."

"Cal."

Heather cleared her throat. "Mrs. Foster, you're right on time. Let's get the girls in the exam room."

"What are you doing here?" Lauren asked as soon as Heather and Mrs. Foster disappeared. "Is everyone all right?"

"Everyone's fine."

"Marlena?"

"In an addictions program, believe it or not."

"Wow. How'd you get her to consent to that?"

"It was her idea, actually. She's finally got it together."

"That's good," Lauren said, meaning it. "And Zane's tests?"

"Doctor says he has an ulcer, but Delia seems to have

291

taken up the challenge of keeping his diet on the straight and narrow."

"Zane and Delia?"

He grinned. "Looks like it. There's a big age difference which Zane isn't crazy about, but he's fighting a losing battle."

"How do you feel about that?"

Cal shrugged. "It's one way to keep a good cook, I guess."

"Then Zane's staying?"

"Yeah, I think I talked him into it."

"What about Brady? Does he know his father used him, then planned to kill him?"

"'Fraid so. I'd have spared him that last bit, if I could, but there was no way to keep it from him. He's just too sharp."

Poor Brady. "How's he taking it?"

"Better, since I put him in touch with my lawyer to see about a potential claim on Harvey's estate. Kid might wind up being the youngest cattle baron in Alberta."

She smiled at that. "And the ranch?"

"That's the damndest thing." Cal shook his head. "After the field day the media had over Harvey's death, I'da thought folks would run screaming from us, but they're coming back."

She felt the weight of that concern slip away. Between Zane Taggart's financial contribution and the renaissance of the guest ranch, Cal's future looked solid. "I'm glad, Cal."

"Thanks."

An awkward silence fell. Okay, Marlena was fine, Zane was fine, the ranch was fine. She was running out of reasons for him to be here, except the one she didn't dare hope for.

She licked suddenly dry lips. "So, what brings you here?"

"I thought we might go for dinner."

Despite her anxiety, she laughed. And was he actually blushing? "You crossed the country to invite me to dinner?"

He smiled, but she could see the tension in him. "I crossed a continent to talk, but dinner seems like a good idea, too. I realized on the plane that I don't remember the last time I ate."

Him, too? Lauren's food had tasted like sawdust since leaving Alberta. The idea that he might be suffering, too, gave her courage.

"Dinner would be nice, but I have Cagney and Lacey."

He blinked. "Cagney and Lacey?"

"The poodles," she blurted, lest he think she would brush him off to watch reruns of that old cop show. Of course, maybe she *should* if she knew what was good for her, but she wouldn't.

"Afterward, then."

"It'll take a little while," she warned.

"I'll wait."

"Okay," she said, smiling. "Okay."

It took all of Lauren's professionalism to get through the next thirty minutes. Afterward, she ducked into the restroom to fix her lipstick. One look in the mirror made her groan. Had she looked like that to Cal? All eyes and nervous excitement?

She took five minutes and did a total face repair. He'd know she'd had to bolster her confidence with makeup, but it was preferable to facing him looking like an apprehensive child.

Stomach leaping, she strode back into the waiting room, only to find Cal gone. She stood looking around the empty room in disbelief. Had he come this far only to chicken out?

"He's helping Mrs. Foster with the girls again." Heather must have come from the back room. Purse under her arm and car keys in hand, she was ready to leave. "Lauren, sweetie, is there something you neglected to tell me about your western vacation?"

Only about a million things. Lauren couldn't have faced Heather's endless questions, which was why she'd delayed coming back to work until her bruises healed well enough to hide.

"I may have omitted a thing or two," she allowed.

The tinkling of the door announced Cal's return.

"You'll have to rectify that Monday, you realize," Heather murmured before heading for the door. "'Night, Mr. Taggart."

"Goodnight, Miz Carr."

Lauren felt Cal's gaze on her as she wrestled with the suddenly stiff lock. Or maybe it was just stiff fingers. Finally, she managed to secure the door.

"So, where to, cowboy?"

"Doesn't matter. I think I'm too jittery to eat anyway."

She felt another zing of adrenaline at his words. That was twice he'd verbalized a vulnerability in the last hour, which was twice more than he'd done in all the time she'd known him.

"Would you like to go home with me? I can fix us a sandwich, brew some coffee."

His eyes lit. "Yeah, I'd like that."

They didn't speak in the car. Traffic was heavy, and Lauren needed to keep her wits about her. The heat in his eyes when she'd invited him home gave her plenty enough distraction.

Twenty minutes later, she pulled up in the drive of her tiny house with its weathered shingles in an older neighborhood.

"Nice," he said, climbing out of the car.

"It's bigger than it looks. Come on."

Ten minutes later, she put a plate of deli sandwiches on the table, along with a carafe of strong black coffee.

"There," she said with satisfaction. "Food at last."

Cal pushed his chair back suddenly. "Will you marry me?"

It took her a few seconds to process the bald words. "That's not funny," she said, sinking onto a chair.

"It wasn't meant to be. I love you, Lauren."

His words were like a fist in the gut. "You love me?"

"Yes."

Joy, disbelief, and myriad other emotions churned in her chest. She did the only reasonable thing she could think of.

She burst into tears.

"Lauren, sweetheart . . ." He got to his feet, then pulled her into his arms. "Oh, baby, don't cry."

Her tears ran unchecked, staining his leather vest as she pressed her face into his warmth. Beneath her ear, his heart pounded like a distance runner's.

In his arms. The one place she needed to be. The haven she thought she'd never know again. She couldn't believe it.

"You love me?" She spoke the words against his chest, not daring to look at him. He gave her no choice in the matter, however, tipping her chin up with a gentle finger.

"I really, really love you."

She searched his eyes. They were shadowed with anxiety, yet somehow clearer than she'd ever seen them. "You pushed me away."

"I know. I'm sorry. . . ."

"You practically bundled me onto that plane."

"You wanted to go home," he protested.

"I wasn't ready." With an effort of will, she pulled out of his arms, taking comfort in his obvious reluctance to let her go.

"Lauren, honey, when you came back to see me, you were on your way to the airport."

The agony of that parting was a fresh wound. "What was I supposed to do? You made it clear you expected me to decamp."

"I may have expected it, but I sure as hell didn't want it."

"You did a pretty good impression of it. 'Think of me when you dust off those moves with the next guy.' "

He blushed. "I only said it because I could see you were already on your way. And you were going to lean over that bed rail and kiss me good-bye. I couldn't have borne it." He shoved a hand through his hair. "I never wanted you to leave. I just didn't dare hope you'd stay once your mission was done."

Lauren's heart thudded like a wild thing in her chest. "What about us? You didn't think I might want to hang around to find out where it might take us?"

"You'd only just reminded me that you were quite capable of enjoying sex for the sake of sex," he said carefully. "You said you were cool with it, that saying good-bye would be no problem."

"Of course I said that! Those were *your* rules, remember? 'No happily-ever-after. No bride and groom on a wedding cake. Just sex.' I was just trying to play by them."

"I didn't mean it," he said, stepping toward her.

"You *did* mean it," she contradicted, backing away, afraid to believe him, yet needing to desperately.

He caught her arm, arresting her retreat. "Okay, maybe I did mean it at first, but I changed my mind."

Lauren dashed new tears from her cheek. "Oh, Cal, you were so afraid I'd find something in you worth loving."

"You're right."

"You wouldn't let me say one positive thing. . . ." She stumbled to a halt. "Wait a minute, I'm right?"

"You're absolutely right."

Something that felt terrifyingly like hope stirred to life.

"The only thing scarier than the prospect of your finding some redeeming qualities in me was the prospect you wouldn't."

Here it was, the nub of it. "Why wouldn't I?" she asked. "Cal, there are lots of things about you people value."

His Adam's apple bobbed. "Yeah, three of them."

Oh, God, he'd inventoried them. And she'd bet they weren't the same three she'd name. "Okay, let's hear them."

"Number one—on a given day, I ride bulls just about as well as anyone in the world. Leastways, I used to."

"Number two?"

"I'm a good rancher, present circumstances notwithstanding."

So far, he'd named only things that he could *do,* things which, if he did them well enough, would earn him the respect of his peers. But nothing about his truly remarkable qualities, like strength, resilience, a deep sense of responsibility, compassion. Lauren could easily have cried again. "And number three?"

"I can please women in bed." The hand gripping her wrist flexed, but she was sure it was involuntary. "I know where to touch them and how. They take one look at me and know it."

A wave of jealousy at the thought of those other women rocked her, but she forced herself to concentrate on his words.

"It's instant recognition. They see right through to my dirty little soul and realize they don't have to hide a thing."

She shivered. "You can't really believe that."

"Tell me you didn't consider an anonymous roll with the cowboy within days of our meeting," he challenged.

She held his gaze while a flush worked up her neck, remembering the awareness that had so quickly stirred the air between them. "I can't," she admitted, "but if you think that's all I saw in you, you're even dumber than I thought. I wouldn't have gone to bed with you unless I saw a lot more than—"

"I know."

She blinked. "You do?"

"Yeah, and it scared the hell out of me. I was afraid I couldn't live up to all the good things you thought about me, even as I memorized every nice thing you said."

"You've got a real problem, you know that?" She was crying again, the tears coursing down her cheeks.

"I know." He grasped her face between his hands and used his thumbs to wipe away her tears. "But I'm working on it."

She gazed up at him to find a suspicious sheen in his eyes. It was enough to startle her own tears into drying up. He must have read her surprise, because he smiled self-mockingly.

"I know, me and sober introspection aren't what you'd call best pals, but I figured out some stuff."

She brought her hands up to cover his in case he had thoughts about removing them. "Oh, yeah? Like what?"

"Like my mother might not have left us if I'd been a better kid."

"Left you?" Lauren's eyes widened. "I thought she died?"

"She did, of cancer when I was five, but I guess I figured she should have fought harder to stay with us. I thought that if I'd just been better, she wouldn't have succumbed so easily."

"That's just not true!"

He actually laughed. "I know that, but the trick was figuring out that I thought it in the first place."

"Then there was your father, who didn't notice you unless you were raising hell. And Marlena, who rewarded you with her love only when you were winning."

"You're starting to get the picture." He brushed a thumb over her lip. "Throw in the prostitute who took me in when I was seventeen and fed me until I found my feet, add the rodeo Annies who rounded out my education and you pretty much have it."

Yes, she got the picture. What a strange trip he'd had.

But she was getting another picture, too. *He really did love her.* Nothing less would have propelled a man like Cal down this path of self-examination. Lauren turned her mouth into his palm and kissed it, keeping her gaze trained on his. As she watched, his pupils dilated and his breathing shallowed up.

"Don't you want to know what else I figured out?" he rasped.

"Of course." She turned her attention to his other palm.

He dragged in a breath. "Lauren, you're making me crazy."

"I sure hope so."

At that, he pulled her into his arms, his mouth fixing on hers hungrily. Within seconds, the hunger swelled to a pure, incandescent need that threatened to engulf both of them. Then he tore his mouth away, breathing heavily.

"I don't know if I can be the man you think I am, but I want to try." His fingers were busily undoing the buttons of her shirt, with her assistance.

"You already are." She shrugged out of the shirt and attacked his while he worked her bra off.

"Lord, I missed you." He took quick nips at her mouth as she tugged his shirt free.

"Me, too." She fumbled with his belt.

Clothes fell until Lauren and Cal were naked in her kitchen. When he pulled her into his arms, body to body, she gasped. She was like the desert and he the rain she'd been too long without. "That should make a hissing sound or something."

He lifted his head from an exploration of her neck. "Huh?"

"Never mind. Just love me." She pulled his head down and kissed him with all the yearning and despair of the past weeks. His response was an echo of her own desperation, but when she writhed against him in invitation a moment later, he pulled back.

"What?" she asked.

"You won't laugh?"

"Promise."

"I feel like we should have a bed for this."

She laughed. She couldn't help it. She was dizzy, happy, light. "I can grant that wish, cowboy. Any others?"

"Yeah, but I don't know if they'll be so easy."

"Try me."

"I want the lights on."

"Done."

"I want to look into your eyes while I love you. I want

you to look into mine. I want you to say you love me when I'm inside you."

Cal heard his own words resonating in the ensuing silence.

Okay, this was hard. Harder than anything he'd ever done in his entire life. He felt naked in a way he'd never been before. He'd just asked Lauren outright—no, begged her—to please love him, and she seemed to be struggling with her reply.

What if she couldn't say it? What if she couldn't love him? Then he saw the glint in her beautiful, slightly red-rimmed eyes. For the third time tonight, tears shimmered like diamonds on her lashes.

"Cal Taggart, if you think I'm going to wait that long to finally say I love you, you've got another think coming."

His knees almost buckled, which would have been extremely inconvenient given the way she hurled herself at him. But he managed to catch her and keep his balance, too.

"Bedroom?"

"Down the hall, second left."

Twenty seconds later, they were tangled on the bed. There was no practiced technique, no careful building and falling of desire. Just an urgent joining. But she kept her gaze locked on his as he filled her, letting him see the stark need, the naked love in her eyes. He knew she would see the same in his eyes. It was the most intimate thing he'd ever experienced and he wanted to draw it out forever. She was already coming apart, though, and he was helpless to do anything but follow her.

* * *

Home, he thought, as he lay on his back looking at Lauren's ceiling. Beside this woman, wherever that might be.

He settled her against him and she grew quiet. Too quiet? He tipped her chin up. "You okay?"

"Better than okay."

She smiled, but something in her eyes made his heart stumble. What now?

"So, how's this going to work?" she asked, not lifting her gaze past his chest.

He tried to swallow down his fear. "Any way it can, I guess, but I'd like for you to make an honest man of me."

"What about that pesky psychic thing?"

"What about it?"

She plucked at the sheet. "I think Garrett was afraid I could read his mind or something."

He snorted. "Now, there's something I'm not worried about."

She glanced up, her eyes fear-filled. "No?"

He smiled. "Sweetheart, if you could read my mind, you'd have given up on me."

"I could have another vision. In fact, I'll probably have lots of them. I usually have a new one every year or two."

"Then we'll deal with it," he said, "just, please God, not the way we dealt with this one."

"I get vibes off of animals. I can feel when they're frightened or angry or in pain."

"So that's how you knew what was wrong with Cosmo."

"No, I had to figure that one out myself. I never saw him in sunlight so I never got that vibe off him."

"Of course."

"You don't think that's weird, the animal thing?"

He laughed, a short, sharp burst of amusement. "Honey, I think it's *very* weird, but pretty useful in your line of work."

She drew herself up on one elbow to examine his face. "You're really okay with this stuff?"

"Of course. It's part of you and I love you."

She leapt on him. Again. He could get used to this.

"Cal Taggart, I love you."

"Mmmm, say it again," he murmured against her mouth.

"As often as you want to hear it," she promised.

"What if I want to hear it every day?"

"That could be arranged."

He felt himself stir. She felt it too, seeing as she was now straddling him on the narrow bed. They'd have to get a queen.

"Marry me? And before you answer, bear in mind that's the third time I've asked you today."

She grinned, raking his chest with the tips of her nails. "Okay. You wore me down."

He ran his hands lightly up the outsides of her arms. "Could we maybe look for a little fixer-upper farmhouse outside of town? I saw quite a bit of arable land from the plane."

"What?"

"I'll need to do something. I can hardly let you keep me," he said mildly. "I've been thinking for a while about getting into breeding bucking bulls. It's something I know, and nothing says they can't be bred here on the East Coast. I could buy a couple of good heifers, drop some money on a few straws of semen from a Yellow Jacket or a Whitewater and we'd be in business."

303

"But what about the ranch?"

"Dad and Jim can handle it between them. Dad's taken to the guest ranch part like a duck to water, by the way."

She stilled again, that hushing of soul and body. "You'd do that for me? Move here?"

He cupped her face, his eyes as earnest now as hers. "Sweetheart, I'd wear a suit and sell used cars if I had to. Of course, I'd rather do this other thing, if it's all the same."

She poked him in the ribs. "Sorry, I can't let you do that. There just isn't enough wide open space here for a man like you. You'd suffocate without your big prairie sky."

His body tensed. "You're not getting rid of me."

"I should hope not!" she exclaimed. "There's a very good chance you just impregnated me."

Oh. *Oh!*

"I meant I'll go back with you. We can live at Foothills."

He shook his head to dislodge the pregnancy thing. "But your practice . . ."

"Can be sold in about a minute. I just sold half of it to Peter Markham last week even though he was in the market for more. He'll be delighted to relieve me of my share."

Cal's heart felt as though it had gotten too big inside his chest. "You'd do that for me?"

She kissed him once, very sweetly, then straightened her spine again. "Sweetheart, I'd wear a uniform and say, 'Would you like fries with that?' if I have to, but I'd rather put my skills to work with your herd, if it's all the same."

Cal pulled her back down so she was cradled against

304

his body, the urge to bed her temporarily subjugated by this tenderness. "Lauren Townsend, you are my heart, my blue sky, my rest."

She smiled into his eyes. "And you, Cal Taggart, are mine."

EVELYN ROGERS

More Than You Know

Toni Cavender was the toast of Hollywood. But when a sleazy producer is found brutally murdered, the paparazzi who once worshipped Toni are calling her the prime suspect. As a high-profile trial gets under way, Toni herself finds it hard to separate fact from fiction.

When an unmarked car tries to force Toni off a cliffside road on a black, wet night, the desperate movie star hires detective Damon Bradley to find the truth. Someone is out to destroy her. Someone who knows the lies she's told . . . even the startling reality that lying in Damon's arms, she feels like the woman she was destined to be. Yet Toni can trust no one. For she has learned that hidden in the heart of every man and woman is . . . *More Than You Know*.

No More Lies
SUSAN SQUIRES

Dr. Holland Banks is head of the Century Psychiatric Hospital and president of the Schizophrenia Research Foundation . . . but is she going insane? The rest of the world seems to be. There's a sniper on the loose, she's being stalked, her father is conducting deadly experiments, and she's begun to hear voices: other people's thoughts. But a man was just admitted to her hospital—one who searched her out, whose touch can make her voices subside. Is he crazy, too, or a solution to her fears? A labyrinth of conspiracy is rising around her, and Holland's life is about to change forever. Very soon there will be . . . *No More Lies*.

Sleepless in Savannah
Rita Herron

Sophie Lane puts her heart on the line and convinces Lance Summers to appear on the matchmaking episode of her talk show—as a contestant. With a little behind-the-scenes maneuvering, she and the sexy developer will end up together. Then Lance pulls a fast one on her, and Sophie vows not to lose any more sleep over him.

Lance's attraction to Sophie threatens his treasured bachelorhood, so he performs a little bait and switch of his own. Now he is free, but Sophie is on a date with someone else! Tortured by images of her with another man, Lance developes a terrible case of insomnia—one only a lifetime of nights tangling with the talk show hostess will cure.

KATHLEEN NANCE

THE WARRIOR

Callie Gabriel, a fiercely independent vegetarian chef, manages her own restaurant and stars in a cooking show with a devoted following. Though she knows men only lead to heartache, she can't help wanting to break through Armond Marceux's veneer of casual elegance to the primal desires that lurk beneath.

Armond returns from an undercover FBI assignment a broken man, his memories stolen by the criminal he sought to bring in. His mind can't remember Callie or their night of wild lovemaking, but his body can never forget the feel of her curves against him. And even though Callie insists she doesn't need him, Armond needs her—for she is the key to stirring not only his memories, but also his passions.

___52417-1 $5.99 US/$6.99 CAN